Dedicated with love to CNG

www.mascotbooks.com

Ten Elephants Ten Memories

For more information, please contact:
Mascot Books
620 Herndon Parkway, Suite 320
Herndon, VA 20170
info@mascotbooks.com

Library of Congress Control Number: 2018903212

CPSIA Code: PRFRE0818A
ISBN-13: 978-1-68401-880-2

Printed in Canada

TEN ELEPHANTS TEN MEMORIES

Ellen Gordon

Contents

Aunt B

Throughout Cate Kingston's young life her Great Aunt B thrilled, entertained, and sometimes terrified her with tales of exotic travel, an extravagant lifestyle, séances, and mysterious deaths. The old, fading black-and-white photos that Aunt B shared with Cate were proof that a once young and enormously rich Aunt B had indeed led an eclectic, worldly life. Aunt B's soft gravelly voice drew Cate into remarkable memories of her adventures—whether foreign or here at Chartres, Aunt B's once splendid, rambling summer home. Now the wealth and the lifestyle were long lost. Yet Cate's eccentric aunt held on to Chartres, and it overflowed with memorabilia from an era that Cate could only dream of. So it was with little wonder that Cate could sit mesmerized, surrounded by the past, hearing firsthand stories of bullfights, elephant rides, fancy dress parties, or the disappearance of Sally the maid. Most of Aunt B's stories were spiced with romance, colorful characters, and sometimes danger, filling Cate with a longing for adventures of her own.

Petite Red

I

Chartres was like a second home to Cate as far back as she could remember. Her mom, June, was very fond of Cate's Great-Aunt B, so visits to Chartres were a frequent adventure. And while toddler Cate spent most of her days attached to her veterinary father, Ken, at times an emergency call made it impossible for her to accompany him. Somewhat reluctantly, Ken would leave his tiny only child in Aunt B's enthusiastic care for a few hours. He had to admit Cate was always happy to run to her aunt for a cuddle, but he wondered just what this larger-than-life Aunt B would be sharing with someone so young.

Toddler Cate knew that being alone with Aunt B at Chartres meant eating thick slices of pound cake with chocolate syrup, maybe catching the lazy black-and-white cat while it slept on the kitchen counter, and always hearing Aunt B's voice almost whispering to her. Two-year-old Cate seldom understood what her aunt had to say, but she would follow her aunt's soft voice as she pointed to a painting or sat on a long over-stuffed sofa, running her veined hands over the fabric. As Cate grew, Chartres came alive with Aunt B's constant reminiscing, and Cate soaked up every almost unbelievable detail. What she never understood was why Aunt B never shared these amazing, daring tales with anyone else. When visiting at Chartres with her mom or neighbors, there was only talk of the weather or local events. It was like Cate and Aunt B shared a wonderful secret—the secret of her aunt's life thirty years ago.

Cate pieced together the story of how Chartres came to be, partly from Aunt B's tales and partly from what her mom knew as fact. Aunt B and Uncle Claude were married in 1919.

Uncle Claude supposedly had close connections with the Rockefellers and the oil industry, but since Aunt B refused to ever talk about his work, no one knew the full history.

What Cate's mom did know was that B and Claude were extremely wealthy. With an apartment in New York City and a five-bedroom terrace home in New Orleans, the restless couple longed for a fashionable summer retreat where they could beat the heat and entertain their endless list of friends.

While on business in Cleveland, Claude was told of a small village and lake not far from there. He knew B's family lived somewhere in that general direction and thought if he could find a summer house it would be the perfect birthday surprise for B. It took just one afternoon for Claude to fall in love with the quaint, quiet community of Chippewa Lake. The problem was a lack of anything for sale that would match the expectations of a perfect retreat for the couple's multitude of friends.

"B, I'm going to build us the most elegant yet rustic cottage that Chippewa Lake has ever seen," a jubilant Claude exploded to B over white Russians in their New York apartment. And he did.

The ten-room, two-story, yellow stucco "cottage" with a front porch to seat twenty was built for summers full of fun. Aunt B named their new abode Chartres. Besides being a town in central France that B had once visited, it was also the street name of their New Orleans home. The terrace home and the New York apartment were long gone by Cate's time. Chartres was all that remained of Aunt B's fortune. Once old enough and brave enough, Cate began to explore this house that felt more like a museum than someone's home.

Even as a youngster Cate's favorite place to be inside Chartres was the huge hall that occupied half of the first floor. It felt safer than the dark of the basement or the unknown that lurked up the steep stairs for tiny feet. Rectangular in shape, this area would have been sitting room, game room, and parlor to Aunt B's crowd of friends.

Even now it was overflowing with Aunt B's unbelievable treasures, and Cate never tired of seeing them. At the far north end rested an elaborate 1917 wooden pump organ that no longer played, although young Cate would give it some loud pounds to her aunt's amusement.

Above the keyboard sat a fascinating row of fifteen pullout tone changers, and above that rose the intricately detailed wood carving of panels and arches. This woodwork masterpiece continued all the way up to the twelve-foot yellowing plaster ceiling. The wonderful rich cloth that covered the foot pedals was well worn, as if all those ghosts of parties past had left their footprints for all time.

Close by, a colorful array of couches and chairs formed intimate sitting areas. The fabrics were worn smooth and the colors faded, but Cate spent hours curled up reading in the overstuffed loveseats. For years Aunt B's obese long-haired cat named Cat curled up for a sleep as Cate read. The Persian carpets, thrown casually over the hard oak floors, though old and a bit threadbare, still displayed their reds, blues, and greens in intricate patterns. As Cate got older she imagined the parties, where beautiful people sat around in merry clusters planning their next game or outing or affair.

On the east wall of this extraordinary room was a fireplace so large that for years Cate could stand inside it and play or read during the summer, enjoying its cool, almost damp tiles. The tiniest detail of carved trees in the wooden mantel of the fireplace made Cate think of the woods on her family farm. As if the mantel wasn't enough to engage Cate, what it held delighted Cate even more. A lifelike, lively family of five extraordinary ebony and ivory elephants strode the length of the mantel. All five had their carefully carved trunks held high. Thick ivory tusks (ivory was legal then) on the mother and father were miniaturized down to the tiniest baby elephant. Their shiny ebony black bodies showed great contrast to the bright white ivory of the tusks, eyes, and feet. Aunt B explained that the huge flapping ears made them African elephants, while Indian elephants' ears were smaller.

Cate would look up at them and make up stories about their lives in wild Africa. By the age of six, Cate and Aunt B had given each member of the elephant family a name. Between books read together and stories Aunt B told about untamed Africa, Cate's imagination was opening up.

Amadi was the proud father, which meant "free man;" Amara, meaning "grace," was the matriarch; Ayo and Anuli meant "joy" and were the proud sons. It was tiny Adanna, meaning "father's daughter" that Cate loved the best. Maybe she loved Adanna the best because she loved being her father's daughter so much. Sometimes Cate would share her made-up stories with her aunt, who would listen intently and always encourage her to expand the stories.

As told to Aunt B by six-year-old Cate:

One day tiny Adanna wandered off and was lost in the thick African savannah. Her father, Amadi, was terrified that a hyena would eat her, and he was angry with her brother Anuli for losing his baby sister.

Amadi raised his trunk high in the air and trumpeted little Adanna's name. All the savannah heard the great elephant's call. All the other elephants started to look for the baby elephant.

The hyenas and the lions looked for Adanna. They wanted to eat her. But the giraffes and the zebras did not want the baby elephant to be hurt, so they looked for her in the thick acacia trees. When excited, zebras give a bark or a yip. And when a friendly zebra family found little Adanna asleep under a tree, they barked as loud as they could.

When Adanna slowly woke up, her family, as well as the zebras and giraffes, were all smiling at her. She trotted to her father, and he wrapped his huge, thick trunk around her in an elephant hug.

After hearing the latest story about the elephant family, Aunt B smiled at her imaginative young grand-niece and promised, "Cate, one day I will give you this set of elephants so that you can go on and on with their stories." Cate was thrilled with the idea that she might own such wonderful elephants but kept silent in case Aunt B changed her mind. Cate so cherished the bond between them that she would never tell anyone else about the stories or the elephant family she loved.

Sometimes Cate would admire the elephant family from one of the two stretched and worn black leather chairs with small white enamel tables by each that occupied the far end of this magical room. This was where Aunt B and her second husband, Carl, would sit in silence each night. In all her years visiting, even spending summer nights, Cate seldom heard them speak. Carl was a cleaner at the local high school. Ten years younger than an already worn and weary Aunt B when they married, it was rumored that he thought he was marrying a wealthy woman. The silence between them began almost immediately when he learned the once beautiful house and her magical treasures were all the wealth that remained. He was never mean to Cate but rather ignored her as he ignored her aunt.

Behind the leather chairs where Aunt B and Carl spent their silent evenings were two recessed knickknack cases, with four shelves each and glass doors. Inside, the shelves held the most amazing collection of small treasures that a young girl could possibly imagine. And if she were very careful, Aunt B let her hold them. There was a small glass container that held a flea circus from Mexico, with the fleas in festive gear. Claude bought this for B for a peso from a girl about Cate's age on the back streets of Tijuana. There were tiny cloth dolls dressed in the finest Argentinian clothing, with minute details of headgear and shoes. Claude and Aunt B had stayed on an estancia owned by a wealthy polo player, and his wife had given B this as a reminder of their stay. There was a bean that held six tiny carved elephants. On safari in Kenya, tribesmen sold these to tourists, and B's guide bought them for her. There was also a ceramic Lord Fauntleroy miniature figure in full short britches and coat that came to Chartres with B's great English friends one summer.

Hours were spent with this magical collection, with mystical Aunt B thrilling Cate with stories to match each piece. Why wouldn't a child develop a sense of yearning for adventure, for being outrageous, for not wanting the ordinary, after growing up with an Aunt B?

Reluctantly leaving her favorite room, Cate occasionally stepped through the break between the worn leather chairs and knickknack shelves into the equally spacious dining room. The polished antique oak table seated twenty guests comfortably, though Aunt B insisted that more guests found space to eat in the sunroom off to the left. Against one wall behind guest chairs was a glass cabinet filled to the ceiling with crystal plates, bowls, platters, wine glasses, and goblets, now never used or washed. Just locked away with Aunt B's memories.

II

The architect who designed Chartres crowned it on the high point of the property, giving it a perfect view of Chippewa Lake. The lake was a three-by-five-mile private lake and in Aunt B's time a playground for wealthy visitors and locals alike. Cate, ever the tomboy growing up, loved the surroundings of Chartres almost as much as the inside. Young Cate defied grass stains by rolling down the gentle slope of lush green grass to the lake shore then racing back up with the brisk lake breeze behind her. Cate Kingston's vivid imagination never had a problem seeing the ghosts of the Gatsby-like folk who spent long playful summers on this cool, lush lawn, when Aunt B was the toast of Chippewa and some of the world. When looking at old photos of a boisterous-looking crowd dancing on the lawn, Aunt B would often call them by name, as if they might come back to life on the green carpet.

Aunt B, when feeling her best, shared stories to match the playful black-and-white photos of the frivolous group of friends from all over the world coming to entertain themselves at Chartres. The photos were clear reminders of formal sit-down dinners with laughing people dressed in elaborate costumes from around the world.

How this costume collection came into being was yet another B legend. Not long after their marriage, Claude and B embarked on a one-year adventure around the world. Everywhere they explored B insisted they not leave until she had an authentic outfit to create a one-of-a-kind costume collection. She did not buy from a tourist shop but preferred to get a local resident to give up their clothing! Sometimes she would trade for something she owned or negotiate a price, or as she confessed to Cate, sometimes she took things off a clothesline. By now Cate felt like a partner in crime when her aunt told her of her many misadventures. She would never tire of reliving her aunt's former life.

Occasionally Aunt B read some of the poems this mischievous group concocted for one another. They were not brilliant poems in Cate's mind, but they were often inside jokes on the recipient and a bit too risqué for her. When Cate was older she began to fully understand that the morals of this collection of friends would not pass muster with her mom, yet the intrigue of steamy affairs gave teenage Cate something to ponder.

Fortune telling was an exciting, if not a bit dangerous, pastime. At meals that stretched for hours, the well-lubricated party might be asked to each tell the fortune of the person sitting across from them. Sometimes outrageous, sometimes frightening, depending on the relationship of the person sitting their opposite and how much wine had been consumed, it was always entertaining. Aunt B was so good at fortune telling, many of her friends believed that she had the gift, and her guests often sought her out for a séance or a reading of tarot cards. The more Cate studied the photos and absorbed the outrageous tales, Cate began to long for this wonderful, free, fun lifestyle that her aunt had so enjoyed. Would she ever be that free?

Leaving the lush green of the lawn, Cate wound through the thick shrubs that formed a deep semicircle around the lake side of the house. So deep and lush were the shrubs that Cate could find places to hide where no one could see her. She often set up tea parties for her favorite dolls when young and later found the seclusion perfect for an afternoon of teenage daydreaming.

When she tired of the hiding places in the shrubs, Cate faced a long row of steep red brick steps that would lead her back into Chartres. The steps ended on a black-and-white-tiled porch that stretched the full length of the house. The tiles were so big that as a toddler Cate could easily sit on one of them. Every summer bright red geraniums would be brought up from the basement to bloom yet again, to line those worn steps and brighten up the porch. Every summer the walls of the porch were newly whitewashed, even as the walls began to peel.

The porch was full of all sorts of intriguing choices for sitting, chatting, and enjoying the lake view, but Cate best loved the pair of ancient peacock chairs. Aunt B shared the adventure of purchasing them in Hong Kong with a devilish twinkle in her eyes. The first time she told the story Cate was only seven. She had bartered hard, she told the wide-eyed Cate, with an owner who had no intention of selling the pair from his own home. Aunt B was a guest in his home when she sat in them and was instantly determined they should adorn her front porch at Chartres. The reluctant host tried to explain that not so long ago these chairs could only be used by royals. Naturally that sparked B's determination to have them. Due to Cate's young age, the negotiating process may not have been fully explained that day, but as she got older, she remembered the devilish twinkle and knew there was more to this story!

Cate could remember having to get on tiptoes to pull herself into one these extraordinary chairs. The colorful batik cushions were soft and faded but so comfortable to curl up in. Intricate weaving of beads and fabric in the five-foot fan back, even in their old age, was engaging. Peacock chairs would go out of fashion for decades, only to be revived and reproduced in the swinging sixties and seventies, but none could ever match the authentic pair of Aunt B's.

III

Cate never met Aunt B's first husband, Claude. He died at the end of the Stock Market Crash in 1929. Aunt B would not talk about his death and only glared at Cate if she asked questions. There were no pictures of him, no sign in the house that he ever existed. Fortunately Cate's mom remembered her Uncle Claude clearly. She saw Claude and Aunt B and their lifestyle before the crash through the eyes of a child. When barely ten and staying weekends with her aunt, she would be banished to a tiny bedroom down the long hall away from the party-goers as soon as the parties grew loud or outrageous. Still there was plenty of opportunity to watch and listen to the glamorous crowd.

Cate's mom looked like she was far away as she recounted how Friday afternoons the cars would start rolling in to park on the large vacant lawn next to Aunt B's. There were Auburns, Nashes, Dusenbergs, and the more common Fords. She could clearly describe Uncle Claude racing in on a Friday afternoon in a brand-new wood-and-steel Auburn Roadster. Soon champagne would flow, there was always music and laughter, and the party usually continued to Sunday afternoon. Cate's mom didn't know all the details, but like so many, Claude lost all his money, including his business in the Crash. Aunt B had yet to know that they were nearly penniless when Claude climbed the steep stairs to the large second-story room where rows of beds once held the merry guests and put a bullet in his head. No wonder Aunt B didn't want to talk about him, Cate thought. She was sure Uncle Claude's ghost was roaming up there and was terrified of the ghost from the day her mom recounted the sad story.

At around ten, Cate began to help Aunt B clean her house to earn pocket money. Aunt B was certainly just being kind, because Cate had no idea how to clean, and the house was huge. Unfortunately, by now Aunt B had stopped caring about the cleanliness of the kitchen or anything else. The past was where she wanted to live, not having to deal with the crusted cat food on the electric can opener, the silent husband, or dust accumulating on the hand-carved table in the grand dining room. When Aunt B was rich, the parties in this house and on the lake were legendary. Cate often tried to imagine what it would have been like if Aunt B were still rich with lovely friends and lots of travel. This later life had dragged her down.

One day when the pretend cleaning was finished, Aunt B and Cate sat on the porch, each comfortable in the peacock chairs, discussing their latest project to tackle the second floor. Cate was not keen on this project, as the second floor had terrorized her from the first time she toddled up the stairs at age three. A door at the top of the long staircase was ajar when her tiny legs had finally reached the landing. Curious, toddler Cate pulled open the door and immediately howled in alarm. There were dolls with no heads, bits of old clothing strewn all over, stacks of old magazines, and long sabers on the floor. An older Cate learned that all the hats, costumes, props, and magazines were part of her aunt's lively plays and games that the young Aunt B and her friends had performed over the summers. Still, that initial trauma and later her knowledge of a suicide and a murder made Cate shudder every time she climbed those stairs.

The twelve-foot walk-in closet that had scared Cate years ago was still untouched, and clearing the contents both scared and excited Cate. To the right of the infamous closet was the dorm-like room where Uncle Claude had solved his financial worries with a bullet. But years before his death summer guests, who seldom really slept, would come to rest on the rows of single beds between their games, or as Cate later imagined, to meet secret lovers.

On the other side of the mysterious closet was a hall leading to three other bedrooms. The tiny one at the end of the hall belonged to a maid named Sally. Sally had survived two summers of coping with Aunt B's demanding guests and was well liked by all. Which is why when Sally suddenly disappeared during the Fourth of July festivities in 1922, it was more than a popular topic of discussion. Some said she just ran away, tired of the work, but most, including Aunt B, were convinced that she was murdered. In the séance that followed her disappearance Aunt B told the ten holding hands around the table that she heard Sally crying. All her personal things, including a stash of money, were still in her tiny room, giving credence to the murder theory. Yet the police were never called. When Cate was older and thought of Sally again, she was convinced that Aunt B knew more about the maid's disappearance and was protecting someone. So the parties continued, and no one ever knew for sure what happened to the young maid.

While Cate should have been listening to Aunt B's plan of action for the second-floor rooms, Cate was miles away thinking once again of the mysterious past of her eccentric Aunt B. One of her very favorite stories that Cate had heard many times by the time she was a teenager was about the wooden

Ellen Gordon

rowboat that the merry party groups used every summer on the lake. Towards the end of summer one year when most of the guests had spread back out around the world and it was nearly time to put Uncle Elmer, as the boat was named, away for the winter, a freak storm hit Chippewa Lake, and Uncle Elmer was dashed to pieces up on the lawn, broken beyond repair. Immediately Aunt B sent urgent messages via telegrams to friends everywhere, "Come quickly. Uncle Elmer is dying." And they came. Over twenty-five guests arrived to cremate Uncle Elmer on a huge bonfire on the lawn!

Even more romantic to a teenage Cate were stories about the young college student chauffeurs Aunt B hired every summer to take her friends and herself wherever they wanted to go at any moment. Two perfect Bentleys were parked in the stand-alone garage near the home. Upstairs was a well-appointed studio with full facilities for the young drivers to live for the summer. No expense was spared for anything Aunt B did or wanted thanks to Uncle Claude. Cate sighed as she daydreamed about the past glory of this home and Aunt B's handsome chauffeurs.

Suddenly Aunt B startled Cate out of her reverie, "It's important that every young girl collects something as a hobby, Cate." Indeed, Aunt B had collected the miniatures in the glass knickknack cabinets, costumes, men's smoking pipes, dolls, and elephants from all around the world. The dolls were so well known that Aunt B would give talks on them at mother/daughter banquets, which were quite popular back then. Cate would go along and hold up the dolls as Aunt B described where they had come from, and there was always a story to be told on how the doll came into her possession.

Cate thought a bit about what she might like to collect, but Aunt B already had a plan. "I think you shall collect elephants, Cate. When their trunks are up they are good luck in your home, and they are a magnificent animal." Aunt B had been on safaris in her younger days and ridden both African and Indian elephants. With that, Aunt B got up and went inside, coming back quickly. In her hand was a small red roly-poly elephant with a tiny flexible trunk. "Here is your first elephant. I used to be very involved with the Republican Party, and this was a party favor at one of their dinners in DC. What do you think?"

Cate knew this little fellow well. He was one of Aunt B's miniatures in the knickknack cabinets behind the leather chairs. She loved him as she loved all the little treasures in the cabinets. That day Aunt B made it quite clear that she would not buy elephants for herself. "You'll see, Cate, people who love you will want you to have them to remember them by or a time spent with them." She was correct. Cate would never buy an elephant for herself and eventually would have hundreds. Cate's life would become nearly as eccentric, or at least as erratic, as her magical aunt, and every elephant added along the way would have its own story.

That day was special for Cate, and she would always remember it vividly. The little red elephant, lovingly called Petite Red, would indeed travel far, yet ten-year-old Cate couldn't know that. She did know that her aunt had given her something very special, part of her aunt's very special past.

Ellen Gordon

IV

Time spent with Aunt B would taper as Cate's love of horseback riding with her dad and her part-time job at Chippewa Lake Park competed for her summer hours when she reached high school. Yet while she was no longer engaged in the cleaning process, by now Aunt B needed more professional help to keep the enormous home at least livable. She would walk to Chartres to catch up with her favorite aunt and hear more stories of the past after she finished a shift at Kiddieland. Or Cate would surprise her aunt on warm summer evenings sitting in the peacock chairs to catch the lake breeze. The stories were still their secret. Cate had never told anyone all that B had shared over the years.

Sometimes June and Ken wondered if letting Cate grow close to the once wild Aunt B was a mistake. They had no idea of the full extent of the relationship or all that Aunt B had told the impressionable Cate. Yet there was no doubt that Cate's endless curiosity about the lifestyle that B embraced had shaped her imagination to dream of something different, new, and far away.

They really questioned their judgment when a slightly tipsy Cate returned home one evening explaining how Aunt B used to drink white Russians in St. Petersburg with a czar. "He had taught Aunt B how to make the perfect drink, so Aunt B let me try one," Cate giggled. Her parents looked at each, half in amusement and half in concern.

Just as she was about to start her junior year in high school, with the park closing for the winter and visits with Aunt B coming to an end for the season, Cate sensed a change in her aunt.

"Are you okay, Aunt B?" Cate asked with raised eyebrows. "You seem a little distant today. I know, you're just going to miss me too much when school starts, right?" Cate tried to make light of the feeling of foreboding creeping in.

"Don't forget, Cate, the ebony and ivory set is to be yours one day." Aunt B ignored Cate's comments and hugged her tightly.

"Don't worry, Aunt B, I'd never forget that, but you keep them safe for me until I'm grown up and have my own home," Cate declared. "Maybe I'll grow up and buy Chartres from you, then the elephants can stay right where they are!" she added more seriously. As she left the large living room, she moved slowly and took in every detail. Just as she was about to step into the long hall, she had one last look at the splendid ebony set before reluctantly going out the back, past the garage to her where she'd parked her mom's black Chevy convertible.

Cate never saw her aunt again. Later that night, after the silent husband was fast asleep, Aunt B marched into the garage that once held Bentleys but now just held her husband's old beat up red Ford pickup. She started the truck, climbed in, and closed the doors. As she fell into her last sleep, no one would ever know that her last thoughts were of Cate and the ebony elephant family. The thought gave her peace to believe they would sit in Cate's home one day.

Ellen Gordon

Star

I

High school was a bit of a blur for Cate Kingston. Years later she would try to recall what she was like at sixteen. She remembered having a lot of close girlfriends, all of whom were the most popular in her class. At slumber parties these friends discussed in detail their budding or ending romances, how far they let their dates go, who got a class ring, or where were they going on Saturday night. They all loved Cate but did notice that she never had anything much to contribute in the sex experimentation department. They knew Cate had male friends, but they were more like buddies who went horseback riding, water skiing, or running with her.

Cate's few real dates in high school included the senior geek, who threw up on her parents' antique Persian carpet before the date even began (some sort of flu, or so he claimed). Then there was the guy who dressed in black (they called them "Hoods" in those days), who drove a tricked-out GTO. None of her few actual dates were with any of the cool guys or ones from the "in" crowd. Yet Cate didn't care, or maybe in reflection she just didn't notice. She was well liked, a bit eccentric, and a bit of a loner compared to her girlfriends. So while her ancient high school diaries tell her that she enjoyed the four years at Franklin High, there was no mention of any romance worth sharing at a slumber party.

It wasn't until high school graduation was only a few months away when Cate seriously thought about her life so far. Why didn't she have a real boyfriend? Some of her best friends were already in serious relationships and "doing it." She knew she was shy or maybe not shy, just content within herself. While she liked being around her friends, when she thought about it, she was most content on her own. When Cate was most honest with herself she knew she was happiest on the family farm, horseback riding alone or with her dad. How odd was she?

Thinking about her dad made her smile. They were so much alike in so many ways. The shape of her ears, too big for her appreciation, and the ski slope nose were identical to his. The physical similarities stopped there, for Cate inherited her Aunt Peg's bright red hair, while her dad's was jet black with threads of silver. Although he told Cate that if he ever grew a beard it would be as red as her hair, she never quite believed him. People often commented on Cate's eyes that could change from a startling green to a pale gray, but she wished hers matched the bright sky blue of her father's.

The true similarity was in their personalities. While Ken, her dad, had a few good friends who he hunted or rode horseback with, he was most at home on the farm. His practice, Kingston Veterinary Services, gave him a great deal of time to tend to his own farm and stock. He wasn't shy, or anti-social—he mixed well with their friends—it's just that he was very comfortable being alone. So more than anyone else in the world, Cate felt her dad understood her best.

The Saturday before graduation Cate joined her father in their hundred-year-old barn that Cate's great-great-grandfather built. The original outside boards needed another coat of white paint, which was on the schedule for that summer. Inside Cate inhaled the smells of hay, oats, manure, and her favorite smell of the horses themselves. Five stalls housed five very different breeds of horses. Cate loved her six-year-old quarter horse, Jack, and had helped train him the past three years. Jack now hung his head over his stall expectantly, always eager for a run.

"Can I take Jack out this morning, Dad, or does Sparky need a run?" Cate questioned her dad, who was busy cleaning his favorite saddle. He kept the black leather western saddle with silver trim just for special occasions like parades, but it needed attention on a regular basis.

"I'll take Sparky and ride with you if you can hold on five minutes," Ken grunted as he lifted the hundred-pound saddle from the wooden horse to its place in the tack room. Sparky was a palomino mix that Ken had been training in hopes of a good sale for him in the summer. Except for Jack, Ken bought and trained a variety of horses in a year as a side business. Cate was never sure what horse might appear for her to try out. This side business created a special bond with dad and daughter as they assessed each new horse for its potential for a profit.

Cate was content greeting all the horses and giving each a small sugar cube. Ken, being a veterinarian, wasn't really keen on sugar treats for the horses, but he knew Cate would never overdo it and knew how much she enjoyed chatting with each horse as they crunched the tiny morsel.

Within minutes they swung simultaneously into their western saddles and walked north from the barn toward the open fields. Both were equally savoring the quiet of the morning, broken only by the gentle clop of the hooves in the soft dust on the lane.

"I'm glad I decided not to go too far from home to start college, Pops," Cate declared, breaking the silence. "I wouldn't be able to do this on weekends or when I have no classes. I would be so lonely away from here."

Ken didn't answer for a few heartbeats—he also was very relieved at her choice. He knew someday she may move away, but he was not ready for that yet. And hopefully she'll never move too far, he thought to himself. He smiled at the way she just blurted this out to him, almost in embarrassment. She had always been like this. Not a child of many words, but when something was on her mind out it came, ready or not.

"Union State College has an excellent reputation, and the teachers section is particularly strong. And I'm glad you'll be commuting, at least at first. When you meet some handsome jock in your physical education classes, we'll see little of you then."

"I've never even had a boyfriend, Dad. Do you think there's something wrong with me?" Cate sighed, suddenly very serious.

Now Ken was at a loss for words. These were not the kinds of conversations he and Cate had. They usually talked horses and the farm and the weather—not boys, damn it.

"To me you're perfect." An embarrassed Ken cantered ahead, leaving a bemused and a bit amused Cate in his dust. They really were alike, she thought, as she urged Jack after him.

She had decided not to go away to college but rather go to Union State College, which was about two hours from her home. She knew a huge part of that decision was her dad. She couldn't imagine going out of state and leaving the farm or him. Yet she was glad that high school was over and that only the summer stood between her and the adventure of college. She wanted change, she wanted some action, she wanted a guy.

Don't they always say be careful what you wish for?

II

Michael noticed Cate seconds before she literally ran into him at the local bowling alley, the first week after her high school graduation. As he stood in the next lane waiting for her to take her turn, he watched the small-framed redhead grab a bright pink ball and with great speed and concentration send the pink blur hurtling into the right gutter.

The hoots from the herd of girlfriends behind her grew louder as she stomped a small foot, turned, and smacked straight into Michael James Scott. The feisty bravado faded fast as Cate's ears turned bright red with mortification.

"Sorry," she whispered and slumped into a seat next to her best friend Sue.

"Wow. Lucky you, I'd bump into Michael Scott any day," Sue teased.

Of course everyone knew who Michael Scott was. Although four years older than the girls, in a small rural community of two thousand, anyone who had lettered in three sports all the way through high school was a legend. And that was Michael, the dark, handsome, and a bit mysterious hero of his day. He finished an associate accounting degree at Wooster College and was working at the Ohio Farmers Insurance Company located in Wooster. The commute was about an hour, but for now he preferred to live at home, and he quite enjoyed the peaceful, country road through Ohio farmland that took him back and forth.

Cate couldn't help peeking at the object of her humiliation, but she made sure never to be bowling beside him again. To add to the embarrassment, he caught her looking at him once and gave her a small smile. He wasn't as tall as she had thought a great athlete would be, but the wide, strong shoulders and neck and the narrow hips showed how well he was keeping that high school body. Cate felt an unfamiliar, almost uncomfortable bump from her ever-changing hormones. Too shy to ever tell anyone, she had started to touch herself when tucked safely in her bed, when the hormones grabbed her, causing a tingle in her breasts and a sense of urgency between her legs. Then the slightest touch down there gave Cate wonderful guilty pleasure.

Now, here of all places as Cate tried to concentrate on her game, the familiar tingle and then the familiar wetness startled her. Cate squirmed in her seat until she couldn't take the intensity and headed to the ladies' room, where she gently held herself between her legs while locked in a stall. The instant release was wonderful and embarrassing for the naïve Cate.

Returning to the alley, Cate's impatient friends called out for her to hurry up. "We only have three more frames, then we can head to Cook's and check out who has a date tonight," an enthusiastic Sue demanded.

Cate obligingly grabbed her pink bowling "weapon," then stole a quick glance to her left before her "toss" down the alley. She took a small misstep when she saw Michael corralled by a pretty girl in tight shorts. Someone she had never seen before.

"Huh, Why should that bother me?" Cate huffed to herself then threw the only decent roll of the night—knocking down every pin.

"Where did that come from?" a disbelieving Sue cried out to her.

Cate didn't answer. She just wanted the game to be over and wasn't even sure why. She didn't wait for the others to finish; she headed for the checkout counter.

As Cate plunked down the awful green-and-red shoes on the counter with a thud, she thought again of what a strange night it had been. She turned quickly to head to the exit before any of her buddies invited her to Cook's for hamburgers. As she picked up the pace, she saw Michael coming towards her, ready to deposit his shoes. When they were face to face he said almost sternly, "May I take you home tonight?"

Cate's head nearly flew off her shoulders. Michael Scott wanted to take her home. Tonight. Michael, in his car, wanted to take her home tonight. Now she was beginning to feel stupid because she hadn't uttered a word in response to his question. So she nodded a yes.

They'd driven straight to Cook's Drive-In, where several cars with either Michael's or her friends had already ordered. Cate felt that they were all staring at them, and Cate couldn't think of a thing to say to Michael, so they just sat there in silence until someone came to take their order.

"What would you like, Cate?"

"Uh, just a cherry Coke, please," Cate muttered.

"Same for me, thanks. That's all," Michael thanked the carhop.

Actually Cate would have loved one of Cook's fantastic King Burgers with the works, but she was sure if she had one she would manage to drop it all over herself. She was feeling very self-conscious and was sure Michael must have thought she was a mute or just stupid.

"What are your plans now that you've graduated, Cate?" Michael groped for topics to get this pretty young girl to talk to him. He was no extravert himself and was usually more comfortable with chatty girls who took control of the conversation.

"I'm commuting to Union State College. I plan on becoming a physical education teacher, hopefully in an elementary school somewhere around here. I'm really looking forward to college and meeting new people." Cate finally took a breath and stared straight ahead. Why was she babbling?

Thankfully, Rod, a good friend of Michael's and his girlfriend Jill came over to the car while they sipped their cokes.

"I've seen you before; you're Doc Kingston's daughter, right? He's a hell of a vet. I'm Rodney, and this is Jill," Rod enthused.

"Nice to meet you both, and I agree. Dad's a super vet!" Cate matched his enthusiasm at the mention of her dad. This outgoing couple would soon become constants in Michael and Cate's time together. They always had lots of stories and gossip to share and seemed to be in constant need of activity.

That first night didn't go as smoothly as Michael or Cate would have liked. He sensed that this was a special person, one he wanted to see again. His past relationships had never lasted long. Being a jock in high school meant there was always someone who wanted to be on his arm, but nothing ever really clicked with any of them. Cate was cute and bright, yet she seemed distant on that first date, like she wasn't sure she wanted to be there. Still he was determined to try again.

As for Cate, she was in such awe of this older, popular, handsome man that she could hardly talk to him at first. As the evening progressed, she did come out of her trance, but she was convinced that he would never ask her out again. At least she had something to write in her boring diary!

They both survived the somewhat awkward start to become a bit of an item that first summer after high school graduation. Cate felt so grown up. Michael was falling in love.

III

Michael turned out to be a bit quiet and a bit moody to Cate's a bit quiet and a bit eccentric. It seemed to both his and her friends that it was a good match, though. The new couple enjoyed boating, water skiing, picnics, and softball games with a variety of friends. In a small community like Franklin everyone knew everyone, and they usually played nice. It would only be later when Cate would learn how tough this community could be to someone who dared to be different.

He was a virgin, and she was a virgin. Cate often wondered if Michael got himself "off" like she was now doing on a regular basis. It just wasn't something they could discuss. Their fumbling in the backseat of his Ford Fairlane was pretty innocent that summer, and at times Cate wondered why.

The summer of 1968 saw Michael and Cate growing a some-what colorless but comfortable relationship with only one part that niggled at Cate. This budding romance was infre-quently punctuated by bursts of jealousy on Michael's part. Cate maintained her close relationships with her girlfriends, especially since some would be going away to school. And it was true some of her harmless male friends still dropped in occasionally or saw her at Chippewa Lake Park's Kiddieland, where she still worked part time. She wasn't sure if he was more bothered by the relationship with the girls or the guy pals. Whatever it was it sent him into bouts of temper followed by silence. The silence was the worst and should have been an early red flag to Cate.

"Why do you care if I spend the night at Sue's house? Aren't you going out with the guys after the ball game?" A baffled Cate asked a stewing Michael.

"Because every time you go to Sue's, Gary, Fred, and Lord-knows-who show up. I don't like you around other guys."

"Okay," Cate sighed. She was not ready for another fight. She knew Michael was already starting to see them as a permanent couple someday. She knew several of his friends were already married and he was at that settling down age. This put Cate into a bit of a panic, with a sprinkling of excitement. Could she be Michael's wife one day and stay there in Franklin forever? It was all very confusing, but if she was giving up her girl's night out and her parents were out for the evening, she had a plan.

"Hey, my parents are out with the Jacobs tonight." Cate started to make her pitch when Michael cut her off.

"Oh, and I suppose Andrew is with them tonight, and they asked you to dinner as well. Is that where you're really going, Cate?" he exploded.

Cate actually laughed, which did little to stem the anger Michael was building up. "If I hooked up with Andrew it would be like incest. You know I've told you before, he's like the big brother I never had. Besides, he's even older than you!" she sputtered. It was true the Jacobs were her parents' best friends and they spent a lot of time together. Growing up, Andrew, like any real big brother, pulled her hair and teased her endlessly, but as they got older, they got closer. Cate felt she could always confide in Andrew, well, about most things anyway.

"As I started to say, with my parents out, want to come back to my room for a while?" Cate hoped she sounded sexy and enticing, but to her ears it was more Mae West.

A surprised Michael followed her to her pale blue room with gingham bedspread and curtains. They sat side by side on the bed. After a few deep kisses, Cate tried to get Michael to lie down beside her. His resistance began to irritate Cate. "Don't you want to do it?" she stammered.

The look of shock on Michael's face said it all as he jumped off the bed. "No, I don't want to do it, well, not now, not here, not like this. I hope we'll be married one day, and that should be soon enough, Cate."

Now thinking he'd made a fool out of himself, he fled the room, slamming doors as he went. Cate heard, not for the first time, his tires throwing limestone as he flew out of her driveway. Wait until they're married? Was he serious? Cate didn't know whether to laugh or cry. Was that a sort of proposal? What she couldn't deny was the warmth down below, and with one touch she knew the ecstasy of the warm explosion between her legs. What a night, a confused and disappointed Cate thought.

IV

Just before Cate was to start college, a group of friends went camping at Cumberland State Park. Most of the couples were Cate's high school buddies, including her best friend Sue. Michael knew them all well and fit right in. As soon as the tents were up the guys were off to fish and drink beer. This left the girls to set up for the night and chat about their futures.

"Todd and I plan on getting married right after college graduation, if I don't get pregnant first," Debbie giggled after a few glasses of Boone's Farm apple wine.

"You won't get pregnant unless you want to," scoffed Karen. "Jamie and I might get married next year, right after our freshman year."

"No way," all the girls shouted at once.

"Yep. We're thinking about it. My folks said Jamie and I could live with them until we finish college. We already talked about it with them."

Cate stared at her friend in a combination of disbelief and a touch of envy." Why the heck would you do something like that so soon? You guys are already doing it." Oops, thought Cate. Why did I say that?

Now the girls stared at her.

Ellen Gordon

"Just because you're a virgin, Cate, doesn't mean you can look down on us," spat Karen.

Cate's face flared. It's true; she was the only virgin on this camping trip, except Michael of course. What was wrong with the two of them? They'd never gotten beyond second base or whatever it's called when a guy touches you down there fully clothed!

Maybe it's time for Michael and I to have a serious talk about "doing it," Cate decided. The evening was ruined, as she still smarted over the discussion she'd had with her friends.

Tucked into their two-man sleeping bag in their tiny army tent, the pair lay on their backs side by side. Cate leant over the drowsy Michael for a good night kiss then let her hand slide tentatively down to his penis. Startled, Michael pushed her hand away. "Go to sleep, Cate. Big day tomorrow."

Cate took the rejection badly and flipped onto her side with her back to him without another word. Maybe she would just go off to college and find someone new, she thought angrily. It would take her almost a year before that flight of fantasy would come to fruition.

Michael feigned sleep but actually stayed awake most of that long night. He wanted Cate more than he ever wanted anyone or anything, but he knew in his heart that if he had sex with Cate now, she would never stay with him. Cate was too independent and spoiled. If only he could just keep this new relationship different from what all their friends had until she grew up a bit, he was sure they had a future together. He was using the excuse that they should wait until they were married, but he was pretty sure that wasn't going to fly with Cate for much longer.

If either Cate or Michael had more open, confident personalities, that night might have gone very differently. If Michael could just express his doubts and Cate could just say what she wanted, which was to at least discuss having sex, they may even have laughed about their innocence together. Unfortunately, neither had the confidence to share their doubts with the other. And typical of the pair, the next morning neither mentioned it to their friends, who assumed by their manner, that all was well between them.

Michael was at Cate's home the evening before she started her first week of classes. Both were a little tense, knowing that this would be a major change for them.

The summer had been busy for both, Michael focusing on his career and baseball with his buddies, and Cate working in Kiddieland, hanging out with her girlfriends, and horseback riding with her dad or her new friends Randall and Richard.

Yet the two were still considered an item and were together at least a few times every week. Mostly they spent time with Michael's friends, Rod and Jill, or with a group of Cate's high school friends.

"Cate, I know we just started dating this summer," Michael began.

"It was a really good summer, Michael," Cate interrupted, not sure where this was going.

"It's just I want to be sure that you're my girl and that you won't be looking for someone else at college," an embarrassed Michael exploded.

Michael had never said that she was his girl, although it was implied by their time together. It felt good to Cate. She felt a love that she hadn't felt before for him. She saw a future, back here in Franklin, surrounded by her friends and never being far from her beloved farm or her dad. She was now sure that was what Michael saw as well.

"I love you, Michael," she blurted without even thinking.

"Oh God, Cate, I love you too. I've been afraid to say it in case you didn't feel the same," an elated Michael declared. He grabbed her in a bear hug and swung her around. He felt so strong and sure of himself just then.

So he forced himself to smile at her as they kissed good night, but there was a lump in his throat at the thought of her starting a new part of her life that he may not be a part of. He knew her well enough to know that she had a lot of growing up to do, and he only hoped that he could be part of that process. She was such a daddy's girl, at times it seemed tough to compete. He feared if given a choice of a horseback ride with her dad or a date with him, he might just be on the losing end.

V

The first few months Cate was at college, things were fine with them. The two-hour commute back and forth to college four days a week and all the studying kept Cate pretty tied up until the weekend. So the pair settled into a routine making the most of their Saturdays and Sundays. Cate was excited about her new college girlfriends; they seemed so different from her high school friends. When she tried to explain to Michael why she enjoyed them so much, he listened and wondered what that meant exactly. Were these new friends better, more interesting, more worldly than Cate's friends here? But he said little, just listened. He too had plenty to share about his work, where he had already received a nice promotion. Between that and the start of his basketball fixtures, he was active during the week but lived for the weekends with her.

The first sign of a small rift brewing came when Cate was home for the Christmas break. They had both been looking forward to two weeks to spend together. Two days before Christmas Karen and Harold Jacobs were coming to Cate's parents for a holiday toast. To Cate's surprise Andrew showed up with them. Cate was delighted; she hadn't seen him since she started classes. Andrew had always been driven to be the best at all he attempted. He wasn't an athlete like Michael, but he was class president right through high school, followed by president of his fraternity. There was something very charismatic about Andrew that easily drew people to him, including Cate.

"Let's go to the Tavern and have a Christmas drink, Cate," Andrew declared as he stepped through the front door. "I want to hear about all your new girlfriends at college; maybe there will be one for me," he joked.

"Love to, but I'm not setting you up with any of my friends, you wolf," she countered.

As Andrew was helping her with her coat, Cate thought she wished Michael did that for her. Uh oh, she suddenly thought. Michael. They didn't have any set plans, but there was always a chance he would pop over after his basketball practice. Oh well, too late and Cate was looking forward to time with Andrew.

At the Tavern the two sat facing each other in a booth, both leaning in so they could be heard over the jukebox. Both were

Ellen Gordon

eager to share their news and excited for each other. Why was it so easy to talk with Andrew and tell him everything? Well, not everything. She probably wouldn't tell him that she's a virgin and that it bothered her.

Michael finished a tough basketball practice at the high school with Rod and a group of guys. Some he knew and some were new to the team. They were all headed to the Tavern to wind down, and Rodney was giving Michael a bad time. "Come on, guy, you are not going to let that little redhead keep you from a beer with the guys, are you?"

Actually, Michael would have preferred to go home, shower, and head to Cate's place, but saying no to Rod was not worth the effort. "One beer and I'm out of there," Michael conceded.

All eight guys clamored into the Tavern at one time and headed to the bar to order. Chad, one of the new guys, made a quick comment about the chick in a booth. All he could see was the perky face and the bright red hair of Cate. All seven turned to look at the center of his attention. There was an audible gasp from behind Chad.

Michael's face turned ashen as he saw Andrew nearly head to head with Cate. "What the hell, Cate?" He breathed out slowly. Before anyone dared to say a word, he turned on his heels and fled. He sat for several minutes in his car fighting rage and tears. How could he ever face his friends again if he had been so betrayed by Cate this way? And with Andrew of all people. She knew how he felt about him.

Call it jealousy if you will; he just knew Andrew liked Cate as more than a little sister, and tonight just showed it's true. How could he be such a fool?

Just then Rodney tapped on his window. Glad that it was dark, Michael reluctantly rolled down the window. "Hey, I talked with Cate. You know she's always been a family friend with Andrew. Sure, he's everything you're not—oh come on—I'm just kidding. Want to go get drunk at my house?" Rodney offered.

Andrew leaned even closer to Cate. "Let's get out of here before I'm lynched." He grabbed Cate's hand, and they flew out the side entrance. The pair couldn't help themselves as they burst into fits of giggles when safe in the car.

"Cate, you can't be serious about this guy," Andrew declared when the laughing had subsided. "Why didn't he just grab a beer and join us? Why would he be jealous of us?"

Cate wasn't sure how to take that last comment. Hadn't Andrew ever thought what it would be like if they dated, even just casually, once in a while? She liked being out with him tonight, but obviously he had never seen her in the same light. Cate sighed. Now she had probably blown it with Michael, and Andrew saw her as no more than his little sister.

Jolted out of her thoughts of Michael and Andrew, Cate realized they were not headed towards her home. Andrew had gone in the opposite direction and was grinning.

"Hey, Cate, it's still early and our parents will still be gabbing away. Let's go by your Aunt B's place—just to see how it's holding up."

Cate wasn't sure how to react. Sure, she still missed her aunt, especially last summer when she worked at Chippewa Lake Park again and knew Chartres was just a short walk away. How many times a few years ago had she left work to sit on Aunt B's porch and get her first introduction to a white

Russian? The strong concoction of vodka, Kahlua, and heavy cream went down too easily for a novice drinker. A nap often followed before heading home.

"Well?" asked an impatient Andrew.

"Yes, okay, it's just hard for me to believe she's gone sometimes and even harder to believe she took her life like that. I haven't been to Chartres since her death." Cate physically shuddered at the memory.

"Your Uncle Carl still lives there, you know. My buddy Alex sees him still driving around in that beat-up pickup truck. How could he still drive it after she died in it?" an insensitive Andrew wondered aloud.

Cate was silent. She knew Andrew had often been at Chartres with her parents and his folks. A seven-year-old Cate had been proud to show him the miniatures in the knickknack cabinets and the ebony elephants on the mantel while the adults enjoyed beverages on the porch.

Once, before Cate could stop him, Andrew raced up the steep stairs to the second floor. Cate was not keen on the second floor. There was the disappearing maid's room and the dorm-like room where Uncle Claude shot himself, both of which continued to haunt the nine-year-old. Yet to let Andrew think she was afraid was not an option at that age. She quietly told him all the stories that she knew, even about the closets full of old clothes, shoes, accessories, and props for presenting elaborate plays.

"I'm going to park at Alex's house, then we can walk over to Aunt B's and have look," Andrew declared as he was pulling into the driveway of someone Cate had never heard of before.

Cate felt like she was nine again and didn't want Andrew to know that she was afraid. Coming back to Chartres felt strange, maybe wrong. Aunt B wanted Cate's mom to have Chartres when she died and said so in her will. Unfortunately, Ohio marriage laws at the time sided with the husband. Cate's mom was given a small amount from the estate but not the house or the contents.

Andrew took hold of Cate's hand as they couldn't help but tiptoe down the long driveway. Before they even got to the house they had to pass the garage. Cate felt close to tears and tried hard to focus on the house. The two antique lamps that dangled precariously from the side of the house threw off enough dim light to show the neglect of Chartres. Two windows were missing and boards were in their place. The outside had not been painted in some time, so instead of its soft yellow, it was a patchwork of white bare spots.

Andrew pulled Cate around to the porch on the lake side of the house. She tried to pull away when they came to the oh-so-familiar red brick stairs, but Andrew held on. The two of them stood at a large, lead-framed window that looked into Cate's favorite room. She shut her eyes to squeeze back tears as she imagined Aunt B in the worn leather chair sitting silently through the evening with Carl.

"Andrew, you are crazy. The kitchen light is on; he's still up. Let's just go, please."

Reluctantly Andrew came away from the window. "I just love this house," he sighed.

A surprised Cate looked at him in the dim light. "You love this house? No, I love this house, Andrew. I spent so much time growing up here." Cate couldn't quite understand her sudden anger with him.

"Okay, okay, take it easy. I know you were close to your aunt; it's just I've always dreamed of owning a house as special as this one."

Cate took another look around. Since it was winter, the peacock chairs and all the wonderful summer pieces were carefully stored in the basement rooms. Or at least Cate hoped so. Then she thought of the ebony elephants on the mantel. Boldly she stepped back to the window, hoping for a peek at the exquisite elephant family. The mantel was empty.

As she gasped at the realization that they were gone, Andrew grabbed her around the waist and pushed her to the stairs. "Carl saw you, and he's coming. They say he's a mean son of a bitch now." Cate and Andrew ran all the way to the car.

Neither had much to say on the drive back to Cate's home. Both were lost in their own thoughts of Chartres and what was happening to it now. Cate had so hoped to see the elephants on the mantel.

As they went to the garage to greet their parents, who were just saying good night, Andrew held Cate back to whisper, "I think you're too good for Michael, Cate. Don't let him control you. If you ever need to talk just give me a call."

VI

Michael woke up slowly the next day with a pounding head and a sense of gloom and doom. Why did he ever let Rodney talk him into getting drunk? Hell, he wasn't even sure Cate was worth the drama anymore. Why not just cut his losses and get on with his life? Maybe she was better off with Andrew.

As the Sunday wore on and the pounding in his head slowed down slightly, Michael began to think a little more rationally. What if Cate didn't really have a thing going with Andrew? What if it's really just friendship as she always claimed? But why out at his favorite bar? The more questions he had about Cate, the fewer answers he had. Should he call her? Should he go over and do what?

He'd learned that yelling at Cate had no effect whatsoever. In the end he did nothing that day. There was a pick-up basketball game at the high school at 3:00 to take his mind off Cate.

VII

Christmas Eve arrived, and Cate and Michael had still not made up. Both too stubborn to call the other, yet neither wanting to spend Christmas apart. Cate had bought Michael a new leather wallet to replace the worn out, beat-up money holder he'd had since he was a teenager. And Michael was sure he found the most unusual elephant that Cate had ever seen. He'd been in a small antique store in Wooster, not sure what he was looking for to get her for Christmas, and there it was.

Around lunchtime Cate's dad asked if she wanted to brave the cold air and take a ride. Anything to get her mind off Michael sounded good to her. They both were bundled in thick coats and gloves, but while Cate had a toasty beanie pulled low over her ears, her dad was never without his cowboy Stetson, no matter how cold.

"Don't your ears freeze, Dad?" Cate insisted.

"Never," was the quiet reply.

Before they rode twenty feet, Cate burst out with, "Michael and I had a terrible fight because I was out with Andrew, and I don't know what to do."

Ken was silent for a few minutes, considering what Cate wanted him to do or say. Secretly he had enjoyed a couple days of Cate around the house instead of tied up with Michael. He knew that wasn't fair, but true.

"Do you think it's over? Do you want it to be over?" Ken finally asked.

"No, I think I love him, Dad,"

That was the end of the conversation about Michael. Yet Cate just felt better saying it out loud. I love Michael. I love Michael. That felt so good that Cate knew she would find a way to get him back.

After the horses were cooled down and the tack carefully put away, Cate kissed her dad a thank you and ran back to the house. She knew in two hours Michael would be at the high school gym with his buddies for one more practice before a big game the next week. With her pride swallowed, Cate called Jill to see if she was going to watch the practice and if she could go with her. Cate hoped for a little moral support when she showed up at the gym.

"Well finally, one of you two very stubborn creatures is making some sense. I'll pick you up just before the practice, but I bet I won't be taking you home," Jill predicted.

The guys were already racing up and down the gym floor when the girls arrived. As usual there was a lot of shouting and sweating and laughing amongst the guys. Rod actually saw Cate before Michael and couldn't resist an elbow into his friend's side. "Well, well, look who came to watch me practice today," he teased.

Michael stopped so fast when he saw her that three men plowed into him, almost knocking him over. When solid on his feet again, he gave Cate a weak wave and a weaker smile. *What the hell am I supposed to do now?* he wondered.

"Five minute break, guys," Rodney shouted.

They stared at each other for a few moments then started walking towards each other. Neither Cate nor Michael had much experience with breaking up and getting back together, so they rather awkwardly hugged. The pair was so aware of everyone staring at them, they were speechless until Cate whispered, "Will you take me home after practice?" Blushing, Michael gave her a gentle squeeze.

Michael woke on Christmas morning with a huge smile on his face. His parents were relieved to not have him moping around the house as he was the last couple days. They had a Christmas breakfast of pancakes, bacon, eggs, corned beef hash, and toast while they opened their presents.

As usual Michael's mom saw Christmas as an opportunity to bolster Michael's supply of boxers, socks, and T-shirts. The best surprise for Michael came from his dad. He took Michael out to the garage, where a ten-foot St. Croix fishing rod was hidden behind the cupboards.

"Dad, that's the best! Guess I won't be using it for a while, but, wow, that's going to catch some serious fish next summer," Michael exclaimed. He wasn't all that close with his dad, who wasn't much into sports like Michael, but he did love to fish. *Maybe this will bring us a little closer,* Michael thought.

Breakfast was barely finished before Michael kissed his mom, waved to his dad, and headed to Cate's. He had the beautiful elephant carefully wrapped in a box. He didn't want anything to happen to it before he got to see Cate's face when she opened it.

Cate and her parents had finished their gift sharing and breakfast when Michael arrived looking like a little boy with a big surprise. Ken and June greeted him amicably then faded into the family room to give them space by the twinkling tree in the living room.

As soon as Cate opened the box, her first thought was how could she have given Michael a wallet when he had given her something so absolutely amazing.

This magnificent specimen of an African elephant was over twelve inches tall and twelve inches from his proudly held trunk to his perfectly curled tail. Star, as he would be named shortly, was a swirl of green, yellow, red, and blue glass while the eye was drawn to his proud chest where a burst of clear glass appeared as a star. When Cate carefully held this intricately detailed glass wonder, she examined the perfect toes, four each on the front, and five each on the rear. Who but Cate would know to look for such detail? Star was heavy to hold, so Cate soon put him down to continue her admiration.

The trunk was stretched high above his head, and even the carving of his eyes showed strength and wisdom. When the time would come for Cate to leave America, Star would be one of the few elephants she couldn't bear to leave behind. During her many adventures Star's magnificent trunk would be snapped off more than once but always carefully repaired, and she only loved him more.

By the time Cate started classes again, the pair were madly in love again. Michael wasn't happy to be going back to the mostly just weekend time together, but he felt confident that time would fly and was sure that they would soon be making plans for their future.

Pax

I

While Cate and Michael were trying to kick-start their romance that first summer after high school graduation, Cate was equally occupied with her part-time work at Kiddieland in Chippewa Lake Park, hanging out with girlfriends, and getting in miles of horseback riding on Jack. Summer was a busy time for her father's veterinary practice, so Cate often found herself heading out into the cool Ohio mornings alone. Years before major highways made their tiny township a "sleeper" community for Cleveland or Akron, where commuters would enjoy the country living, the open fields belonged to Cate. With her fast and sometimes ornery quarter horse, Jack, she could ride for miles through unfenced land or around large farms without bothering anyone and often not even seeing another person.

One of Cate's favorite rides found her miles west of her farm. With the corn and wheat already taken in a month earlier, Cate urged Jack along a path on the edge of seemingly endless open fields. After nearly an hour enjoying the quiet and coolness of the early morning, Jack stopped abruptly. Cate wasn't paying attention and was deep in thought about a fight she had the day before with Michael. Jack stopped because a sturdy wire fence was in his way.

Cate laughed out loud and petted Jack's neck. "Well, Jack, where the heck are you taking us? We've never been here before."

The fence stretched all around a fifty-acre farm, Cate estimated. In the middle sat a small white farmhouse and a neatly painted red barn. It seemed strange to her that there were no crops growing; it was all open paddocks. When Cate spotted a small herd of ten paints, buckskins, and quarter horses, she was thrilled. Her dad would love to see these, Cate mused. She urged Jack into a canter around the outside of the fence to get a closer look.

Before she reached the horses she noticed two young men mending fences unenthusiastically, not far from where she was now walking Jack to let him cool down. Cate gave a tentative wave and was rewarded with enthusiastic waves from both boys. Cate watched as the boys hopped on a pair of lively paints and galloped towards her. She wasn't sure if she should stand still or race Jack back home.

When the boys pulled up their horses close to the fence that separated them, Cate gave a little gasp. "You're identical? How does anyone tell you apart?" Cate gushed. Until they were up close she had no idea that they were twins. Same wide mouths, now grinning, dark brown eyes with lashes so long they seemed unfair to Cate. They were dark-tanned, and the sun had streaked their unkempt hair. Cate was almost speechless with the look-a-likes, but she recovered in time to ask, "Want to ride with me? I usually go to a little creek back about a mile, but we got off track this morning. I like to give Jack a drink before I head home." Cate was babbling, and not sure why.

"Can't," piped up Randall, or was it Richard? "The folks don't let us leave the property—ever."

"What? That's crazy." Cate laughed, not believing that was possible. They were two strong, tall, and good-looking guys. How could they possibly be forced to stay on the farm? Cate stopped laughing abruptly when she realized the twins were not laughing with her.

It turned out to be true. The twins were raised by their father and stepmother, who had allowed them to attend school but nothing else. When school was out for the summer they were expected to work on the farm. They had no friends, joined no clubs, never played sports, or even attended any games. They had one year of high school to go and then according to them, they were expected to stay and work the farm. The father had great plans to begin planting corn and hay to support the horse farm, and the boys were expected to make that happen. Cate didn't know what to say to them, but she sensed that if they could figure out a way, they would not be working on this farm the rest of their parents' lives.

II

After several morning rides to the twins' farm, Jack was getting used to making stops at the gate of the horse farm. He would whinny as soon as he saw the twins headed his way, always on new horses for Jack to meet. Cate and the boys were eager to chat, Cate often giving them news that they were seldom allowed to hear. She shared movies she had seen and stories about her work in Kiddieland, but somehow never told them about Michael. That day as Cate was telling them in great detail and enthusiasm about a victory for the Cleveland Indians, the trio turned to see their stepmother coming towards them across the pasture. Cate froze where she sat on Jack and watched the tall, skinny, untidy woman march to where they waited.

"I'm Joan Harcourt. Would you like to come in for a lemonade with the boys?"

Cate was nervous and the boys were in shock. Cate wondered if she might be kidnapped or beaten up by the wicked stepmother. "Okay, thanks," Cate managed as she looked at the twins for support.

Yet neither happened. While the boys' dad and stepmother were not particularly friendly toward Cate, it occurred to Cate that they were a bit defensive about how the twins were treated and how they had kept them out of the world for so long. They explained several times why it was vital for the boys to learn not only how to run the farm but also how they can expand it in the future. The pair professed ill health and an inability to assist with many chores. They concluded their declaration of good intentions by saying that when the boys finished high school, they could make a fine living here on the farm. Cate was more than a little dubious of the parents' intentions, especially since the parents looked perfectly fit and healthy to her.

Having not been beaten up, Cate's old foot-in-mouth tendency got the better of her as she was about to leave. "I see how important running the farm would be, but do you think the twins could just ride with me once in a while? Not long, maybe half an hour?" she asked innocently as she prepared to rinse her glass in the sink before departing.

The stepmother scowled at Cate, but their dad rubbed his cheek and slowly agreed. "I guess the new quarter horse and the new paint could use a little extra training."

Probably out of disbelief that Cate had even asked, Richard and Randall did their best not to act surprised or thrilled. They just mumbled a, "Thanks, Dad," before running out the door, pushing Cate as they went.

"I can't believe that just happened," choked Richard. "We haven't been allowed off this goddamn farm in five years, except for school and the occasional trip with them to the store."

Cate wasn't sure she liked the language, but she was delighted with his enthusiasm. Not wasting a minute, in case their father changed his mind, the boys saddled their horses, and the trio rode off towards the creek that Cate had been heading to before the invitation for lemonade. They walked the horses until out of sight of the house and the path widened into a lane.

"Beat you to that big oak tree." Cate fairly squealed with the challenge and nudged Jack into a gallop before the boys knew what she was up to. With the head start Cate had no trouble winning, although Richard's quarter horse was literally at Jack's tail at the end.

All three were laughing with the adrenalin still pumping as they walked their mounts the rest of the way to the creek.

"No fair, you had a head start. My Banjo would have outrun your nag in a fair race," Richard said, still laughing in spite of himself. "Where did you learn to ride like that?"

"I've been riding since I was two. My dad and my mom are both excellent horsemen. Just like your family, we buy, train, and sell stock regularly. Not Jack, though, he's mine," Cate said patting the lathered neck of her horse.

III

As that summer before college flew by, the rides became a frequent part of Cate's hectic schedule. There was work, Michael, and rides with her dad as well as with the twins. It was tough to tell who enjoyed the rides together more—Cate, Richard, or Randall. Cate had gotten to know the twins pretty well and now could actually tell them apart. Richard had a small white scar on his right temple, a reminder of what a fall off a horse next to a fence pole can do to your head. And for some reason Randall's hair was always cut shorter. This seemed odd to Cate because their stepmother cut their hair the same day every month, but why one shorter? Cate laughed to herself, thinking maybe she had never learned to tell them apart so she just kept cutting Randall's shorter each month.

Richard was more outspoken and the one constantly asking Cate questions about her life, her family, her friends, and her plans for her future. Sometimes he grew so serious that Cate wondered what he was thinking and planning for himself. While Cate was falling in love with Michael, she had to admit that she had a little crush on Richard. He was a year younger than her, but it made little difference in their horseback riding relationship. They had a kind of teasing flirtation going on that Cate encouraged.

Ellen Gordon

Randall on the other hand was quiet, shy even. He seemed quite content to let Richard do the talking for the both of him. Cate knew what it was like to be shy around people she didn't know. So far in her life Cate had never mastered the art of small talk with strangers.

Having grown up with the same people all her life, it made Cate insular and comfortable. When forced into social circumstances with strangers, Cate could be totally tongue-tied. Or even worse than tongue-tied, she might blurt out any inane thing that popped into her head. But for some reason it was different with the twins. The trio had become instant friends.

When the trio was watering their horses one day, Cate was watching the two of them give each other a hard time about work that needed to be done by the end of the day. For most of their lives they pretty much only had each other. Not long after their rides started, Richard out of the blue shared that they could barely remember their real mom. When they were three she left the farm, their dad, and them without a goodbye. At the time the toddler twins were distressed, but they had no understanding of where the mom they loved had gone. They always expected her to come back until they were six, and Joan, the wicked stepmother, moved in.

Their dad took them into the rather messy kitchen the month before they were to start school, sat them on the stiff high chairs, and said with a stern look, "This is your new mother. She will live with us now, and you must do whatever she tells you, got it?"

The boys started school, and the pattern for their school years was set. Stay on the farm except for school. Get off the bus and start chores, even as six-year-olds. There was no Department of Children and Families to come knocking on the door to see if the boys were okay or to challenge this parenting style. They were fed, clothed, educated, and polite.

They were straight-A students without any parental support, and their teachers thought them exemplary students, just a bit withdrawn. Cate just couldn't get her head around what their life had been like all those years and what sort of people their parents were.

Cate was becoming obsessed with the twins. It all seemed so unfair that two bright young men could be virtual captives in their own home. This was the first of the social injustices that Cate would encounter and rebel against before long.

IV

Cate reflected on her perfect summer as August slipped away. She graduated from high school and was about to start a new life in college in only a few weeks. She had met Michael, and although they seemed to disagree on a lot of things, they were having fun with their friends, and she was pretty sure she was in love. Her part-time job in Kiddieland at Chippewa Lake Park was easy, and she loved the kids. So the twins and the rides were a bonus to a perfect summer.

Late in August Andrew and his parents were at the Kingston house for a cookout. As usual Andrew and Cate wandered off to the front steps to catch up. Andrew was still enthusiastic about his work at Highland Tractor sales, where he had worked right through college. Selling heavy construction equipment like excavators, bulldozers, or wheel loaders, whether to a large construction fleet or to a single machine contractor, was Andrew's kind of a challenge.

"You should see these machines, Cate. One day you need to come with me to the yard, and I'll show you how to operate an excavator. We have a test center next to the store so customers can actually try out a machine. When you're going to invest thousands of dollars, you want to get it right," Andrew practically crowed.

With his outgoing, easy personality, not to mention his good looks, Cate had no doubt that he would succeed at whatever he put his mind to. She really was interested in his new career and would take him up on the visit to the yard. Yet she could have no idea on this warm summer night in her parents' home just how incredibly successful he would one day be.

Once Andrew wound down on his favorite subject he looked closely at Cate. "You look very content and, I don't know, different. What have you been up to all summer, missy?"

Cate was not about to talk about Michael, although she was sure their moms had kept each informed on the children's adventures. It still stung how Andrew had made it clear that she could do better than Michael. Instead she told Andrew about Richard and Randall. Once she started talking, even she had not realized how important the twins had become in her life, largely because she just could not believe that they never had any opportunities. While that made her incredibly grateful for all she had and her wonderful parents, it just seemed unfair.

Andrew listened, absolutely intrigued by the story about the twins that Cate was telling him. Like Cate, he couldn't understand how it was possible, except with chains, to keep two healthy young men isolated for so many years. Although he had taken enough psych in college to know that young minds can be molded to believe almost anything over time, this did not seem real.

"What the hell are they going to do when they graduate next June?" a still incredulous Andrew asked.

"Work on the farm, I guess. What choice do they have? They have no money, no plan, and at least Randall is convinced that that will be his future. I do think that Richard is trying very hard to imagine a way out of the farm life. He hasn't said it out loud, but he often goes quiet when I'm talking about college."

"No, no, no, that's not good enough. Come on, Cate, what's wrong with you? There are many choices for the boys, if they'll just go for it. We can get them off that farm, Cate." Andrew's enthusiasm was contagious, and soon the two were throwing out options for their future. They were so caught up in options to free the twins, Cate's dad had to come get them to join the others for dinner.

The conspiring pair started at the beginning and shared their ideas with their amused parents. Sure, it sounded like a true fairy tale, but was it at all realistic, and would the boys really want to leave? It may be a sick environment, but that is all they've ever known. Yet the parents soon were caught up in the newly formulated campaign for "freeing the twins."

V

A full year had passed since the first inkling of a plan to free the twins germinated at the Kingstons' backyard barbecue. The first challenge was to just get them off the farm for short periods of time, and it was Ken, Cate's dad, who made the first move. Ken went to the farm to meet their dad, John Harcourt, with an idea that they all knew had to work if they were to go any further.

"Mr. Harcourt, nice to meet you. My daughter, Cate, has enjoyed rides with your sons this summer. They sound like good lads, and that got me thinking. While you have two strong sons, I have one slightly spoiled daughter. I have a vet practice that keeps me busy, but so does our farm. If I could get your sons, say on Saturdays, to help muck stalls, feed stock, that would be a great help. I'll pay them, of course," finished a slightly breathless Ken.

With little hesitation came, "How much will you pay? How will they get back and forth? And I need your word that they will go nowhere else but your farm, Mr. Kingston."

A very relieved and surprised Ken drove home over the speed limit to tell Cate. Cate in turn was on to the phone to Andrew. "Plan A is working. Dad did it; the guys can come work for Dad on Saturdays," a thrilled Cate reported.

So as Cate began her freshman year at Union State College, she would sometimes see Richard and Randall at her farm, cheerfully helping her dad and enjoying the freedom, even for a few hours. Cate and Andrew, with the help of Cate's mom, had begun to gather information about alternatives for the boys, if they could get them away from their parents permanently. Cate loved this time conspiring with Andrew and felt like they had never been closer. Yet no one was yet game to introduce the idea of running away to the twins as the planning continued.

When Ken dropped the boys back one day, Mr. Harcourt stated that he was going to need the boys back there on Saturdays going forward, that they had their own work to do. Ken could see the stepmother standing just behind her husband with her hands on her hips. Ken realized that it was her who was demanding this change, that she was thinking they were losing control of the boys.

"Well, it's your decision, of course, but I was just telling the boys that early spring we will need to do the sowing, and I thought they told me that you hoped that they could start crops at your place next year. I can teach them all I know and provide some seed for you when you're ready." The quick-thinking Ken dangled the carrot.

Once again, the "what's in it for me" won Mr. Harcourt over. "That would be a good thing for them to learn. Okay, they can keep helping you, and if you need them more let me know. School is no good to them, and this is their last year, so let us know." The father agreed. Ken watched as the stepmother stomped back into the house. She lost that round, but Ken was sure she wasn't finished trying to assure the future of the boys on the farm.

By now Andrew and Cate, with approval from her parents, decided that the best option for Richard and Randall would be the army. They had been to a recruiting office in nearby Akron to get all the information they needed for the twins to read. The recruiter explained that after they turned eighteen, had a high school diploma, and were physically and mentally fit, they could join the army immediately. With the very real threat of the Vietnam War looming, recruits were critical.

With six months until the twins turned eighteen, all agreed that Cate should be the one to brave the conversation with Richard and Randall. She found them throwing down hay in her family barn one Saturday morning. She had thought and thought about where to begin and then did a "Cate" and said, "What do you think of the idea of you running away from home and joining the army after you graduate from high school in June?"

Richard stood completely still for no more than ten seconds before charging Cate, scooping her up like the hay bale he had just tossed, and squeezing her. Cate turned her head to see that Randall had collapsed in a heap on the bale he was about to pick up. He looked a funny color, Cate thought worriedly. It took some time for Randall to agree to this daring plan, but following Richard is what he had always done and would again shortly.

VI

When Richard and Randall turned eighteen in May 1969 and graduated from high school in June, the plan that started as just an idea back at the Kingston's barbecue came to fruition. On the day they ran away, Cate's dad picked them up as usual at 7:30 a.m., like they were going to the Kingston farm to bale hay. They each had their usual small duffel bag with a change of clothes, as they always showered before returning home after a day on the Kingston farm.

Not once did either Richard or Randall look back as they drove down the long lane to their freedom. Ken could only imagine what was going through the twins' heads.

They spent that day and that night with the Kingstons. Andrew stopped by on his way to work to congratulate the twins and wish them luck. The Kingstons had organized suitcases for each of them that held everything from the sheet the recruiter had given them. It listed everything required to show up at basic training. With Andrew waving from the driveway, Cate and her parents drove them to the train station in Cleveland. Cate hugged them tightly and for some reason was reluctant to let go. Would they be okay on their own when their world had been so small?

That next evening the twins' father called demanding to know where the boys were and when they were coming home. Cate's mom answered with a perfectly straight face, "I think they've run away."

Cate called Andrew right away that day, full of congratulations for themselves and their mission. It had been great fun working out the details and pulling off the escape with Andrew. Of course, she couldn't tell Michael what she had been up to; he was not a fan of Andrew or of her riding friends. Cate had to admit that now that they were successfully launched, she would miss the time spent organizing the plan with Andrew. They had always been close, but this was different, more grown up and exciting. Not for the first time Cate wondered what it would be like to date Andrew. He had a busy social life, yet he never seemed to have a steady girl.

Ellen Gordon

VII

Richard and Randall stayed in touch through basic training at Fort Dix in New Jersey before they moved on to advanced training at Fort Polk in Louisiana. They came back only once more to the Kingston farm in April 1970. Cate was so excited for the visit and was in the family barn when they arrived. They had already agreed that a ride would be first on the agenda.

Cate had a new horse, Bella, cross tied for grooming when she turned to see Richard and Randall standing in the large barn doorway with those familiar grins on their faces. She felt herself inhale in surprise. They had gone away boys who she adored, but they came back men.

"Oh my gosh, you guys are gorgeous," Cate couldn't help but call out, then laugh at her own reaction.

"Weren't we always?" countered Richard with an even wider grin.

Cate hugged them each tightly, then stood back a little embarrassed and at a loss for words.

"Are we going to ride or what?" Randall recovered first.

The trio saddled up Jack, Bella, and Sparky. Sparky was meant to be trained and sold, but the family had fallen in love with him. The trio headed through the woods at the back of Cate's farm. It was so good to be with them, but all three of them had changed since the twins ran away. Richard and Randall were trained soldiers and nearly grown men now. They were willing to tell Cate about their training and people they had met, but the one subject on all three's minds remained taboo. Vietnam was the black cloud, but the three were determined not to let it ruin their reunion.

As for Cate, she was over halfway through her second year of college, and she had changed also. While still officially Michael's girl to her family and hometown friends, the time spent at college had opened her eyes to the world, and as scary as it was, she wanted to be a part of it. She had been to several impromptu gatherings on campus where anti-war students gave predictions of the devastation in Vietnam and America's growing involvement.

That night Ken and June made the boys welcome for as long as they could stay. June had a few rare days off and prepared a huge turkey dinner to make up for any holidays they had missed. Piles of mashed potatoes, squash, cranberries, corn, turkey, and stuffing welcomed the boys back. Just as the homemade cherry pie and ice cream was being served, Andrew appeared.

"Look at you guys. I think the army fed you well." Andrew laughed as he warmly shook their hands.

It was a good evening, and Cate once again felt close to Richard and Randall. After a boisterous game of Monopoly, with Andrew the winner, of course, everyone was reluctant to say good night around midnight.

In the morning the boys seemed eager to head back to the base. Everyone seemed strangely quiet, but Cate volunteered to get them to the bus station. As they gathered their gear, ready to head to the bus, all Cate wanted to do was hug them and keep them safe. She made them promise that there would be a lot more rides together. The twins just chuckled, always amused by Cate's enthusiasm, but silently they hoped that more rides would happen.

VIII

May 4, Cate was in English class at Union State College when a student ran down the hall screaming. It took her class a moment to catch his words as he continued past their door, but when it became clear what was shouted, all were stunned into silence. Cate felt tears roll down her face, but she didn't bother to brush them away. After a brief silence, pandemonium broke out. "Go," choked Professor Green, unable to control his voice.

Nearly every student in that room knew someone who attended Kent State University. The campuses were only seventy miles apart, and the two shared many activities. The news that four students had lost their lives at the hands of the Ohio National Guard did not seem real or possible. Cate and her classmates poured out of the classroom and onto the open campus, where the whole university seemed to be huddled in disbelief.

Since December 1 last year, when the Selective Services held their first draft lottery for 1970, there had been unrest on campuses across the country. The Vietnam War effort was unpopular to say the least, and to think that now their young men could be forced into the army was tearing the country apart.

Cate had listened wide-eyed as someone she knew explained the draft to a small group of protesters on campus one beautiful spring morning. "If your birthday was September 14, you were the number one pick for the draft in the nation. From there, your draft status was determined by your initials. It was bad luck if you were born September 14 and your parents named you Alexander Anderson," he explained.

So Kent State was not so very different than most campuses holding mostly peaceful demonstrations and rallies against the draft and the war. But when President Nixon announced the Cambodian Campaign in a televised speech on April 30, after he had let the nation believe there might be an end to the war in sight, more serious protests erupted. Some said outside agitators had come to the Kent campus to stir the students into more violent protests, though that was never proven. It was reported that in the village of Kent itself there was some violence, causing bars to close early a few days before the 4th.

A planned May 1 rally got out of hand, and after the ROTC building was burned to the ground, the governor, James Rhodes, called in the National Guard. All further rallies were banned. Yet on that black day in Ohio history the word had spread that there would be a rally in spite of the government order.

At the time of the confrontation there were about 3,000 people on the Kent State Commons. Only about 500 were hardcore protestors, supported by about 1,000 "cheerleaders." Keeping their distance, 1,500 spectators watched the events unfold. Only about 100 National Guard members were standing their ground when it happened. Was it fear of the large group of students that prompted the 61–67 gunshots that exploded into the crowd of students in just 13 seconds?

Cate and her three best buddies, Lynn, Barb, and Patty, sat in silent protest with most of the numb students in front of the administration building on the Union State campus. Soon that building would be taken hostage by the protesting crowd demanding answers for the killings. Many Kent students forced to leave the campus joined ranks to sit, cry, and protest with Union State. Bursts of yelling and blaming were followed by bouts of tears, fears, and disbelief.

The more Cate got caught up in the anti-war movement, the more she thought about the twins. She was so afraid for them, and yet she was so proud of them. She may not have supported the war, but she supported those fighting it. She was relieved that the men she cared about were not drafted in the first round. Michael simply missed because of his birthday, and David had a kidney issue that made him exempt. Andrew, with his folks' support, hired an attorney to plead his case for exemption on an old injury to his leg. While Cate was glad he didn't have to go, somehow it didn't feel right that a healthy man with the financial means could find a draft dodge so easily.

A letter from the twins came in June, just a month after the Kent shootings. It was brief and it terrified Cate. They were headed to Vietnam. They had both trained on the M60 machine gun and were to be helicopter gunners. Later Cate would question the wisdom of the army letting twins be machine gunners in the same helicopter, one of the deadliest jobs in the war. Yet she knew that Richard and Randall would have asked to be together, no matter the danger.

Cate and her dad were trying out two new Tennessee walkers that Ken had just purchased. Their unusual gait and high spirits were a challenge to both. After an hour the pair started to settle down, and Cate pulled up next to her dad.

"You were in the army, Dad. What was it like? I just can't imagine what Richard and Randall are going through."

"It was different for me. Because of my crushed shoulder I couldn't fight in World War II, but I told you, I was assigned to administration work in Macon, Georgia, for two years before the war ended. I did feel guilty that I was safe and so many of our troops died in that war, but I had no choice."

"I'm glad you didn't have to fight. Just think, if something happened to you then, you wouldn't have met Mom in the hospital and gone home to marry her, right?"

As father and daughter were cooling down the horses after a two-hour ride, Cate was still thinking about war, Richard and Randall, and her dad and his desk job.

"Do you think this Vietnam War, if you call it a war, is right, Dad? I'm so confused. When I'm with friends on campus who are vehemently opposed to the war, some even willing to go to jail or Canada rather than face the draft, then I think we have no business being there. Then I think of Richard and Randall risking their lives every day for us, and I feel like a traitor when I listen to the protestors."

Ken sighed and looked over his horse's back at Cate. When did she get so grown up and serious, taking on the problems of the world? Where was his tomboy tagging along with him everywhere he went? What advice could he possibly give her when he couldn't understand this war any more than she could?

"All I know, Cate, is that we are in it, and we can't let our troops, like Richard and Randall, think they are fighting for nothing," was all Ken could muster for his worried daughter.

IX

A tiny package arrived for Cate in December 1970. When she saw it was from Vietnam she was at once thrilled and terrified. The twins must have been okay if they're sending her something. And if it was bad news, it wouldn't come in a little box, right? Trembling hands opened the precious package to unveil a tiny ivory elephant with pinprick sad black eyes.

Hoping there would be peace soon and the war would end, she named this tiny piece of joy Pax. There was a very short note in the box from the twins. "Okay so far, on R&R for two more days. Hope to be stateside in two months if all goes well."

Cate put the miniature African elephant on her nightstand by her bed. Every night she would say a little prayer to keep the twins safe. She told the little pachyderm that she planned on lots more rides with Randall and Richard when they were home. She had written them several times inviting them to stay with her family when they had leave after Vietnam. She could only hope that her prayers would keep them safe.

White Cloud

I

For the small-town girl, Cate's college freshman year was a true eye opener. The freedom of campus life where no one knew her felt both strange and exciting. Going to classes the first week without knowing a single person was surreal to Cate. She had known every person in her classes from grade 1 to 12, keeping her in her comfort zone all the way through graduation. So, when she stepped into freshman English for the first time, she couldn't believe there were a few hundred unfamiliar faces scattered around the theater-like classroom. Cate sat in the very back row and watched eager faces interacting with each other. How was she ever going to meet anyone?

After three weeks of classes and not a single interaction with another person, Cate began to think she made a mistake coming here. If she had gone to the community college near Franklin, she would be with most of her high school friends, and she would see a lot more of Michael. So just as this thought was getting her down while she was waiting for her anatomy class to start, Cate was suddenly surrounded by a trio of fellow phys. ed. majors Cate had seen in her Fundamentals of Health class.

"We know you—you're one of us," announced a tall attractive blonde peering down at Cate. "How come you never introduced yourself?"

Cate swallowed then looked at the blonde and her two companions. "I'm Cate."

"Good to know. I'm Barb, this is Lynn, and this spitfire is Patty. Good to meet you, Cate."

"Hey, we're off to the Chuckery after this class; come and tell us all about Cate," insisted the other tall blonde.

Cate just smiled at them, but it felt so good to be asked. Heck, it just felt good to have someone talk to her. From that day on it felt like Cate was adopted by the trio and she never quite knew why, although she suspected that she must have looked totally lost those first few weeks, and they were rescuing her.

The four girls never ran out of topics to explore, debate, or explain as soon as they got together. The discussions were often serious and heated one minute and silly and imaginary the next minute. This was all new to Cate. They debated the most effective contraceptives, right along with what Patty would do if Bobby had to go to war. Sometimes Cate felt she could hardly keep up with her new friends.

The conversations with her Franklin girlfriends usually concerned what was going on in their community. It was more like gossip about people they knew rather than what was going on in the world. While Cate sometimes missed the comfortable routine that she shared with friends she'd known all her life, she felt so much more grown up and sophisticated with her college crew.

II

"Who the hell decided that to be a phys. ed. teacher you had to memorize every stupid bone in the human body?" exploded the fiery Italian classmate, Patty, to Cate in their anatomy class. Patty was loud and brash and confident and not to be messed with. She came from the Cleveland area but was living in a dorm on campus. Her boyfriend of many years, Bobby, was also a phys. ed. major. Cate had never learned the fine art of effectively using curse words, but Patty was the queen of them. Red-haired Cate and curly black-haired Patty were only similar in their diminutive size. Neither would reach 5'5" in combat boots.

Patty, Lynn, and Barb were naturals for becoming physical education teachers. Lynn and Barb were excellent basketball players, and Patty was lethal on the hockey field.

Cate, on the other hand, had been a bench warmer on the high school basketball team, was a cheerleader for only one season because she couldn't do a decent cartwheel, and ducked when the volleyball came at her. After a particularly rough basketball class Cate limped back to her car to head home, again questioning her own insanity for choosing phys. ed.

III

Before Cate even got to high school her mom, June, started planning her future career. "Be a teacher, Cate. That way you'll have your summers with your kids. I never had that privilege with you. That's why you always tagged along with your dad," June said wistfully as the two of them looked at college brochures.

Cate's mom had chosen nursing as her career, which had kept her in a stressful, hectic work environment at the local Franklin hospital. She wanted Cate to choose a career with more freedom. Cate knew that her mom, even after all these years, only had a few weeks of vacation each year. She also knew there was some resentment about the closeness of father and daughter, the result of all their time together as Cate grew up. Eventually Cate just came to accept that teaching would be her focus. She really had no other passion to pursue, and it felt good to see her mom satisfied with the decision.

"Is teaching what you really want to do?" Cate's dad asked one day when they were out riding. Secretly he had hoped that she would follow in his footsteps and be a veterinarian. He knew how much she loved animals, especially the horses. He daydreamed of her taking over his practice one day.

"I guess so, Dad. It does make sense. If I do get married someday, it would be nice to have my summers off." Cate decided she sounded just like her mother now. The hardest part of this teacher business was deciding what kind of a teacher to be.

"What I can't see, Pops, is me teaching a high school English class or a first-grade class full of rug rats."

Not long after that talk with her dad, Cate finally decided what kind of teacher she wanted to be. She may not be a "jock," but she did not want to be cooped up in a stuffy classroom with the same children every day. At least with physical education she could spend time in a gym, a pool, or better yet outside. Of course, that meant she had to actually pass the physical components of the program. Becoming a phys. ed. teacher, even with her new friends for support, was not always easy. Field hockey classes caused serious black and blue legs. Diving off the pool's highest platform was not an option for someone terrified of heights, which Cate was. That refusal dropped her swimming course to a C and made that instructor furious. Yet her high marks in the academic classes balanced out the challenges of the physical.

IV

"Lesbians are just fine with me unless they try to come onto me. I've had a couple give me 'that look' a few times in the locker room but no big deal." Barb laughed at the wide-eyed expression on Cate's face.

To Cate's knowledge there were no lesbians in Franklin, and if there were, they certainly would not come out of their closet. Cate had classes with some very butch young women. Campus life had begun to give Cate what she craved—a look at a world bigger and more diverse than Franklin.

The more she learned and grew, the more she realized how insular her world had been the past eighteen years. Right now

Ellen Gordon

she was content to hold on to her old world, including Michael, but who would have thought she would get to know lesbians!

Cate wanted to talk about everything with her new friends. Barb and Lynn were from Akron and were rooming together in an apartment off the Union State campus. Cate wasn't sure that was legal for freshmen, but they seemed to get away with it. The pair had been best friends since elementary school and practically finished each other's sentences.

Cate knew that all three—Barb, Lynn, and Patty—thought she was naïve. Why on earth did they want to be friends with such a country bumpkin? Plus, Barb and Lynn had each other, and Patty had Bobby. Why were they always so nice to her and so much fun to be around? Sometimes they all got in trouble for laughing out loud in class, just like they were back in high school, and other times there were serious talks about politics and war. Cate loved her time with them and sometimes wished she didn't have to head home every day after classes finished. Especially tough was saying hooray for the weekends. When they reconnected on Mondays Cate never seemed to have anything exciting to tell about her weekends with Michael. At least not compared to the stories from Barb and Lynn about their romantic and ever-changing encounters with the opposite sex.

Before Cate started spending time with the trio she had never really compared herself to others. Now with Lynn and Barb both various shades of blonde and both built like athletes, tall and solid, she sometimes felt like their little sister. They always seemed at ease with themselves and comfortable wherever they were and whatever they were doing. Cate was convinced that she would never be that sure of herself and often shrank back and away from new situations. Barb and Lynn couldn't help but notice this hesitation to join in on Cate's part and seemed determined to get her out of her shell.

Growing up with the same kids since she was little, she got a sense of security within the group. Was she the prettiest—no, that was Marcie. Was she the sexiest—no, that was Wanda. Was she the smartest—no, that was Barbara. But she was Cate and people, especially her good girlfriends and now Michael, liked her just fine. So why was she scrutinizing herself now? Why did she want to be someone else?

Cate found herself wondering what it would be like to be Patty, with a steady boyfriend, a tough exterior over a heart of gold, and a future all planned. She was funny, good at sports, and tomboy pretty with her dark eyes and black curls. Cate decided that Patty was a lucky girl.

Or what if she were like Barb and Lynn, tall, fit, a bit crazy, and all-American-girl pretty? Cate just couldn't figure out exactly who she wanted to be or what she wanted to look like, but the restlessness and the longing for change were beginning to wear on her.

One evening out of the blue Michael said, "You really are very cute, Cate, do you know that?"

Since Michael was not given to compliments on a regular basis, Cate was quiet for a moment. "Do you really think so?" was all she could think to say. He only smiled at her. Well cute was okay, but maybe she'd try some make up and let her bright red mane grow longer and straight like so many on campus, including Barb and Lynn, were doing.

V

So, with summer break only weeks away Cate was still Michael's girl. And even if things weren't great with them, neither knew how to fix it or how to break up. After a challenging but interesting first year of college, Cate did look forward to a lazy summer working part time in Kiddieland at Chippewa Lake Park, getting closer to Michael, and catching up with her high school friends again.

There would be some serious horseback riding with her dad, of course, but it made her sad to think of Richard and Randall and the long rides they had together last summer. It was still so hard to believe that they were headed to the army.

Lately Michael was talking about their future together as if it was sort of a given. Cate listened to him and tried to get caught up in this future he described. But Cate was starting to feel a tiny tug between her life with Michael and their old friends and the people and the lifestyles she was experiencing on campus. This tug was no more than a blip on the path to Michael and Cate's future until one single night turned the blip into a cliff drop for Cate.

Barb had spent most of the last weeks of college before summer vacation trying to get Cate to go out with the girls. The Three Musketeers—as Cate liked to think of Lynn, Barb, and Patty—had a favorite little bar, Wildwood, not far from campus, and Barb was determined that she would get their country bumpkin to join them at least once. Her freshman year was almost over, and although Cate felt she had grown up a great deal, that little ache for a big adventure wouldn't go away. More than once she wondered if she didn't have Michael would she have had that adventure her freshman year?

"Please, please, please," Barb effused, "say you'll come out Thursday night, stay with Lynn and me, and we can go to biology together in the morning. "

Cate had never accepted their invitations. There was the two-hour drive home and there was Michael. It seemed to her that he was keeping her on the straight and narrow, and ever more narrow, as time went on.

"Lynn and Patty are tied up until later with a study group, and I can't go to Wildwood alone. Please, please, please come with me. You'll love it there!" Barb continued to badger.

Cate had to laugh at Barb's enthusiasm. "Oh, great, you'll hang out with your new love, Joey, and I'll do what exactly?"

Barb totally ignored her and went on planning their adventure. "Bring your gear on Thursday morning, then we can go to Skyway for burgers before we hit Wildwood."

Now all Cate could think about was what she would tell Michael. She could lie and say they were going to study for the anatomy final, which was probably a better idea than Wildwood, or she could just tell him she was going out with the girls for a night. Oh boy. She could only imagine that fight. Yet here was her best new buddy asking her to go out, have some fun, and spend the night. What harm can there be in that?

"Okay, but you promise not to leave me standing in a corner by myself while you cuddle with Joey?" She knew Barb was far from being a virgin, which made Cate a little envious. Her own total inexperience was wearing a little thin. Michael was still holding back, still saying waiting for marriage was what he wanted. Secretly she wondered if this was his ploy to get her

Ellen Gordon

to marry him sooner rather than later. She had gone on the pill two months ago, hopeful that Michael might lose control one time and she would be ready.

Driving home from campus that Tuesday after English, she was both excited and apprehensive. She was seeing Michael for dinner and planned to tell him about Thursday night. She also knew to anticipate an explosion. That crazy, jealous temper. *As if he's ever had any reason to doubt me,* she thought, *I must be the most boring, loyal girlfriend on my campus.*

Michael picked her up promptly at 7:00, as always coming in to say hello to her mom and dad, who were just about to sit down to their dinner. "I won't keep her out late," Michael assured a somewhat amused Ken as he followed them to the door.

"Just be safe and have fun," Ken called after the pair.

Ken looked at June with raised eyebrows. He knew Cate well enough to know something was up. She even forgot his good night kiss on the way out.

VI

Dinner was at one of their favorite places, Norton Gardens, where fried chicken, mashed potatoes, a side of seasoned rice, and coleslaw were what they ate every time. Always crowded, they managed to squeeze into one of the small wooden tables. The red-and-white checked tablecloth and napkins had been a part of the country-style décor since they opened twenty years before.

While they waited for their food over a couple Budweisers, Cate debated how to broach the subject of girl's night out. Her stomach was so churned up she couldn't enjoy the meal like she usually did. She finally decided it would be better to discuss it when they were alone in the car on the way home rather than start a disagreement in the restaurant.

"I'm going to spend the night at Barb's place Thursday night and go straight to biology class Friday morning," Cate blurted out in one breath half way between Norton and Franklin.

"Why? Why would you do that? Don't you play euchre with Sue and the girls every Thursday night?"

A prickle started up the back of Cate's neck. One, she was so sick of the Thursday night euchre game where they gossiped the same small-town gossip week after week. Cate had stopped going months before. And two, why did she have to explain everything she did to him? The next words tumbled out of her mouth before she could think any better.

"Barb wants me to go to a bar with her, and some of the other girls are joining us later. She's been asking me to go out with them for some time—so I'm going."

"The hell you are, Cate."

The anger in his voice silenced her. They rode in cold quiet until they pulled up at her home. Cate prepared to jump out—only wanting to be away from him and his anger.

"Stop. Wait. I'm sorry I spoke like that. It's just that you can't just say 'hey, Michael, I'm going to start going to bars with my new friends' and not expect me to lose it. What's this all about, Cate?"

Cate sighed. "Nothing. I just really like Barb and Lynn and Patty. I like being with them. They talk about all sorts of interesting stuff. I'm just bored with the same ol' stuff here in Franklin."

That put Cate's foot firmly back in her mouth, and she knew it.

"Just get out of the car. Have fun with your new friends. I'm quite happy with our boring old stuff."

The car door was barely shut before Michael reversed fast, spraying the small limestone rocks of Cate's drive in all directions.

"Whoa, what was that all about? Not sure I want Michael or anyone tearing up our driveway. Another tiff, Cate?" Cate's dad inquired with a frown.

Once again Cate wondered what her dad really thought about Michael and her as a couple. Did he assume they would find their way through this stormy relationship and get to the altar one day? Or did her dad know Cate better than she knew herself? She looked carefully at her dad. While neither of her parents was very demonstrative to each other or to her, the pair had been married a long time. She'd never heard them raise their voices at each other. They must love each other, right? Cate wondered.

"Oh, Michael's mad because I'm spending the night with girls I've met at college. We're going out with a group of friends," Cate exaggerated.

"Good for you, kiddo," was all he said before going back to his nightly ritual of reading the Cleveland Plain Dealer cover to cover.

Cate didn't hear from Michael and she was glad. Let him stew for a few days. Thursday, she headed to afternoon gymnastics class before meeting Barb. She had butterflies as she flew along 224 toward campus. She didn't know if they were from excitement or fear.

To pass gymnastics she had to do a routine on two pieces of equipment. Cate was fairly confident that her routine on the trampoline would get her a solid mark, but the parallel bars were a bit riskier. Her routine was simple—swing legs up, lean into it—legs back—swing up and repeat before performing a turn—same routine back and dismount. Even in practice her arms would shake with exertion, and the insides of her thighs were black and blue. She landed with an unladylike thud, and while the instructor was not overwhelmed by her performance, she did give her a pass.

The torture was over and a lighthearted but nervous Cate went to meet her friends in the Chuckery, the favorite campus hangout. They all teased her about her first night out, but Cate took it with good humor. If only they knew about the hundred butterflies that were definitely taking over.

"Wow, where did you get that cool outfit?" Barb exclaimed.

Cate was proud that she finally got up the courage to get a mini skirt. The skirt and the army style jacket to match were khaki green. With a simple white T-shirt and white knee socks, it made quite a statement. She was as ready as she would ever be to show up at a bar with her friend.

You had to be eighteen to drink 3.2% beer and twenty-one to drink anything heavier. It was no surprise to Cate that nineteen-year-old Barb had a fake ID and could drink what she wanted to.

Many college kids had fake IDs, especially to show they were eighteen and could get into bars. Not Cate. When she showed her Ohio driver's license to the guy at the door, he smiled. "Oh my—an honest kid. Welcome," he said as he stamped her hand.

As they moved through the little bar, Cate looked back over her shoulder to see the door guy still watching her. Seeing who Cate was looking at, Barb explained, "That's George. He owns this bar—well his parents do, but George and his brother Louie mostly run it now. Ha, he's still watching you. Be careful, he's a fast one."

They were lucky to find two seats at the far end of the bar. Joey wasn't there yet and Cate was relieved. She felt so strange here as the bar filled up and the music got louder from the jukebox. Three Dog Night blared "Mama Told Me Not to Come." Cate thought that a bit ironic! Barb in the meantime had started up a conversation with the dreamy-looking guy next to her. "Love the one you're with," sighed Cate.

Honestly, she didn't mind sitting there, safe at the corner of the bar. It was new to just be sipping on Buds and watching people. All new people. Long hair was now in for men, and Cate observed the good, the bad, and the just plain ugly on a variety of heads. She chuckled to herself trying to imagine Michael growing his shiny black hair down to his shoulders. Never.

After some time and three Budweisers, Cate became fascinated with one guy who seemed to move easily amongst the now very crowded bar. She turned to ask Barb if she knew who he was, but now Barb was leaning in close to her new-found friend. When she turned back the stranger was leaning against the back wall and talking rapidly to a group seated at the table below him.

Cate couldn't get over what he was wearing. Brown suede coveralls over a bright orange T-shirt that hung on his skinny, well over six-foot frame. His long, perfectly straight naturally blond hair didn't look exactly well shampooed. Since he never seemed to look her way, Cate continued to blatantly stare at this bizarre human being.

Barb tapped her on the shoulder, and she turned in her seat to face her. "Are you okay? Sorry, but Chad and I are just hitting it off!"

Cate smiled at her liberated friend. "I'm just fine—have fun."

When Cate turned back in her seat, she found the strange man in coveralls standing right beside her. She gave a tiny gasp at his nearness.

"Do you know me?"

Cate stared into the most unusual eyes that she had ever seen. They were steel gray with bright yellow flecks. They reminded her of some of their barn cat's eyes, but she'd never seen anything like them on a human. Cate's mind was spinning and asking herself, What kind of a pick-up line is "Do you know me?" Conceited for sure!

She could only blurt, "Why should I know you?" already feeling stupid for such a lame comeback.

"Well, you've been staring at me for some time, so I decided that either you know me or you want to know me. Which is it?" he said in a soft voice that was almost drowned out by the music.

Oh my God, oh my God, oh my God. Cate panicked. *Just go away. No, don't go away.* She thought her head would explode.

"Well?" he said again in that same low husky voice.

"I'm sorry for staring," was all Cate could manage. She looked down, away from the captivating eyes and watched his strong, calloused hands as they moved slowly into the deep pockets of his coveralls. She did not want him to go away, and he seemed to sense it.

"I'm David, and I want to know you."

That was it. Over the cliff Cate would jump. Not full flight that night, but the steps towards the edge were laid that night as they talked for two hours. Not pickup talk, not boring Franklin talk, but talk of the war and the destruction of trees and of communes. She sat wide-eyed, asking him questions and telling him little about her life. *What's to tell?* she thought.

Then he simply got up, preparing to leave. He took Cate's phone number and simply said, "I want you to come see me soon."

"What was that all about?" Barb giggled as she assessed her friend's expression. "That guy comes in here a lot, I think. He's like the resident hippie of Wildwood. He seems to know a lot of people, but man he is one strange-looking dude. What on earth did you talk about for so long?" Barb asked.

"Oh, just bar chat."

As if Cate had any idea what normal bar chat was, but she didn't want Barb to laugh at her if she told her the truth. Cate knew that night that she was headed for trouble because she knew one thing for sure, and that was she wanted to see those crazy eyes again.

The weekend dragged for Cate. There were no cell phones or voicemail or caller ID yet, so if she wanted to get David's call she needed to be by their home phone. There were two phones in their home, the beige one in the family room and Cate's pink princess phone.

To stay near a phone there were little white lies to tell her parents, and thankfully Michael was still not talking to her. On a normal weekend, Michael and she would be having cookouts or going to the movies with their friends. Thank heavens it was exam time, and Michael was pouting.

When Monday came and no word from David, Cate began to wonder if she imagined the whole episode. She had to get back to classes and the real world. At first, she was embarrassed that he didn't call, but by Tuesday night she was angry. If he didn't call by the next night, Cate was going to patch it up with sulking Michael and pretend she never met the gray-eyed stranger.

At 10:00 Cate was curled up in bed writing in her diary. She'd kept a diary since she was twelve, and right now she was printing unkind words about her mystery man. When the phone rang, it startled her so that she threw the pen across the room. She picked up the phone quickly in case one of her parents was still up and near the phone. She knew it was David and suppressed a giggle at the thought that she was just writing out her frustration.

"Kingston residence, this is Cate speaking," Cate recited her mom's preferred phone etiquette for answering as calmly as she could.

"Well, Cate Kingston, this is David speaking, and I want you to come to my place tomorrow."

No chitchat here, Cate thought before she could think of any way to respond.

"Are you there, Cate?"

Ellen Gordon

"Yes, I'm here. I have classes tomorrow, so I'm not sure that's possible," she mumbled while she thought what Michael would think if he knew what she was thinking of doing. If she went to David she wasn't sure she could face Michael.

"Come see me, Cate. Write down my address. I'm only twenty minutes from your campus, just outside Union City," he directed.

Cate slid off the bed to retrieve the pen and obediently wrote down the address and directions. She knew he had no phone of his own and could tell he was on a pay phone.

"See you around 2:00—looking forward to it." Click.

A gentle tap on her door meant a parent was awake, and she wasn't surprised to see her dad with a book in his hand. "Everything okay, peanut? It's a little late for Michael to be calling, isn't it?"

"It's fine, Pop, it was a college friend. We're getting together tomorrow to work on a project."

"Good, get some sleep."

"You too, Pop. Don't you ever get tired of those Agatha Christie mysteries?"

No way Cate could sleep now. Her stomach was doing flip-flops. *What am I doing? Why do I want to see this strange man? What about Michael?* These questions kept her up until after 3:00 when she fell into a troubled sleep.

Cate paid little attention to what her math or history professors had to say that day. The conflict between betraying Michael and the thrill of seeing the gray-eyed hippie again kept her mind fully occupied. Yet when the last class finally ended Cate didn't hesitate to toss her books into the backseat and jump into her little VW bug named Bluey and head off campus. The navy blue VW was a high school graduation gift from her dad. It was a good thing she grew up driving tractors on the farm, because the gear shift was just like the old Ford tractor that her dad taught her to drive on.

There was no GPS or MapQuest then, so as Cate entered an enchanting circle that surrounded a small park full of flowers and trees, she hoped she had gotten the directions correct. She missed the small brick road the first time and had to go around the circle again. The small wooden sign, Perin Drive, was visible the second go-round, and she had no trouble finding David's house. It was exactly as he had described it. It was painted navy blue with a bright orange door and trim. It sat far back from the road and peeked out through blue spruce pine trees. Splashes of red geraniums surrounded the one tall oak tree.

When she pulled into the long gravel drive, she didn't shut off the car because now she was in full-blown panic. Cate was frozen at the wheel, and when she saw David standing in the doorway watching her, she still couldn't move.

Go, Cate, run, Cate, her mind kept repeating, but she didn't.

David opened the car door, leaned in close, and shut off the engine. He handed her the keys, took her hand, and said, "Let's walk."

"I'm glad you came, Cate," David spoke in that same soft yet controlled voice as they headed to the park.

Cate nodded and gave him a thin smile.

"Let me tell you about this park." And he did. For the next thirty minutes Cate loved listening to the somehow sexy voice explain how the park came about, the community that supported it, and the names of the flowers. Cate relaxed as she listened. Suddenly out of nowhere came a loud thunder clap, and seconds later they saw a huge bolt of lightning come down close by. The skies opened in a torrential downpour before they could even stand from their grassy seats.

"Run," David laughed. Hand in hand they raced across the park. The lightning was both terrifying and beautiful all around them.

Inside the tiny hallway, the two stood dripping on the wooden floor of David's home. "Stay here," he directed and disappeared. He returned with a large towel and gently pushed her into the little bedroom off the hallway. "Take your clothes off and put on something from the closet in there. Toss out your clothes, and I'll get them in the dryer. Hurry, you'll catch a chill." Slam.

Cate was starting to shiver, so she got out of the soaking shorts and T-shirt, panties, and bra. Part of her was terrified that he would come in while she was naked, but the familiar ache between her legs betrayed her good intentions with David.

Dressed in someone's PJ bottoms held up by a string and an old Ohio State sweatshirt complete with holes, Cate peeked out the bedroom door. "Better?" David called from across the hall in a large furniture-less room. The floor was littered with brightly colored pillows and rugs. Somehow this room was so "David."

"Yes, thank you," Cate replied rather formally. "Yet I wouldn't have thought you to be the pajamas type." The words popped out of her mouth before she realized how that sounded. This foot in mouth was getting to be an old habit, she decided glumly.

"I'm not," David roared, "haven't worn them since I was twelve. They belong to Fred, my sometimes-housemate.

What Cate remembered most about that first afternoon was that David didn't even try to kiss her. They just talked about the world and what was going on with Vietnam. Time flew by. Cate saw it was 5:00, and she had the two-hour drive to get home. After two glasses of Boone's Farm apple wine, she knew she had to get going. Back in her dry clothes, David walked her to the car.

He leaned in the window and very quietly asked, "Have you ever smoked pot? And will you sometime, when you're ready, let me make love to you?"

Cate's eyes grew huge with surprise. She put Bluey in reverse, prepared to race away, when out of her mouth came, "No and yes." She couldn't look at him again and started down the drive, but she did hear him say, "See you next week at the same time."

David stared after the little blue car long after it disappeared. "What on earth are you playing at?" a slightly bemused and amused David asked himself. What he saw was a sweet, slightly naïve young woman who was looking for the kind of trouble he could give her.

VII

David made no excuses for the life he was now living and enjoying. He had tried a career as a shop teacher in a high school in Pennsylvania, but a relationship with a student ended that career before it barely got started. He had no regrets leaving the silly teenage girl or the school. It was 1967 and the place to be was Haight-Ashbury in California.

Once entrenched in the hippie culture of drugs, sex, and rock and roll, a year went by that David could barely remember. Fortunately, after a horrific experience with LSD, he realized that he needed to get out of California or he would be lost. Back in Ohio where he grew up, he found a little workshop to rent and began making cabinets, chests, and specialty furniture.

He made more than enough money to support his casual lifestyle, which involved marijuana, no more hard stuff, sex, and the accumulation of a great many friends. He had a low-key charisma that people gravitated to. He spun wild stories about his time in California, and young people like Cate couldn't get enough of what he had to say.

Cate did see David the next week and several more times before classes finished for the summer. On their last afternoon together, David made love to a terrified Cate. He was gentle and kind and didn't hurry her through her first sexual encounter. But when David came inside her with a small yelp of pleasure, Cate couldn't believe it was over. It hadn't hurt like she thought it would, but she didn't get off like she did when she touched herself. She sat up on the pile of blankets David had strewn of the living room floor and gave him a weak smile.

"Remember that you told me you would have sex with me some day and that you would try marijuana with me as well? Today is the day for both, my special Cate," David said as he reached behind the pillows for a small brown leather pouch.

Maybe because she was still trying to process that she just had sex with a casual acquaintance that she may never see again, but she didn't shy away from taking a few hits off David's expertly rolled joint.

Cate sank back down on the pillow and closed her eyes for just a moment. "Whoa, I'm spinning. It's like I just had three glasses of wine," Cate murmured. Then she promptly fell asleep for an hour.

A grinning David greeted her when she woke up. "I think you handle making love and marijuana like a pro," he teased.

Cate looked at him as she gathered her clothes and prepared to leave. The conflict over what just happened and the fact that she was headed to a summer with Michael overwhelmed her.

She wasn't sorry it all happened, but now what? This man still scared her. He seemed to have a control over her that was uncomfortable. There could be no future with him. He made his living doing carpentry, and though he seemed very good at it, he had little interest in money. Cate had listened to his plans for a commune in Pennsylvania so many times she could sometimes see herself in that life with him. Then she would shake herself and think of Michael and that life, which seemed much safer.

Yet there was no way to hold on to the old world of Cate after that day with David. When she drove home she tried to only focus on her summer with Michael. If there was going to be any hope for their future together, she needed to give it a real try. Maybe she could get him to sleep with her this summer. She had a moment of panic wondering if he could tell that she wasn't a virgin before remembering the old story that girls who rode horses from an early age often had broken the hymen before sex.

Ellen Gordon

"Well, goodbye, David," Cate called out loud as she drove back to Franklin and Michael. Yet some little voice in the back of her head warned her that she may just see the strange man with the weird gray eyes again.

VIII

That summer had its ups and downs for Cate and Michael. It was nearly impossible for her to totally forget David or what had happened between them. He had given her just a taste of a wholly different lifestyle, and if she were honest with herself, she liked the wildness, the freedom of being with David. She spent the summer working, riding, and trying to hold on to the love she had for Michael. The arguing followed by silences followed by making up had become their norm. Secretly Cate was glad when the summer was coming to an end and she would be headed back to the campus. She had missed her friends, and yes, she wondered if David would seek her out again.

She wasn't totally surprised and secretly pleased when the first week back on campus while rushing for an English class, David suddenly stood in front of her. He looked just the same, yet the long hair was shiny and clean, and jeans replaced the suede coveralls. Before either said a word, he gave her a big bear hug, lifting her off the ground. When he let her go he reached into his flannel shirt pocket, put his hands behind his back. "Guess which hand," a grinning David requested.

Cate tapped his tough calloused right hand, and it unfolded to reveal White Cloud. To date, Cate had about twenty-five elephants and would eventually have hundreds given to her by people who were touched by her. Yet no one would ever understand how each elephant, enormous or tiny, old or new, sank into her heart forever. Little White Cloud was old, and the white paint on the metal was chipped and dirty. Tiny red dot eyes seemed startled to Cate. She chuckled to herself—that was how she usually felt around David—startled.

IX

David would often disappear from her life while he found religion in Maine or joined a commune in California, then he would reappear as if he had never left, wanting Cate back in his life. Throughout Cate's sophomore and part of junior years at Union, David wove in and out of her existence. Cate was never sure how he funded all these excursions and probably didn't want to know. But he was part of the growing up and growing aware process in Cate's life, and she would never regret knowing him or losing her virginity to him. Even though their last encounter would be ugly for both.

Sometimes she was convinced that she would never have left Michael or the little community of Franklin behind if she had never experienced her time with David. He fed her a sense of wanting more and wanting new. She often thought that David should have known Aunt B—what stories they could have told each other. White Cloud would be tucked in her suitcase when it was time for Cate to cut ties with all she knew and run away from her old life.

Ellen Gordon

Hubert

I

Although Michael and Cate had enjoyed their time together during Christmas 1969, by the end of her sophomore year of college, Cate started spending less and less time at home and less and less time with Michael. They were still dating but not as steadily as Michael wished. He had learned to back off on any talk of their future or marriage. He could see her tense when the subject came up. He thought if he let her get this wildness, this restlessness, this desire for something new and exciting out of her system, then she would eventually settle down with him. Truthfully, Cate still wanted to believe that would happen also. If only she could just be content with the life Michael was offering.

David was still in her life when he blew into town full of tales of his new adventures. She still found him to be one of the most controversial, interesting people she knew. He was always so full of ideas to save society and challenge the war and, of course, there was the sex.

Equally distracting was her close friendship with the friends whom she called her Three Musketeers. Patty, Lynn, and Barb continued to surprise and delight Cate in their solid friendship and sense of fun. She even began to spend the occasional night at Barb and Lynn's apartment, much to Michael's disapproval.

As summer break of 1970 approached, Cate found herself more than a little conflicted. While still reeling from the Kent killings, Richard and Randall heading to Vietnam, and knowing she wouldn't be seeing David and little of the Three Musketeers until fall, Cate was sad to see term end. Yet she still had her wonderful job lined up again in Kiddieland, this time as part-time manager.

She looked forward to hours of riding Jack, hopefully with her dad. And in theory she would have more time to spend with the man she was supposed to love, and she was looking forward to trying to make it work with Michael. It had to work. She could never move away from the farm, her dad, or the little community of Franklin. Could she?

It was times like this that Cate wished so hard that Aunt B was still with them. It had been several years since she took her life, but she was the one person she could share this terrible sense that she was missing out on something. There was no way she could go to her mom, or especially her dad, and try to explain the confusion she felt over what she wanted. She tried to talk to the ghost of Aunt B and ask her what she should do. She even went to Chartres and sat out of site down by the lake and dreamed of Aunt B's past, the parties, the excitement, the travel. That only made her more confused and restless. She was sure a young Aunt B would tell her to dump Michael and run away with David for a year or two while she was still young and free. Thanks, no help there.

II

At times Ken, Cate's dad, felt a bit like Michael. He felt he might be losing his daughter to a strange and maybe even dangerous world. The Kent State murders had terrified him as a dad and as a citizen. How was it possible to slaughter kids? It had never been his nature to pry into his daughter's affairs, and he wasn't going to start now. But when she showed up one summer Sunday morning to ask if he felt like a ride, Ken was delighted. He hoped that maybe she would share a little of what was going on with her and maybe what her future might be.

Ken didn't dislike Michael; he just didn't think that he was enough of a challenge for his precocious daughter. When they were together there always seemed to be a tension between them, and if that was true love, Ken felt bad for them both. The only real reason Ken might be pulling for Michael was that if they married they would stay right here in Franklin. He would get to see Cate often, and then there would be grandchildren for him to spoil. Still he wouldn't want Cate to marry Michael if she weren't really in love and wanted to be with him.

Ken reflected on his own marriage of twenty-eight years. He loved June and that was that. He would never want anyone else or anything else. Was it always exciting and did they get a lot of time together? No. Between her busy schedule at the hospital and his veterinary business, their lives were a bit separate. Neither were either of them very demonstrative partners, which Ken sometimes wondered what Cate thought about how her his parents seldom kissed or held hands like some couples their age. Yet they both adored Cate and early on had decided that they only wanted one child. Even now Ken wasn't sure how that came about and wondered if Cate wished that she had siblings.

Cate had started to stay in town with her new girlfriends, who Ken and June had not yet met. She always let them know ahead of time when she would be back, but they couldn't help but wonder what she was doing in Union with her new college friends. And there was this tiny, niggling feeling, that neither Ken nor June would verbalize, that maybe there was some man, other than Michael, in their daughter's life. For Ken's part, he didn't want to think of his daughter sexually with any man at this stage, let alone a stranger to him. June on the other hand knew Cate well enough that Michael's determination to wait until they married was not what Cate wanted. It was a rare mother-daughter conversation when Cate shared that she was a virgin. June just hoped she was smart about birth control and aware of a disease she had read about recently. She wished once again that she had a closer relationship with her headstrong daughter.

III

"How about you take Sparky this morning, Cate? He hasn't had a run in almost a week," Ken asked as they reached the cool of the dark barn one summer Sunday morning. Six of the wild cats and kittens rubbed against their legs, hoping it was feeding time. These cats came in cycles.

Just when it looked like the barn was overrun with them, distemper would come through and wipe most of them out.

Even though Ken was a veterinarian, he believed in the normal cycle of life for these felines and never wanted them to be pets. Their job was to keep the mice and rats out of the grain. Although when Cate was growing up, she occasionally begged him to let her keep one as a pet, then Ken would dutifully vaccinate it.

"Great," laughed Cate, "but we better lock up Jack. He gets pretty jealous when I ride another horse."

Father and daughter skillfully threw on their western saddles and bridles in almost synchronized movements. "Where shall we go, Pop?"

"Just for fun, let's ride up to the Jacobs' and talk them out of a lemonade. I've been wanting to catch up with Andrew to see how his new enterprise is panning out."

"What enterprise is that?" Cate asked, somewhat surprised and somewhat put out. How could Andrew be starting something important and not tell her about it? But then she had to admit that she hadn't been around as much as she used to be when their parents got together, so she hadn't kept up with Andrew's news. Now she remembered all the times they had spent together helping Richard and Randall escape, and she missed her big brother. Why hadn't he told her about this new enterprise, whatever that was?

Ken went on to explain that he didn't know much, but that while keeping his sales job at Highland Tractors, he was renting a small plant in Akron and making a new construction bucket for wheel loaders. He should be careful because he is somewhat in competition with his boss, but he's not ready to go out on his own until he has a decent product. "Anyway, hopefully we'll find out more when we see him."

The trail to the Jacob's was well worn, and Cate cheerfully followed her father down the narrow path. The quiet of the early summer Sunday made it easy for the pair to carry on a conversation. Yet it took a while for Cate to speak, and her dad sensed there was a reason for her silence.

Then out of the silence Cate opened with, "Dad, I'm going to move out at the end summer. My junior year is going to be rough, but this would make it easier to study. I've saved enough to share an apartment with Lynn and Barb, and I'm sorry, but I really need to do this."

Ken almost laughed at her earnest plea. Cate never was one for subtlety. Although she was a quiet one, when she had something to say it seemed to just leap out of her mouth. He knew this was hard for her to say because she knew he would be a bit hurt and a bit sad to see her go, but he knew someday she would want her space.

"It's okay, Cate, but your mom and I will need to see the apartment. We know your friends a little, but we would like to get to know them a bit better. Are you sure you can afford it? Your mom and I can probably pitch in a bit. If you'd gone away to college from the start the fees would have been higher."

Cate urged Sparky up next to Sable, her dad's mare, and threw her arms around his neck. "You are the very best, Pops. Thank you."

For the rest of the ride to the Jacobs' they remarked on the blackberries that were almost ripe and would make an amazing pie soon. They crossed a small creek, splashing and scaring the small black tadpoles lining the edge. Cate's head was spinning with the realization that soon she would be living near campus with her friends and finally on her own.

Ellen Gordon

Now the only tough talk would be with Michael. She decided to tell him, and it was true, that the commute every day for classes was getting tiresome, especially in winter. Barb and Lynn's apartment was close enough to walk to the campus.

The fact that David, that on-again, off-again hippie, lived only a few miles away from the apartment was not something she would be mentioning to anyone, least of all Michael.

With horses tied up in the Jacobs' empty barn, they headed to the large brick house. Andrew's father, Harold, owned a business in Cleveland and with the commute and responsibilities he was not going to be a farmer. He bought the home in the country more for Andrew and Karen. It proved to be a safe, quiet place to raise their only son.

After the customary hugs, Karen and Harold settled the two into comfortable chairs on the back lawn and went to get refreshments. When they returned, Andrew was with them. As always, looking so comfortable with himself, no matter what he was wearing, suited him. Cate gave a smile of approval at his white T-shirt, worn jeans, and loafers with no socks.

As the adults eagerly started their own topics of discussion—the economic cost of the war, Nixon, the price of gasoline—Andrew and Cate sat apart on the bench under the sprawling oak tree. "Remember when we used to climb this tree, Cate, and you got stuck halfway up?" Andrew teased, looking up through the sturdy branches.

"I think you dared me to do it, even though I've never seen you get up as far as I did, smarty," Cate boasted.

The two bantered back and forth with their comfortable brother/sister one-upmanship. Then Cate told Andrew that she was moving into Union to be closer to the college. Andrew just looked at her for more time than made Cate comfortable.

"What's going on, Cate? I know you well enough that it's not the commute, and you're spoiled rotten at home. What's up? Are Michael and you finally finished?"

That one stung. Andrew was hitting way too close to the truth. Yes, her parents did spoil her, and living at home had been great her first two years of college, but how dare Andrew suggest that this indicated the end of her relationship with Michael? A stony silence followed.

"Okay, sorry, none of my business, but, Cate, you better not get caught up with some hippie, pot-smoking idiot out there. You're way too good for that scene. Let's drop it, do what you want to do." After a moment he began, "I want to tell you a little about my business."

Cate was more than a little relieved to move on, as the picture of David, her pot-smoking lover, was a bit too vivid, and she was genuinely interested in what Andrew was up to. While still in college Andrew worked for a local John Deere dealer. At first it was mainly washing the machines, cleaning up the sale yards, and eventually learning to drive the wheel loaders, excavators, and backhoes around the yards as needed. He liked the construction company owners who came to look and buy the machines. They were usually rugged, hardworking men, competing in a tight market. They might be road builders or homebuilders or pipe layers. They may have a company with a fleet of three machines or three hundred machines, but they all had a passion for the machines and how they performed.

Andrew graduated with a degree in mechanical engineering, but he didn't have the interest in the kind of jobs offered to a new graduate in that field. Just as he was about to graduate, his boss at Highland Tractors Sales asked him if he would like to join his sales team. Roger liked Andrew and his work ethic in the three summers and other part-time work he had put in with the company. The other sales team and contractors alike enjoyed his enthusiasm for the machines and the work they could do. Andrew didn't hesitate; he accepted his first and last job.

Before the ink was dry on his diploma, Andrew was shipped off to Dubuque, Iowa, to the John Deere training center. For five days, he was trained on all the machines that John Deere Construction Division manufactured. Although he had moved a lot of the machines at Roger's company, he never worked the machines in the field. The scraper training was darn-right terrifying, and some of his classmates bailed out without finishing the round.

They were asked to fill the scraper with dirt then drive on top of a hill to distribute it. Andrew was proud that one, he didn't roll the one-million-dollar machine and kill himself in the process and two, he was only one of three in the class who managed to do it correctly. Half of the men in the class were salesmen in training like himself, and half were actual contractors in training. To everyone's surprise there was one female in the class, and she also managed the scraper exercise, putting many a man to shame.

By the end of the five days in Iowa, Andrew struck up a friendship with Jack, a construction company salesman from New Jersey, that would last a lifetime. They had both managed to pass the course with flying colors and enjoyed the camaraderie over a few glasses of wine at the end of a grueling day on the machines.

For two years Andrew continued to learn the sale of heavy equipment and found he liked it a lot. It didn't hurt that he was very successful. By the second year he was on a full commission basis and was making a good living for someone so young. Part of his success was that he would go out into the field to demo a machine, at times covered in mud, to show a machine's capability. He didn't need a heavy sales pitch; he believed in the Deere machines and it showed. It didn't take long before some of the largest construction companies sought out Andrew and the Deere machines when they were ready to expand.

"So, if you're doing so well, why this new adventure, which sounds pretty risky?" Cate asked, questioning his sanity over this business endeavor.

"Now that I know the machines so well, I've been looking at the couplers and attachments that are available as options on the wheel loaders. Do you know what a wheel loader is, Cate?"

Offended, Cate scoffed. "Of course I know a wheel loader. When I visit farms with Dad, the farmers sometimes have one to do everything from cleaning stalls to moving grain."

Andrew spent the next half hour explaining how he knew he could build better attachments than the ones John Deere or others offered. The quality was just not there. He was convinced that he could build a better front-end bucket as a start. It didn't take much to rent a very small plant in a commercial part of Akron, and he had some buddies from his college days with knowledge of the engineering and manufacturing of the product.

Cate wasn't totally convinced that her pseudo big brother hadn't lost his mind, but she couldn't deny the determined look in his eye or the careful planning he had done so far. "Okay, I'm glad you're going for it, Andrew, and someday when you have a huge manufacturing empire, I'll come to work for you." Neither of them would believe that would ever happen for so many reasons, but they were in for a major surprise one day.

Ken and Cate tightened the girths on their saddles, gone slack as the horses rested, and waved goodbye to the Jacobs. Cate told her dad about the conversation with Andrew and was surprised that he was so supportive.

"Now is the time for Andrew to go for it. There's something very special about that young man, and I just know he'll make a go of it."

How funny it would be if they both knew what the other was thinking as they trotted their horses home. Cate was imaging Andrew with his own company, fancy cars, big home and, yes, Cate by his side. She knew it was a ridiculous daydream. She never thought of Andrew that way before, but he was awfully good looking! And right in front of her was Ken, thinking how it would be the best of all worlds if Cate and Andrew fell in love. He was quite sure that Andrew would be successful; he always was, from the time he was a little boy. Whether it was chess or academics, he always excelled. So, what if the families were joined by these two good-looking, smart, young people? If only his Cate would settle down a bit. He just wasn't sure about this move to Union. Then Cate broke his reverie.

"Thanks for the ride, Dad. I wish Richard and Randall were here this summer. They just have to be okay and come home to us." Cate sighed. It would be another eight months before they received a letter from Randall. On this perfect day, Cate needed to believe they were safe.

"They'll be fine, sweetie. Don't they always look after each other? Hey, don't you work today?"

"Not until 5:00. There is a group from some church coming in for the rides and a picnic. Janet, my boss, thinks there will be lots of little kids," Cate enthused. This was her third summer working at the park, and she loved it once she got there. Kiddieland only had eight little rides, including a train that ran around the fence line. A lot of the time Cate was the manager, responsible for letting the other staff know which rides they would handle. Of course, everyone wanted to run the train, and the airplanes were a little awkward lifting the kids in and out, so she was careful to spread responsibility around fairly. She had no idea that this innate sense of fairness would bring her success in a future career.

Cate also liked it best because the work was outside. A lot of her friends, both high school chums and new college buddies were waitresses during the summers. Cate couldn't think of anything worse than delivering food in a silly uniform.

Maybe they made better money with the tips, but she wouldn't trade her summer job for any other. From 5:00 to 9:30 that Sunday, Cate rotated staff between boats and trains and airplanes with a sense of accomplishment when she saw the smiling kids and parents.

IV

Michael, understandably, was not as easily accepting of Cate's plan to move to the college. He tried threatening to break up, plenty of yelling, the silent treatment, and left her alone for three days to change her mind. In the end, he realized that he couldn't stop her and if he wanted to keep her, he would have to find a way to make this distance thing work. Michael suggested that he could start coming into Union and he could get to know her friends better.

He said he would like to see her apartment and explore the campus a bit. In all the time they had been dating Cate never even thought to ask him to the college. She had managed to keep these two parts of her life separate.

Cate outwardly agreed that Michael coming to Union would be great, and she made up some things that they could do. On the inside Cate cringed. She hadn't told Barb and Lynn that she was still seeing Michael, and they assumed, especially now that she was moving in, that it was over. It was getting more complicated to keep her different lives separate. The girls knew she met and occasionally saw David, but they would never have thought that Cate would lose her virginity to a wacko like him. Cate didn't like hiding things from anyone and never had in the past. Now she was not upfront with Michael or her parents or her high school friends or Barb and Lynn. What was happening to her? Where was the "goodie-goodie two shoes," as she was often called in the past?

She just wished there was just one person who she could be completely honest with. She needed someone to understand how she always wanted more, always wanted to see what else was out there, and it sure wasn't in Franklin. Now even Andrew seemed to disapprove of her move to Union. If only Aunt B were still at Chartres. Cate was sure she would understand the chaos in her life.

Her mom was surprisingly more supportive than Cate would have imagined. So much so that she began to suspect that her mom might be pleased to see her move out so that she would have her dad all to herself again. It's true that one of the reasons Cate didn't want to go away to college was because at that time she couldn't imagine living anywhere but on the farm. She was very attached to her high school friends then, and she had just started her time with Michael. She knew her mom loved her, and Cate loved her back, but maybe it was time that they gave each other some space.

Yet how she would miss 5:00 a.m. breakfast with her dad. Plus, it meant not being around on weekends as often, so there would be more stress on her relationship with Michael. Yet as she prepared to move to this big adventure, she was feeling close to Michael and almost sure that their love would last.

"Cate, do you need to think about going on the pill now?" June asked as they started packing a few of things for the move. "I know Michael and you have been dating quite a while, and now that you have your own apartment, I just thought you might want to be prepared."

Cate let the shampoo bottle slip from her hands when she heard her mother's words. Cate was already on the pill thanks to the clinic at college, but she never, ever thought she would hear her mother bring up the subject. "Maybe?" was all Cate could think of to say. She was twenty years old, and most everyone she knew, even her high school friends had been

Ellen Gordon

sexually active for several years. Yet Cate appreciated her mom's openness, so she let her go through their family physician for a prescription.

As close as she was to her dad, they could never discuss sex! When her summer job at Kiddieland finished in late August, Cate packed up her little blue VW and with a double supply of birth control headed to her new adventure in Union to start her junior year.

V

Cate had been out of the house for four months when her dad found himself sitting on a hay bale talking to Jack, who hung his head over the stall door as if he were really listening. "We sure do miss her, don't we, Jack? She'll be home for Christmas break soon, and if the weather holds I bet she will take you out a time or two."

It was just too quiet in the house now. Not that Cate was even home all that much before she moved out, but bacon and eggs without her in the morning just didn't seem right to Ken. Maybe it's time he tried something healthier every morning, like the oatmeal that June ate religiously. Thinking of June and her daily oatmeal routine made him chuckle.

He had to admit that when Cate moved out their sex life took a sharp turn for the better! They hadn't had that much sex in a very long time, and he wondered why Cate's leaving correlated with June's definite increase in libido. No complaints on Ken's part, but it did make him wonder just what sort of relationship mother and daughter had. Sometimes there was an undercurrent that perplexed him. He couldn't love either one of them more than he did.

He did recognize that what he had with his daughter was very special. It started from the time she was born. With June's erratic, heavy rotation at the hospital in Franklin, Ken became the primary caretaker early on. His business as a large domestic animal veterinarian gave him some flexibility in his hours. If there was an emergency birth of a foal, it was not unusual for the farmer to see Cate in a car seat in Ken's truck.

Quite often the farmer's wife would whisk Cate into the house until Ken finished, or she would sit in a stroller safely away from the action but content to watch. By the time Cate was walking, the whole little community was used to the little red-haired shadow of her father.

Ken was startled out of his reverie when he saw someone standing in the barn entrance. Ken hoped that whoever it was hadn't heard him talking to Jack!

"Hey, Mr. Kingston, I was driving by and thought I'd say hello," a hesitant Michael offered to a surprised Ken.

"Cate won't be here until the twentieth, Michael," a slightly annoyed Ken stated.

"Oh, I know. It's just that I'm worried about her or rather worried about the two of us," Michael gushed.

Ken looked closely at the young man. It looked like he hadn't been sleeping much. This all made Ken very uncomfortable. He didn't want to be discussing Cate with Michael or anyone else. Yes, he had seen a change in her also, but he believed in her and that ultimately she would make good decisions with her life.

"Michael, you need to talk with Cate, not me. I can't speak for her." He spoke a little more sternly than he meant to.

"Sorry, Mr. Kingston," Michael apologized, "it's just by now I thought we might be thinking of getting engaged, but I'm pretty sure that's not going to happen this Christmas and maybe not ever." He spun on his heels and headed for his car. *Now I've made a fool of himself in front of Cate's dad,* he thought as he started to run.

"Give her some time, Michael," Ken called out, a little more kindly this time.

It was some time after Michael left that Ken was still sitting on the hay bale. There was plenty to do this afternoon before he went to the Clark's farm to check on a new calf. The cow had a difficult birth, and the calf had not responded as immediately after it dropped as it should have. Ken wanted to be sure it survived the first twenty-four hours, the most dangerous time for newborns. Yet he continued to sit and finally admitted to himself that he just didn't have the same old energy. At fifty-six, he was sure he was too young to be slowing down, but he felt tired more often now. Then he chuckled again; maybe it was too much sex.

VI

Cate bounded into the family room and flung her arms around her father, nearly tipping him over. This Christmas break would turn out to be tough on Cate, Michael, and her parents, but upon seeing her dad, Cate felt that somehow her junior year would straighten itself out. Why did her dad seem so serious?

"I am so very glad to be home. I've got two whole weeks to do nothing but eat, sit by the fire, and beat my father at Yahtzee," Cate announced, then added, "and I'm never missing another Thanksgiving without my family." Cate had opted to join a large group of David's friends, who decided they would make a Thanksgiving feast the old-fashioned way on someone's farm. The food was a disaster, Cate was not into acid or other serious drugs, and she missed her family terribly.

Father and daughter were both equally happy to be together again. Ken looked at his smiling daughter and thought that maybe they had worried about her unnecessarily. She was thinner and more...what? Different. Her red hair was long and flat against her head with some sort of beaded band securing it. Did they call those pants bell-bottoms? They made petite Cate look somewhat out of proportion.

"Cate, are you a hippie, or do you just like looking like one?" Ken half teased.

"I'd never be a real hippie. They don't wash, and they say they don't need money—ha—that is not your daughter, Pops." Again, the guilt crept into Cate's mind. She knew her parents would not approve of her lifestyle on campus.

The two of them built a roaring fire, so when June returned from the hospital they had hot chocolate and popcorn all ready for her. The three sat in front of the fire and caught up on each other's news. By 10:30, June was exhausted and kissed the two of them good night, knowing they would be up for hours yet. Maybe she did feel a little jealous sometimes, but when she saw them together talking about everything from

Ellen Gordon

Ken's latest patients to Cate's trouble with French, June knew how very much she loved the two of them.

Growing up, Cate pretty much had everything a young girl could want. She had her own phone in her room long before any of her friends did. And like many of her friends, her mom often found an unusual elephant for Cate when she traveled or for Cate's birthday.

By now Cate had thirty-eight elephants in all shapes, materials, and sizes. Some were just fun elephant gifts meant to remind Cate of an enjoyable time. Like the green elephant key that Michael bought her to unlock the animal descriptions at the Cleveland Zoo. When Cate saw that one it hurt a little, remembering how very close they were that first summer they got together.

Yet knowing Cate's obsession with elephants, Ken had never bought one for her. The gifts from him to Cate were almost always related to the horses or the farm in some way. When she was thirteen, he gave her an old Ford tractor that she drove around the farm. Then of course there were saddles and bridles and chaps for their trail rides and western wear for horse shows, but no elephants.

It looked like it might be a good Christmas after all. Cate went out with Michael a few times over the holiday. She tried to let herself be lulled back into her old life.

Catching up with her old girlfriends had not been the same, but Cate wanted to try. They all seemed so settled and content with their lives in Franklin. Many times Cate reflected on her own chaotic life and wondered not for the first time why she couldn't just be content with this life Michael wanted them to have. She knew Michael adored her, and he had a good steady job and future, and they had plenty of good friends together. Besides, if she did settle down with Michael, she knew they would stay in Franklin, which meant staying close to her dad and keeping her horse. Being away from college, David, and her friends for a couple of weeks gave Cate hope that she might be content here. Yet it was not meant to be; the changes in Cate were too deep now.

Ken and Cate did manage to get in one short ride a couple days before Christmas. A light snow was falling, but the wind had died, and for Ohio the weak sunshine was a bonus. They saddled Jack and Sable and decided to head to the back of the farm, over the shallow creek, and into the fifty-acre woods. Over time the cattle, sheep, and horses that roamed in the huge paddock had created crisscrossing paths in every direction.

Although the paths were narrow, the stillness in the forest made their voices sound loud as they talked about Christmas presents for Cate's mom, Cate's grades, a new horse Ken was considering purchasing, Richard and Randall's silence, and anything and everything but the "thing" most on both of their minds. Were Cate and Michael still together, and did they have a future?

As they unsaddled and rubbed down the horses, Cate said out loud but more to herself, "I always want to live in the country and have horses. It's fun living near campus, but sometimes I feel like screaming when I feel so closed in."

"Now you know why I chose being a farm animal veterinarian. I couldn't imagine myself living in a city and taking care of spoiled poodles." He laughed. "I love this farm, and while I know your mom might prefer a newer home closer to Cleveland, I couldn't live anywhere else."

Cate smiled at her dad. They were so alike in so many ways, including temperament. That little speech was the most Cate had heard him talk at one time in quite a while! Not for the first time Cate wondered just what kind of a marriage her folks really had. There was never any fighting, but there was very little demonstration of their love. Cate had never seen them hold hands and the kisses were brief pecks on the cheek when they were coming or going. Was her dad happy with his marriage? Could she be happy with Michael?

"Michael and I are going to hang out with Sue and Andy tonight and grab some dinner at the Old Trail," Cate informed her father. "Sue's not even out of college yet, but they're having a baby in five months. Can you believe that, Dad? I don't want any babies until I graduate, get a job, and travel," Cate blurted.

"Tell them congratulations from us, Cate. It does seem a bit young, but I can't lie; you'll make me a very happy man the day you tell me you're having a baby."

"Well you better stay healthy, because it will be a long way down the road, Mr. Kingston," Cate teased.

On Christmas morning Ken told Cate to close her eyes— no peeking. Patience was not a strong point of Cate's as she wiggled in the living room chair beside the enormous Christmas tree.

"Okay, open," Ken instructed.

"Oh my, oh my, it's unbelievable," Cate shouted as she jumped up and down then ran to hug her parents.

"That is all your adoring father's idea, Cate." June smiled. "He just brought it home one day and said, 'This is for Cate,' like he bought you elephants every day!"

Well, obviously, it was for Cate. It was a dark green ceramic elephant with a flat tabletop. This beautiful elephant had its trunk held high in what Cate thought was a whimsical way, as if it was somehow amused. Her dad bought her this amazing, unique piece of art, and Cate had never loved an elephant or her dad more than at that moment. She would always remember the proud look on his face that he had found something she loved so much. The best Christmas present ever.

"I'm going to call him Hubert," Cate proclaimed the next day. Ken was not amused. Hubert was his middle name and not one he liked being reminded of. *Typical Cate*, he thought, *coming up with a way to tease me. Oh well, I'm so glad she likes Hubert—poor elephant.*

The school break was flying by, and a few days after Christmas June asked her daughter if she wanted to go into Medina for some shopping and have lunch. Cate hadn't spent much time with her mom and was feeling a little guilty.

"Sure, sounds good," Cate agreed. On the way to Medina, the pair passed the sign to Chippewa Lake, which always made them a little melancholy for Aunt B. "Oh, I meant to tell you, Cate. Some investors have purchased Chartres from Carl's estate. They say they that are going to restore it to its original grandeur, but the rumor is they have no money to pull it off. I can't bring myself to go look at it anymore."

Cate flashed back to the last time she spoke with her wonderful Aunt B. She would forever feel guilty that she didn't know what her aunt was going to do. Could she have stopped the suicide? She just missed her so much. And as she tried to untangle her mixed-up life, she could use that free spirit to guide her.

The outing didn't go well for the mother or the daughter. It started when Cate tried on boots that looked like something a biker would wear instead of a college coed. "Cate, those are hideous. You can't wear something like that on campus, or anywhere, I would think," June criticized.

Cate felt herself bristle. Since she'd been home for the holiday, her mom had made her dissatisfaction with Cate's clothes known in a none-too-subtle way. Cate loved the tie-dyed shirts she'd made with David and wore them often with beaten up bell-bottomed jeans. The fact that she appeared without a bra at breakfast one day shocked both parents into silence.

For Christmas her mother gave her a very expensive Pendleton skirt and sweater. When she opened it, Cate couldn't help herself as usual and burst out with, "Where on earth would I wear this, Mother dear?"

After giving up on the boots, Cate and her mom had lunch at Michael's restaurant on the square in Medina. Cate had been here before but was correct in thinking the name was a good segue into her mom asking her about how Michael and she were doing.

June told Cate that she needed to be thinking more about the future, what she would do after college. Secretly Cate thought she was probably afraid that she would come home again. Then felt bad for even thinking that was her mom's motivation for asking.

"If you want to marry Michael someday, you would do well to settle down a bit and stop all this hippie nonsense. And you better not be smoking pot, because I know Michael would never tolerate you trying that dangerous drug."

Cate didn't know whether to laugh or cry at her mother's words. Heaven knew she had no idea at this stage if she really wanted to marry Michael or not. And it was too late for the marijuana; she already enjoyed the occasional smoke with David or other friends at parties.

"Mom, just let me lead my life my way, okay," Cate snapped at her mother. She immediately regretted the tone and the words, but it was too late to take them back.

The two barely spoke on the way home. When he felt the chill in the air as they sat down to dinner, Ken wondered what had happened between his two favorite ladies. Rather than ask, he retreated to the barn as soon as he finished the slightly burned pork chop.

The Kingstons were delighted when later Andrew dropped in unexpectedly for an evening cheers with them. Cate admired his argyle cashmere sweater in blues and greens, looking quite sophisticated with navy dress pants. "Where are you off to, looking so sharp, Mr. Businessman?" Cate couldn't resist.

"Not that it's any of your business, young Cate, but I had dinner with my business partner, Jack, at Ken Stewart's tonight to celebrate a sales order for five wheel loader buckets. We are on our way, and I've come to gloat to my good friends," a very satisfied Andrew boasted. Cate didn't comment on hearing Jack's name again. Jack was a great name for a horse, she thought, not for a grown man.

The remaining week of break flew by. As Cate was packing to return to college and the apartment, she felt a little tug of sadness. She and Michael had a lot of fun, especially with their old friends. It felt comfortable and easy now. He hadn't pushed for marriage. In fact, Cate wondered why it never came up. She braced herself that there might be an engagement ring in her Christmas box that he set under her parents' tree. There was no ring, just tickets to see *Hair* in Cleveland and dinner at Morten's before the show.

Hair was quite entertaining, and Cate was surprised that Michael would even think of such a hippie, raunchy show. Maybe he was trying to let her know that she wasn't the only one up with the times. During the show one of the nude actors ran into the audience and right over Dorothy Fuldheim's seat! She was a popular, though rather old-fashioned TV presenter, so the audience went crazy watching her expression.

Sue and Cate were in the backseat on the way home from Cleveland after an amazing show and dinner. "Come on, Cate, when are you two getting engaged at least?" Jill whispered over the guys' discussion of their next ski adventure. "We have so much fun together, and I'm going to need you to help me with this baby," she whined.

"You and the baby will be just fine; besides, I would probably drop it!" Cate declared, hoping that would change the subject from Michael and her.

The toughest part of returning to school was leaving her dad and the farm. On the night before she was leaving, she followed him to the barn to help with the chores. How many times had she done this? It seems that she had been following him around all her life.

"I'll toss down a couple bales, Dad," she volunteered as she started the climb up the twelve-foot wooden ladder to the hayloft. "Look out below," she called unnecessarily as the first bale flew to the floor and hit with a dusty thump. Cate loved this barn, with the smells of the hay, the horses, the saddles. This was home to her.

"Pop, I am so going to miss this place all over again," Cate declared. "I have no idea when I'm going to get back again this semester—it's a tough one."

"You just take care of yourself, Cate. I know Michael and you have some tough decisions to make, but don't you ever believe that he is your only option."

Cate nearly tripped over the bale of hay. Did her dad just say that? Cate felt unexpected tears forming; she just wanted to go hug him. *He gets it—he really gets it*, she thought to herself. *He knows I think there may be more to life than here with Michael in Franklin.* Maybe her dad knew her better than she knew herself. She knew that he would love her to marry Michael and be here forever, but he was giving her the freedom to decide. Michael had been more than a little distant as they said their goodbyes the night before she was headed back to Union.

So on a snowy Sunday afternoon Cate was ready to head back to college. Cate loved Hubert and insisted it was the perfect name for such a happy elephant. Hubert was loaded into the backseat of the VW with a seatbelt around him as Cate waved goodbye to her folks. Yet she knew they were worried about her and yet did not question her. How did she deserve such amazing parents?

She looked back briefly in the rearview mirror and saw that although her parents were still waving, they'd already turned to look at each other. Something in that look told Cate that they were not happy with her, and Cate knew that they were somehow disappointed in her.

Dumbo

I

When Ken and June agreed to let Cate move in with Barb and Lynn at the start of her junior year, they admitted only to each other that maybe Cate was not quite mature enough to handle the freedom. The summer before the start of her junior year, they noticed subtle changes in their only child. She was seeing less of Michael and her high school friends, grew quiet with worry over Richard and Randall, and seemed preoccupied much of the time. Yet they knew they could not hold her back, although Ken would have liked to try.

Cate moved in with her friends a week before classes started. The new freedom didn't take long to begin to change her. Just months into the fall of her junior year, Cate found herself looking for a new Cate, a more worldly, with-it Cate. The introverted country girl of 1968 just starting college now wanted to be the party girl of 1970. It seemed to Cate that there was so much bad in the world, with the Vietnam War still taking American lives. Richard and Randall were God knew where in Vietnam. Kent was still trying to recover from the shootings. Cate tried to convince herself that free love and a little pot were the way to go. Her roommates and other friends began to wonder about her. "Okay, Cate, exactly how many guys have you slept with?" asked Barb, only half joking, as

Ellen Gordon

they spread out on the living room floor of their apartment, supposedly studying.

"Well, there was David, Aaron, George from the bar, Joseph, and Ed," Cate rattled off with a grin. "I'm not serious about any of them, Barb," she clarified, "I'm just having fun."

"God, I feel like your mother, Cate, but honestly, you're missing classes and smoking a lot of pot."

"Well, the world is going to hell, Barb, and I can't do a damn thing about it, so why not just enjoy my life? And my grades aren't that bad," an agitated Cate retorted.

But her downward spiral continued through the fall. Even though she said she would never miss another Thanksgiving with her parents, she did. She chose to party with some people she met at an "end the war" protest on campus. It turned out to be even worse than the one the year before with David. There was so much anger, and some of their protest plans seemed dangerous and out of control to Cate. She ate very little of the Chinese food they had brought in and left early alone.

Back in the empty apartment—Barb and Lynn were home with family—Cate began to reflect on the most bizarre Thanksgiving she had ever attended. Yes, she wasn't convinced the war had ever been a good idea, but what about guys like Richard and Randall? What would they think if they heard Cate was out protesting the war?

"I am out of control," a depressed Cate admitted to herself in the empty apartment. She missed her parents; sometimes she missed Michael painfully too. Life was so simple once. She would finish college, marry Michael, and settle somewhere near her dad and the farm. That blissful picture only lasted a few minutes. Then Cate realized just how far she had wandered off that safe path. The sex meant nothing, the pot just slowed her down, and now her grades were going down. "I'm a mess," Cate concluded as she sank into the squishy beanbag, trying to decide what to do with the rest of the Thanksgiving break.

Somehow Cate had gotten through Christmas break without falling apart. Her dad had given his only child a most precious gift named Hubert. She looked tearfully at the large green elephant and wondered what was happening to her. Sitting in her bedroom apartment at the end of January, Cate knew she needed to go home. Maybe college wasn't for her after all, and if she continued drop her grade average, maybe she would be out anyway.

When Cate surprised her parents the next Saturday morning, she was greeted by her unhappy father. "What's going on, kiddo?" Ken tried to sound unconcerned, but the furrowed brow gave him away. His lovely daughter looked gaunt and unreasonably cheerful. Had she really changed that much just since Christmas? He and June had been concerned, but this seemed more serious. "College life getting you down?"

There was an uncomfortable silence between them.

"I'll be fine now, Pop. I just needed to get home." Cate laughed as she hugged him tightly. "It's just a real tough semester, and I've had trouble concentrating. I'm worried about Richard and Randall and the war, and everything is such a mess," was all Cate could think to say.

"Cate, we're all concerned about the war and the safety of our soldiers, especially the twins, but you don't put your life on hold and let what is important to you personally just slip away. How does that help anything?" a now visibly irritated Ken reproached his daughter.

"You're right, Pop, and I won't let anything spoil the weekend with Mom and you." With tears forming in her eyes Cate went to her room to unpack. What could she possibly say to her dad? She knew she was on a slippery slope, but she was not going to let it ruin this time with him.

She'd gone out with Michael a few times over Christmas break and knew there were still feelings on both sides. She just felt a terrible guilt that if he knew what she had been up to at college it would be over. The thought of losing him forever still worried her. What was she going to do?

Cate was restless that Saturday night, and so to avoid a long evening watching TV with her parents, she called Michael. While he didn't know she planned on being home that weekend, he was glad that she called. Maybe both had this little voice in their heads saying maybe someday this will all work out after all.

There was a party at Rod and Jill's home that evening, so Michael invited her to join them. It was a winter cookout, so even with the ground frozen and snow threatening, everyone huddled around a large open fire pit or stood giving moral support to the chef beside the huge gas barbecue.

Cate was confident that she could just walk back into this familiar group, and she would still be the adored, crazy Cate that she was just a couple years ago. But this group now felt alien to Cate. The talk was mostly about local football, the race for county commissioner, and of course kids. Cate found herself outside of the circle of these old friends. *When had they gotten so boring?* she thought to herself.

As the evening dragged on and the beer and wine flowed, Cate became more and more agitated. Even Michael paid her little attention. Fueled by frustration and cheap wine, true to form, Cate spoke without thinking. Standing next to Michael by the barbecue piled high with hamburgers, hot dogs, and buttered onions, Cate questioned loud enough for everyone to hear, "Does anyone here have a little pot to spare?"

All conversation stopped, and all heads turned to Cate. There were no pot smokers in this group, and if she had thought for one second, Cate would never have asked that question. Not only did this group never do any drugs—beer and wine were their limit—they all had a pretty clear idea of the kind of person who did smoke it. They knew Cate had changed, but what on earth had happened to the sweet, shy, eccentric Cate? No one spoke until Michael touched her arm.

"Come on, Cate, I'll take you home," an embarrassed Michael breathed in her ear as he maneuvered her to the door. "Sorry, guys," he called over his shoulder as he closed the door.

Cate wouldn't even realize it for another year just how many doors closed on her that night. The small community had concerns about Cate ever since she basically dumped Michael and started running with a new crowd in Union. There were rumors of her wild behavior including drugs and orgies. Later, when Cate learned of all the things she supposedly had done, she could only sadly laugh. "If I did a quarter of the things this town says I did, I'd have been dead long ago," she once shared with Andrew.

"I miss the old Cate very much," was all Michael had to say as they drove away.

The old Cate. Cate looked over at Michael as he drove and realized that the gap between them had widened to where there would be no together ever again. She hadn't meant to humiliate him in front of his friends and just now she was missing the old Cate as well. There were no tears, just a terrific sense of loss. This man was going to be her husband, and those friends would be her friends for all her life. She was meant to settle here, stay close to her dad and the horses. No goodbyes were exchanged, both too damaged to speak.

Inside, Cate's parents were watching Bonanza together. "You're home early, dear," her mother called out without taking her eyes off Hoss and Little Joe.

"I'm just tired," was all she got out before heading to her room. Tomorrow she'd tell them about the party because, in this small town, the fact that Cate was a pot smoker would get back to them quickly. She barely slept that night, haunted by what she had done to herself and Michael.

Cate did tell her parents about the party and what she'd said. They didn't have much to say in response to her confession. For the first time in her life Cate felt that her dad was ashamed of her, which was almost more than Cate could bear. Now she had let down Michael, her mom, and worst of all her dad.

No more was spoken of the incident as a remorseful Cate headed back to campus early Monday morning, determined to find a way back to the old Cate. She hoped that she hadn't totally ruined her relationship with Michael, but that seemed likely now.

II

Cate returned to Union and stuck her nose in the books, determined to get back in her dad's good graces. Her heart was still heavy with concern for Richard and Randall, as their time in Vietnam was soon to be over. Every morning she talked to the precious Pax beside her bed with the note from the twins saying that they should be home soon. Her worry about them was a constant. Blaming the stress, Cate was not quite completely rehabilitated. She still found herself smoking a little pot, and she did let David back in her life momentarily. She convinced herself that this was a good start to redemption, and her friends did see a positive change.

Cate had never expressed an interest in joining a sorority, mainly because when she first started college she was way too shy to ever go to one of the introductory parties. Her close ties with Barb, Lynn, and Patty fulfilled her need for support and companionship. She watched groups of sorority girls and fraternity guys move around campus in clusters—dressing alike, talking alike, and taking most of the roles as class presidents and editors of the paper. Cate was at once amused with their confidence and sometimes a little envious of their dominance on campus. Nevertheless, having never been invited to one of their parties, she had little to honestly judge them by.

Dressed in flared jeans, a thick woolen turtle neck sweater, a soft leather jacket, and combat boots, Cate was making her way through ankle-deep snow on her way to the Chuckery where Barb and her new guy, Curt, promised to buy her lunch.

With too much bounce in her step Cate missed the last step coming out of Cambridge Hall. Both feet were out from

Ellen Gordon

under her, and she sat down so hard on the sidewalk that her teeth made a frightening crunching noise. Not only was she intensely embarrassed, but her butt hurt so bad, she couldn't stop the tears.

"Ouch, ouch, and ouch," came a concerned voice from up above her. Honestly, Cate wished no one had seen the ungraceful crash, and she really didn't want sympathy. "I'm fine—just fine—go away," she ordered in her not-so-brave voice.

"Nope, can't do that. It is my duty as a gentleman and a scholar to put you back on two feet and escort you to wherever it is you were bouncing off to," declared the confident voice from above.

Cate dared to take a peek at the man determined to further embarrass her. Her first thought was, *Oh my goodness, this is the all-American boy next door.* He wasn't all that tall, but there was something about the way he stood that said he was somebody and he knew it. He had on a dark navy blazer, with a light blue shirt and a tie that screamed fraternity. Cate almost moaned out loud, and not just from the pain.

"I'm not going away, and soon you will have a very wet bottom, which will be more embarrassing than your tumble," Cate's rescuer declared. "Here, take my hands and rise up, young lady."

Reluctantly, Cate put out her now-freezing hands and let his surprisingly strong hands easily lift her to her feet. Cate was right. He was only a little taller than she was, but he was sort of stocky, like a high school wrestler, she decided. He held her hands a little longer than necessary then looked embarrassed himself.

"I'm Max. I don't think we've met." He grinned, which made him look like a little boy with mischievous eyes that were intently focused on her at the moment.

"Hi, Max, I'm obviously Clumsy Cate," she said as she returned his stare. Why did she feel so instantly at ease with this guy? He was obviously a Maximillian, with all that goes with it. Oh well, if he wanted to walk her to the Chuckery, why not, Cate decided.

"Don't let this tie fool you. I'm a jeans and sweatshirt kind of guy when I'm not on official business for the student council," Max stated, suddenly serious.

"Really? I picked you for a fraternity kind of guy who drove a sports car and had girls hanging all over him," Cate expounded as if she were angry with him.

"Whoa, whoa, you are all wrong, lady, but if I were you I wouldn't go around stereotyping frat guys. Some of my best buds are in fraternities and just because I'm not, they don't look down on me," Max countered with his own angry tone.

Cate blinked a few times before she knew what to say. "Sorry, wow, that made me sound pretty petty, and I thought I prided myself on being an open person."

"Let's start over," suggested a relieved Max.

Ellen Gordon

III

By the end of February life was going in the right direction. Her grades were coming up, and she'd gained back some of the lost weight, so she looked healthy again. That semester she had both swimming and basketball classes to complete, so she was feeling fit as well. She'd been out with Max several times, and while he wasn't as exciting as David or some of the other men Cate had been "experimenting" with, he was funny and solid, and she loved his mixture of good friends.

So just when Cate saw her junior year looking like one of her best, her dad called on March 15. Cate had just finished classes for the day and was at the apartment with Barb. They were hotly debating whether to go out for pizza or just open a couple cans of soup, when the phone rang. Barb picked it up and turned sharply to Cate as she looked through their pile of food coupons. "It's your dad."

Something in the way Barb spoke convinced Cate that something was wrong. Barb had obviously picked up something in Ken's voice. The girls stared at each other. Cate didn't want to take the phone. Could it be her mom? Could something have happened to Michael? Not once in those few seconds before she took the phone did Cate imagine it would be about Richard or Randall. When she thought about it later, she wondered why she didn't know immediately after all these months of worry.

Cate would remember this conversation for the rest of her life. "Baby, I hate saying this over the phone, but we got bad news today." Cate could hear her dad swallow before he could go on. "Richard is dead, sweetheart. Randall sent you a brief letter saying only that Richard died in an attack while they were on a mission in their helicopter. I opened it, sensing it was unwelcome news, but we'll keep the letter for you."

Both Cate and her father were thinking that Randall had been forced to watch his twin, his other half, be shot and die before anything could be done to save him. "Thanks, Daddy, can't talk right now." Cate hung up with a sob.

"No, no, no, not Richard," was all Cate could call out to a perplexed Barb. When she realized what Cate was saying she rushed to her friend and held her tight while Cate continued to wail. The war was ending; they would be home soon—ready to start their lives for real. Why? Why Richard? Why now when they had both survived so much already?

The Vietnam War would cost the lives of 58,220 military personnel. The names can be found now on the memorial wall in Washington, DC. Yet beyond the deaths, there were thousands who would never be their selves again due to post-traumatic stress disorder (PTSD), physical injuries, or delayed illness due to Agent Orange. Cate would personally know two more who would die, and several of her friends came back strangers who never got back on track with their lives.

Cate tried to hang in there until spring break when all she wanted to do was to go home the very day her dad called with the unthinkable news. She wanted to ride horses with her dad. She wanted to talk about Richard and Randall with him, because he knew and cared about them also. She even wanted to commiserate with her mom and Andrew, who helped them run away from their repressive home life. Sometimes Cate couldn't help wondering that if she had just left them alone on the farm, Richard would still be alive. She knew that negative thinking didn't help anyone, but she just felt more anger towards the war than ever.

She did appreciate the patience and understanding from Barb, Lynn, Patty, and even Max. It was somehow cathartic to tell them all about meeting the twins, the hours of horseback riding, her family's role in their running away, and about Pax, the little ivory elephant that sat on Cate's desk, still bringing on fresh tears.

Spring break did help to heal Cate. Indeed, she did ride Jack a great deal, both with and without her dad. She rode by Richard and Randall's old farm one chilly April afternoon and wasn't surprised to see it deserted. The parents' plans to have the twins stay on the farm and grow crops had failed when the boys disappeared. She wondered if they even knew that one of their sons had given his life for his country. Would they have cared?

After that brief letter telling them of Richard's death, Randall was never heard from again. Cate would wonder about him for years, always hoping he would turn up at the farm looking for her. When Google became available to her thirty years later, she would try to find him that way with no success. Of course, it was possible that Randall died in Vietnam also, but that was too much for Cate to imagine. She hung on to her old hope that he had survived and made a good life for himself. She liked to think that he found someone to love and they had a wonderful son named Richard.

IV

Max was becoming part of Cate's campus and social life now. Barb and Lynn were half in love with him, which amused Cate no end. Even though they were both in relationships of their own, her Max could do no wrong. "Thank God you found someone normal and smart and cute," they seemed to be constantly telling her. Cate decided they were just relieved that Max was not a David-type.

They fell into a contented routine of studying together at least once a week at Cate's apartment, joining friends every Thursday at Brubacker's to watch a game or play pool with a group of Max's outgoing friends, then if Cate wasn't going home for the weekend, there were hikes in the many parks or cookouts with Cate's roommates.

As Cate was catching up on her diary one day, she realized just how much her life had changed in six months. Only occasionally did she miss the wild times of her crazy experimentation phase or the potential of a quiet life in Franklin with Michael. She decided this diary would make one great book one day.

As summer approached, Cate decided to take a job with the Akron Recreation Department and stay in the apartment most of the break. She got home often enough to keep the horses fit, but she was enjoying her time with Max. He was the type every parent hopes their daughter marries. He worked a job in the library, made good grades, and was extremely popular with many on campus.

Plus, she couldn't ignore the fact that he had a great future in his father's accounting firm. When she watched him with

Ellen Gordon

a group of people, she liked his easy confidence. He wasn't movie star handsome by any means, but his sandy hair and freckles were most attractive. Cate often asked herself why she had never asked Max home to meet her parents. She didn't know how to answer that but just kept putting it off.

It was just before they learned of Richard's death that Cate slept with Max for the first time. He came over to take her to a movie, but with her roommates out, they took the opportunity to step up their relationship. By now Cate had had quite a few lovers, and it was obvious that Max was no virgin, but Cate thought the sex was just like their relationship. Solid, steady, normal somehow. Max seemed very content with what they had, and Cate felt no desire to take on any other lover. Cate didn't know it, but there would be other similar relationships to the one she had with Max.

Cate hadn't seen Michael since that dreadful night at Rod's party, but she still thought of him. He had been such an important part of her life. She just wished it hadn't ended like it did, but she was too proud and too embarrassed to contact him.

Sometimes when she was home she would see his car parked somewhere and she'd have to fight the urge to approach him. So it was to her surprise and delight that as she saddled Jack for an early morning ride one weekend, she saw Michael headed for the barn.

"Hey, Cate, your mom said you were down here. I just wanted to say hello. Just didn't want us to end angry with each other," Michael sighed as he kicked around some loose hay.

"Thanks, Michael," Cate looked closely at her ex-boyfriend, never lover. He looked very handsome and very confident.

"You look terrific, Michael," she said, as the tiniest feeling of regret washed over her. "Look, I know I behaved pretty badly for quite a while, and I'm sorry for that. You deserve a lot better than me." Cate gave him a little smile and kicked hay at him.

"You were certainly out of control that night at Rod's, and I'm afraid you burned a few bridges around our little community. You just never could keep a thought to yourself, could you? Imagine asking our square friends for marijuana!"

Cate didn't need reminding of her tendency to blurt out whatever she was thinking, but before she could react to Michael's tough comments, he had his arms lightly around Cate.

"Look, I know it's over between us, Cate, but I would not trade one minute of our time together, even the rough patches. I just wanted to tell you good luck with whatever comes your way. Know that I will always have your back."

Cate gently wiggled out of Michael's arms, not trusting the emotions welling up inside her. Their eyes connected for just a few seconds before Michael officially walked out of Cate's life.

Shaking off what just happened, Cate finished putting Jack's bridle on him, deciding to ride bareback today. She subconsciously rode slowly towards Karen and Harold's, secretly hoping Andrew would be home. Even with his busy new business and work at the equipment company, he still lived at home a lot of the time. Cate liked to tease him about being a momma's boy who couldn't leave home. In reality he was too broke to live anywhere else, although he sometimes slept in his small manufacturing building, at least that's what he told his proud parents.

Ellen Gordon

Cate tied Jack up in the barn and was pleased to see Andrew's old pickup in the drive. In the house she hugged Karen, with Harold still at work, just as Andrew bounded down the stairs and lifted Cate off her feet in a bear hug. Karen gave the two of them cold Michelobs then left to write letters.

"You look very thoughtful. What's up, munchkin?" an interested Andrew inquired as he gently placed her back on the ground. Cate's eyes swept over the tight blue jeans and the plaid shirt hugging his very fit body and wondered yet again how he always looked like someone out of a fashion magazine.

"Well, Michael and I just admitted that it was completely over. I'm dating a man named Max that I like a lot but don't love. I'm about to finish my third year, and with one to go, have no idea what I want in the future. I know I wasted a chunk of my college years being stupid and trying to be someone I'm not. Richard is dead, and we've heard nothing further from Randall. What a life." Cate exhaled as she looked over at her big brother, nemesis, mentor, and usually friend.

"Wow, that was a mouthful coming from you. Your dad and you talk less than most people I know. I can't even tell if you're sad, mad, happy, or just glad to see me," Andrew joked, trying to lighten her mood.

"Forget me, let's talk about you." And so they did for the next hour. His business was growing slower than he liked, but he was putting together a great little group of employees. That included Jack, who seemed to be an important part to the growth of Andrew's company. It had been a risk for both of them when Jack left a high-paying position to take a chance on Andrew.

"You'll meet Jack, Cate," Andrew said. "He is the best sales-man I've ever seen, knows machines backwards and forwards, and is just one hell of a great guy." Cate had seldom seen An-drew so enthusiastic about any other human being, and it amused her. She looked forward to meeting this guy one day.

Reluctantly Cate jumped back on Jack to head home. Why did it always feel so good to talk with Andrew? He seemed so grown up, and their bantering never changed. "What would it be like if Andrew asked me out?" Cate asked an uninter-ested Jack.

V

Towards the end of summer Max lost his maternal grand-father, and although the grandfather lived outside of Chica-go, a good five hours away, Max had always been his favorite grandchild. They talked on the phone at least once a week, and Max would often shoot home for a quick weekend visit. They shared a love of old movies, and just the month before they had watched *Casablanca* for at least the tenth time.

Max stopped at Cate's apartment the afternoon he found out. Cate took one look at the red swollen eyes and the sad-ness in his walk and knew it must be something dreadful to get Max down. They sat cuddled on the couch for some time as Max rambled on and on about his grandfather and all that they had done together. He rattled off the long list of their fa-vorite movies and how they planned on watching *The African Queen* next month.

Cate was genuinely sorry for Max's loss and found that his sadness was bringing her down as well. Cate was still coping with Richard's death, and she didn't want more pain in her life. And for a reason she couldn't explain, somehow, she found herself somewhat annoyed with Max. She said nothing, just held him and listened, but she wished she could get him to leave soon so she could study for the physiology exam. *Why am I feeling so callous?* Cate asked herself. *This is my Max.*

"Cate, please come to Chicago with me for the funeral. My folks are dying to meet you, and I could really use you being there for me." Max was now hiccupping from the crying.

"Okay," Cate blurted before she thought it through. How could she say no to him when he was in so much pain?

Ken and June knew that Cate was seeing someone; she made no secret of it. They even knew his name was Max. But the fact that she never brought him home to meet them had them baffled. They wondered if she was ashamed of them for some reason, or was he so horrible she knew that they would hate him? They had never pushed Cate to give them answers or to tell them all about her life. From the time she was little, Cate had her secret side where even her beloved dad couldn't penetrate.

"You're going to Max's grandfather's funeral in Chicago tomorrow?" asked an incredulous Ken. To be invited to such a family event, Ken decided his daughter must be in a stronger relationship than they had imagined. He badly wanted to demand that they get to meet this guy as soon as possible, but he held his tongue.

"Yea, Pops, Max is pretty shook up. They were close, and maybe I can cheer him up a bit." Even to Cate's ears she sounded pretty unenthusiastic, and a bit unsure.

"Okay, promise to call when you get in and when you're headed back—promise?" Ken relented against his better judgment.

Max's parents turned out to be warm and friendly. Cate liked them instantly and vice versa. While it was a sad occasion, there was still time for getting to know each other and having some fun. Over hot cocoa and a long game of Monopoly, the mutual admiration society was cemented.

A day after the funeral and the day before they would return home, Cate and Max went to downtown Chicago and walked the Magnificent Mile. Typically, it was windy and rain threatened, but the pair were in great spirits. They stopped in front of Cartier and Gucci, pretending they were actually buying something there. When they were passing the Disney Store, Max told her stay there while he ducked inside. A few minutes later he appeared with a tiny Dumbo the elephant, complete with huge ears, a red ruffle around his neck, and of course, the saucy little yellow hat sitting askew on his head. He fit into Cate's mittened hands perfectly.

"Oh precious little elephant," Cate purred, and Max beamed. Dumbo was the first elephant Max bought for her, and it would be the last. Yet for today the couple were very content, and Dumbo just brought them closer together.

"Thanks for being here with me, Cate. I can't tell you how much I appreciate it, and my parents would just like to adopt you, but that would be a little incestuous!" whispered Max.

Max and Cate were an official item from that day. Cate's partying now was mostly with his friends, all future doctors, lawyers, and, yes, accountants. Sometimes at one of these parties Cate would look around and remember the parties just a year ago. All the pot smoking, protesting of the war, sleeping around was the norm. And just three years ago she was a shy Franklin girl who only wanted to marry a local and live there all her life close to her dad and the farm. Well, she still wanted the last bit.

VI

September 1971, Cate began her final year of college. It was an amazing fall day with the leaves still on the trees in reds, yellows, and oranges. Cate took a deep breath of the cool fresh air as she made her way to the administration building lounge where she was meeting Patty, Barb, and Lynn for lunch. As she settled into one of the comfy green chairs, she thought about her three best friends and all they had been through and what was next.

Patty was still with Bob, and they had their future pretty well planned for the next five years. It looked like because of his football playing and coaching skills, unless he flunked out his senior year, several Cleveland schools were actively pursuing him for a teaching and coaching position when he graduated. His negotiations included a position for Patty in a school close by. The pay was not great, but with the extra for coaching, they would be just fine. Then there would be the house and then the three littlies. Cate sighed heavily as she thought of her own future. *What future?* she mused.

What's more, even Barb had a game plan. She was already applying for positions in California in recreation programs around San Francisco. Cate couldn't believe she would just leave her friends and her family for a new life on the West Coast.

Barb was always the most confident and creative of the four, and Cate had no doubt that she would enjoy her new life. *And I'll be sitting here hoping I can find a teaching job somewhere close to home, I guess,* Cate thought. Max would be heading to Chicago to start work with his father, and for some reason Cate didn't seem to mind that he would be leaving

Lynn didn't care where she went after graduation. She was applying to schools all over the country and, without a steady guy at this stage, was looking for adventure somewhere exciting. Cate admired and somewhat envied her open-mindedness and eagerness for whatever came her way after college.

The trio was late as usual, so Cate let her mind drift to her own future. She decided that it was finally time her parents met Max. She thought again that it was possible that she might marry Max someday, right? The thought interested Cate, but she couldn't honestly see herself with Max forever. Why not— the man is perfect. Well, except his eyeteeth protrude a little too far out, and sometimes he talks with his mouth full when he's in a hurry, and he cries more than most men. Huh? She'd never made a list of his faults before. Thankfully the girls arrived, and the discussion turned to midterms and lunch.

Ellen Gordon

VII

Thanksgiving was only a week away, and Cate was beginning to regret inviting her parents and Max to her apartment for the feast. Once again her roommates were with family, so the apartment was all hers. She was staring at the turkeys at the Buehler's grocery, trying to imagine just how much turkey four people could possibly eat. Then there were pies to make, and did she have enough dishes? Finally, she called her mom that night, and they sorted out the menu and who would make what. Feeling a bit more confident, Cate was looking forward to having her parents in her home at last. The only time they had even seen the apartment was when Cate was moving in two years ago.

"Mom, Dad, this is Max, and he's not a Maximillian, just plain Max," Cate announced for no particular reason.

Ken greeted Max with a firm handshake and almost a smile. It was clear that Ken was checking him out closely. June, on the other hand, gave him a little hug and a big friendly smile. "So glad to finally meet you, Max."

It didn't take Ken long to spot Hubert, the green elephant table that he had so proudly given Cate two Christmases ago. Naturally, Cate would have to tell Max yet again how Hubert got his name, just to tease her father. It was an icebreaker, and soon the four were chatting about the kids' upcoming graduation in June, and of course Cate's parents were especially interested in Max's future plans.

"I'm really looking forward to working with my dad in his company," Max explained to June and Ken. "He's making me start out at the very bottom of the business because he wants me to learn just like he did. I'll probably be buried in the mailroom the first year."

"Well, Chicago is not so very far away, Max. I'm sure Cate and you can stay in touch," June interrupted.

Cate was mortified. Was her mom suggesting that Max and she were to be a permanent couple? While Cate had to admit the thought crossed her mind once in a while, somehow the thought never stuck for long.

Quickly changing the subject to the food for the day, Cate asked her dad to help her get the turkey out so it could sit for a few minutes while Cate got out the rest of the dishes. As Cate and Ken headed to the tiny kitchen, Cate wondered what on earth her mom would say to Max next!

"Well, Cate, I must say on first impressions that you have a winner," Ken conceded while he plunked the heavy turkey onto a mat.

"Thanks, Dad. He's a good guy, and we have a lot of fun. I just don't want Mom trying to push it into something it's not and may never be," declared Cate a bit louder than she meant. Ken studied his lovely daughter and wondered for the hundredth time how he ever conceived such a wonderful human being. All he ever wanted for her was peace of mind, which she seemed to find difficult to achieve. Why was she always so restless for the next "thing or person" in her life?

The pair laid out the endless dishes of food that they could never finish, but leftovers would keep the girls eating for a week. It turned out to be a good Thanksgiving Day after all. The food was perfect, and there was no more talk of the future for Max and Cate by anyone. Cate was proud that her parents obviously approved and liked Max. The easy day finished with a competitive game of euchre with Cate and Ken just beating June and Max.

After her parents had gone back to Franklin, Cate cuddled into Max's arms on the couch. "Well, do you think I passed muster with your folks, Cate?" a tentative Max asked.

"Oh I guess they think you're okay for a city guy," Cate teased. What she was really thinking was how would it be if she married Max and had a lot more dinners like this with her parents. While the day had been about perfect, she wasn't at all sure that was what she wanted, or who she wanted, forever.

Julia

I

A thoughtful Cate was sitting alone in her colorful apartment bedroom, which by now was filled with more elephants and other memorabilia from her two years sharing with her friends Lynn and Barb. Christmas break was only a few weeks away and then a scant six months to graduation. "Well, Hubert, faithful elephant friend, what should I do when I graduate? Should I marry Max? Assuming he asks me. Should I head off to California with Barb and have an adventure? Should I get a teaching job close to home so I can still have Jack and see my folks?" Cate stared at the wonderful, colorful elephant. "Wow, Hubert, a whole lot has happened since Dad surprised me with you! And now it's decision time for my future, and I'm clueless. Once again, I could use some help here, Hubert."

II

Cate surprised everyone by choosing a quiet Christmas at home with her parents over a ski trip to Colorado with Max and his family. While Max was still in her life, the excitement of the relationship had started to cool after Thanksgiving for Cate. Was it because her parents thought he was great?

When she drove Max to the airport for his flight to Colorado, neither Cate nor Max had much to say. As Max went through the airport doors at Cleveland Hopkins, he turned back and looked at Cate. What was that look? Cate wondered. Sadness? Confusion? Did Max have his own doubts about them?

She was glad he was away and she could have some time to think. Halfheartedly, she applied for teaching positions around home and in a few larger cities like Cleveland and Columbus. She still thought that Max may ask her to marry him and supposed that may be an answer to her indecision.

"I do still love Max, don't I?" Cate pondered as she carelessly wrapped a set of champagne flutes for her parents. Daydreaming, she could see the perfect wedding and the adventure to follow in Chicago. Yet as it seemed to happen lately, that daydream turned flat in Cate's mind.

"Something has to happen, something has to change to help me make up my mind," Cate demanded as she tangled the tape into an unusable ball. She just wished that there were more options or that somehow her future looked clearer and more exciting.

III

As usual, Ken, June, and Cate were attending the Jacobs' annual Christmas party. Both Cate and June had purchased new dresses for the occasion. Cate admired June's black crepe floor-length dress, highlighted with a ruby necklace and earrings, an early Christmas gift from Ken.

"I hope I look as terrific as you when I'm your age, Mom," Cate sincerely told her mom as they were getting ready to join Ken in the car.

"Ha, enjoy this time, Cate. Trust me, the wrinkles will get you soon enough. And your blue empire waist dress is so perfect with your hair. Excellent choice," June returned the compliment.

Andrew, confident as always, was playing host with his parents. Cate couldn't miss the admiring look he gave her when she entered their living room with her parents. The look made Cate blush, so she hurried to greet his parents. Cate enjoyed the evening catching up with many family friends, hearing of their travels, their children and grandchildren.

Cate and Andrew couldn't grab any alone time until it was almost time for Cate and her parents to leave. Yet Cate couldn't help catching glimpses of him throughout the evening as he charmed everyone he talked to. He had this ability to make anyone feel interesting and worth a chat. Where and when did her "big brother" develop that smoothness? Cate felt a bit jealous, wishing she had his relaxed, comfortable way with people.

Just as the Kingstons were gathering their coats, Cate felt a firm hand on small of her back propelling her forward toward the kitchen. Before she could protest, Andrew turned her around and kissed her firmly on the lips. Cate felt herself swooning a little with the surprise and the warm feeling moving through her body.

"Look up, Cate." Andrew grinned. They were under a huge clump of mistletoe. "By the way, that dress is perfect for you, the color and the style. Hey, let's get together soon."

Before Cate was quite recovered, Andrew gave her a little brotherly hug and was off to make someone else feel special.

Cate was very quiet going home, still savoring that kiss and what it might mean.

IV

Cate and her dad only got to ride one day because of the snow and cold that holiday, but they spent a lot of time cleaning tack, grooming the horses, and just hanging out together. One night, well after 10:00, Cate and Ken were still in the barn checking water lines to be sure they weren't freezing up. Ken had installed a phone line in the barn only a year ago, when he missed an emergency call from a frantic farmer with a dying cow. Yet when it rang that night, both Kingstons jumped as Ken reached to pick it up.

Cate heard her dad's hurried response. "Be right there."

"Want to help your old man deliver a foal?" Ken questioned as he grabbed his case from the tack room and headed to his pickup.

"Yes, please." Cate hurried to catch up with him. "Stop at the house, and I'll run in and tell Mom."

"No time, Cate, the mare is in trouble. We'll call her from the Smiths'."

The mare, a charcoal-colored Welsh mountain pony, was on her side and panting, barely catching her breath between pants.

"How long has she been like this, John?"

"She's been quiet on her side like that for about two hours, but the difficulty with breathing began just as I called you. I've never seen that before. She'll be okay, right, Ken?" a worried

John asked. He had raised horses for years and knew that mares did not like humans around when they foaled. Most foals were born between midnight and 6:00 a.m. Knowing that Mazzi was close, John gave her some quiet time. But when he did a quick check at 7:00 that evening, he could tell she was starting labor. When he returned at 8:30, he was hoping to see her new foal. Instead he started to worry that this was going to be a difficult birth, and by 10:30 knew he needed Ken if he were to save both the mare and the foal.

"Cate, sit by Mazzi's head and try to calm her. I'm going to have to take the foal, and it's in an awkward position."

Cate gently stroked Mazzi's sweaty neck and jowls, softly reassuring her as best she could. "Hang on, Mazzi, almost over. Want a boy or a girl?"

"Okay, I'll make a small incision to help with the delivery, and she's going to be a bit sore, John, but here we go."

As Ken pulled the not-yet-breathing foal from Mazzi, she whinnied and kicked legs in protest. Cate just kept stroking her and talking to her.

As he laid the newborn on the soft hay, the sac around the foal broke, and there lying in a puddle of blood and placenta was a long-legged black filly. As if by magic the spindly legs began to move, and the tiniest of whinnies came from the foal to let Mazzi know that she was here and okay.

"Everybody out," Ken commanded. Even though it was a difficult birth, Ken knew it was now Mazzi's show. Both mare and filly would rest for up to twenty minutes after what they had both been through.

Then if all went well, Mazzi would get up on her feet to start cleaning the miracle baby. During this time, the mare while standing would pass the afterbirth. Only after this very important bonding took place between the mare and foal would Ken return to clean up and check Mazzi.

Cate sat on a bale of hay outside Mazzi's stall with tears rolling down her cheeks. When Ken had finished and was packing up his instruments, Cate gave her dad a big hug. "Pop, that was so amazing. I'm so glad I was here with you tonight." Cate sniffled into his shoulder.

Ken gently pushed her away and looked at his grown-up daughter. "You were a great help. Maybe when you graduate you would consider training as a vet assistant and come work for me," he said, only half kidding with a sigh. He knew all too well that she would soon graduate and start a career in teaching.

The night was pure magic to Cate. That moment when the gangly foal emerged from the sac and came to life was something she would never forget. No wonder he loves his work so much, she thought as the exhausted pair drove towards home.

Feeling closer than ever to her father, Cate wanted more time with him than ever. As they pulled into their driveway, Cate asked, "I have spring break in three months, Dad. Let's see if we can find a trail ride somewhere. You know, like the ones we used to do. Maybe a three- or four-day ride?"

"I would like that a lot, and am delighted that my nearly grown daughter still wants to hang out with her father! I'll start researching what's available and let you know. We have the dates of your break on the calendar. I will find us one fine ride to celebrate spring," he promised.

V

Back at classes, Cate spent time with Max and still occasionally thought of Michael. But after spending time with her dad over the Christmas holiday and looking forward to the trail ride at spring break and then graduation, Cate thought she was finally getting it all together. She wasn't as anxious about the future, feeling that things were going to work out in the next few months. She really wasn't sure why the change, but life seemed a whole lot simpler without the constant questioning.

On a blustery Thursday night in late April, the little apartment found Max, Barb, Patty, Lynn, and Cate discussing the coming weekend. It wasn't warm enough for an outdoor outing, but as winter dissolved, all were tired of movies and basketball games.

"I propose a cookout at the lake. A little snow or freezing temps never stopped us before," suggested Max, who was then greeted by female moans and groans.

"I wonder who that could be?" Cate teased when the phone rang at 4:00. They all knew that Bob called Patty every afternoon before he started his coaching practice. Everyone rolled their eyes as Patty raced to pick up the phone.

"It's for you, Cate," a surprised Patty announced as she stretched the phone cord far enough to reach Cate seated by Max on the tiny worn couch.

"Cate, I um, I, I don't know how to say this to you." Karen, Andrew's mom went silent for a heartbeat. "Oh Cate, I'm so sorry," and a sob escaped before she could finish. "It's your dad...he's gone, Cate. He passed away this afternoon."

Ellen Gordon

Cate sunk to the floor, gently putting the phone on to the carpet. She wasn't sobbing; rather, she sat very still as tears flowed down her face. She turned frighteningly pale.

Max didn't know what was said, but he imagined the worst by looking at Cate's face. He was afraid she was going into shock. He picked up the phone. "This is Max. What's happened?"

"Thank God, Max. Please just bring her home. Her father passed away quite suddenly, and June is falling apart."

He promised. He promised. He promised. Cate would repeat that to herself over and over as the anger and sadness and hurt and pain continued to wash over her.

He promised, and then, before their trail ride together, he died. He died suddenly and alone in the barn that they both loved. Only the horses and wild kittens saw him collapse, with his weary heart stopping before he hit the soft hay of the barn floor.

He promised.

VI

The funeral and the gathering of nearly a hundred of Ken's friends, colleagues, and family followed just a week after his death. Cate was sure she could never cope with the pain, or the sense of loss. Inconsolable and withdrawn, she wanted no one near her. As friends and family filed through the family home after the funeral, Cate stayed as far away from the well-wishers and sympathizers as possible. She watched people hugging her weary mom, giving her their sympathy and support. Cate was too wrapped up in her own misery to consider how devastating the loss of a husband was to her mother. She wanted and needed Cate's support, and she wanted to comfort her daughter, but Cate pulled away.

What about me? Cate thought. *Nobody loved him like I did, and he loved me more than anyone. None of you know how much I'm hurting. I wish you would all go away.* Cate kept to herself the day of the funeral and for many days to come.

Cate's strange behavior was tolerated up to a point, but when she barely acknowledged close friends trying to relay their condolences, there was little sympathy. Yes, everyone knew how close Cate and her dad were. Maybe too close, some narrow minds reflected, but her behavior was not acceptable.

VII

Cate seldom went home after the funeral. She loved her mom but just couldn't help being angry with her for not saving her father somehow. She knew that it was wrong to shut out even her mom, but she couldn't help herself. The house, the farm, the barn, the horses all made her feel lost. How could she ever enjoy these things without her dad?

"Cate, you've got to snap out of it. Spring break is just days away. What are your plans?" an unsuspecting Barb asked, not remembering Cate and her dad were supposed to trail ride over the break. Barb and Lynn continued to try to get Cate out of this funk that had taken her over since the funeral.

Something let go in Cate's mind. "There will be no more trail rides or bailing hay or cleaning stalls or mending fences with my dad. He's gone. And I don't know how to go forward with my life, Barb. So please just back off and leave me alone," Cate snapped and ran to her room.

Barb and Lynn had to give Max credit for trying to penetrate Cate's gloom and despair. He attended the funeral but could see Cate was not happy to see him, so he left and didn't try to see her for several weeks. In reality, Max had planned on asking Cate to marry him just before their graduation, but now he was more than a little uncertain as time passed. The small diamond ring waited in his apartment desk.

Years later, Cate acknowledged that what she had needed was professional help to get through her grief. She couldn't blame her mom; grief counseling was years away from being an accepted course for those suffering depression over a loss. Cate muddled along alone through her final months of college, not bothering to attend her graduation. She was amazed to see how good her grades were, since she barely remembered attending classes those last months.

Patty, Barb, and Lynn couldn't hide their enthusiasm for their futures, even though they tried when Cate was around. Barb and Lynn would be giving up the apartment in two weeks, preparing for the next stage of their young lives. They had no idea what Cate intended to do, if anything, when they all left campus.

"Cate, since no schools have picked up your applications, you need to pack up and come with me to California. We can wait tables if we must, but I think I've already nailed a job with the San Francisco Recreation Department. What do you say?"

"Thanks, Barb. You and Lynn have been the best, and I'm sorry I've been such a mess lately. I just don't know what to do with myself. So no to California, but you guys better stay in touch with me," Cate managed.

"I told Max I wouldn't be seeing him anymore. It's not fair to keep him in limbo, and he needs a fresh start in Chicago. It just wasn't meant to be. I guess I blew that one too," Cate confessed.

Hubert, the last gift from her dad, was seatbelted in the back seat of Cate's VW as she headed back from where it came, Cate's family home. Carefully packed in a box in the trunk was Dumbo, a reminder of a love that almost made it with Max; Pax, the little ivory elephant from Vietnam, reminding her of Richard's death; Star, that magical glass elephant from Michael when they thought they had a future together; White Cloud, the miniature white metal elephant from her hippie days with David; and the start of it all, Aunt B's Petite Red. By now Cate had over fifty elephants, but these six elephants were strong reminders of Cate Kingston's adventures that shaped her life so far.

With a sigh, Cate backed out of the apartment driveway slowly, taking one last look. So much had happened in her four years at college, and now she was headed home to live with her mother?

VIII

It didn't take long for Cate or her mother to realize that Cate being home on the farm, with no future plans, was not going to work for long. June was working through her own grief that summer as well as trying to shut down her husband's business and organize her own financial future. Between her job, which was a lifesaver right now, and Ken's life insurance, June would be comfortable in her eventual retirement. What to do about the farm and the livestock was still up in the air. June knew she did not want to discuss options with a moody, unresponsive Cate right now.

One day, out of loneliness and frustration, Cate called Michael. She had heard he was with someone now, but she hoped that he would understand how lost she was without her father. They had been so close only a few years ago.

To her relief, he came to see her one warm July evening. Cate knew that some of the people in their small town thought she was being some kind of prima donna or martyr about the loss of her dad, and after the incident with the marijuana at Rod's party, a lot of her old friends were pretty much done with her.

"Michael, I'm so lost without him. I don't know what to do with myself," Cate cried as soon as they were seated on the back porch with a cold Pabst. "What do you think I should do?"

"Get a job, Cate, and just stop feeling sorry for yourself," Michael lectured in a tone Cate didn't like at all.

"Is that what everyone thinks? That this is all about me?"

"Cate, your dad would be miserable if he knew that you were giving up on your future because of him," Michael bluntly stated. After a few minutes he finished his beer, gave Cate a kiss on the top of her head, and left, leaving Cate more miserable than ever. *It just isn't fair,* she fumed to herself. *No one will ever understand.*

The final blow that turned her life literally upside down and finally put her into motion was a combative conversation with her supposed big brother and mentor, Andrew. They did have that wonderful kiss at the Christmas party, didn't they?

Andrew stopped by late one afternoon when he knew June would be home. The whole Jacobs family had kept June busy when she wasn't at work, and she was coping as well as could be expected.

There was a very close bond between Andrew and her mom that Cate resented just a little. Cate was surprised to learn that Andrew was helping June redecorate Ken's study. She wasn't happy to see some of Ken's things removed and replaced with accessories more with June's style.

Cate walked into the cool farmhouse kitchen to see June and Andrew laughing over something Andrew had said. The two stopped talking and looked with both pity and annoyance at the tears on Cate's cheeks.

"Everyone is done with you, Cate. Grow up and make your parents proud again. You're acting like a two-year-old," Andrew lectured, and he stormed out of the house.

Cate turned without a word to her mother and slowly headed to the barn. She had found it impossible to go there for weeks after the funeral, but thinking of Jack and Sparky without Ken forced her to visit but not ride. How could she ride out alone? Fortunately, June had plenty of local volunteers to look after the animals until she could decide what to do with them.

Ellen Gordon

Sitting on a bale of hay, looking at Jack, who was looking at her, Cate said aloud. "My dad is dead. Richard died in Vietnam, my best friends have abandoned me with their new lives, Max ran for his life after the funeral (although she knew in heart that wasn't true), and now even Michael and Andrew don't like me."

Cate stood, walked to Jack's stall, and buried her tear-stained face in his neck. "I'll show them all, Jack, I'll leave this petty, mean town and never come back."

IX

When David was in her life, he shared his dream of moving to Australia. "We need to go to Australia, Cate. That is the last frontier—you can homestead, live off the land, and be free in Australia." Cate had heard it so often when they were together that it must have stuck in her subconscious, because not a day after her meltdown with Andrew and her mother, she was back at college investigating teaching positions in Australia. It was her secret, and even if nothing came of it, she was moving again and interested in something.

It turned out that two Australian states, Queensland and Victoria, were recruiting teachers from America due to a critical shortage in both states. An agreement was made between the two countries that those who accepted a teaching position would get a free flight to Australia, which would include family. Both countries also agreed that for the two-year contract, the teachers would not pay taxes to either country.

Cate carefully read the application and all the information that the college counselor had available.

Cate read that the Australian consulate in Chicago was handling applications for Ohio teachers. Cate carefully filled hers out, laughing at how little, well, no experience she had teaching physical education, but she had to try. It just felt good to take the application to the post office and send it certified like they suggested. A week went by with no reply, and it was nearly September. Things were not better on the home front, and Cate assumed there were no positions or she was too inexperienced. She knew it was time to look at other employment opportunities.

One phone call changed all that. Cate was so glad her mom was at work when a Darrel Stonier called from the Chicago consulate asking for her.

"Miss Kingston, we've reviewed your application to teach in Australia, and you are under consideration." Darrell paused to let that sink in. He waited for what sort of reaction he was going to get from this young Cate Kingston. He had heard them all—from screaming with excitement to telling him abruptly, "Oh I don't really want to go to Australia."

"Are you there, Miss Kingston?"

"Sorry, I'm just so surprised, I mean happy, I mean, yes, I'm here." Cate held her breath.

"You'll need to come to the consulate for an interview. Would that be possible next week?" Darrell continued quickly.

He sounded very young to Cate, and she tried to imagine someone in his position, changing lives with a phone call. "Yes, I'll be there. Please give me a date," a more confident Cate accepted.

Cate arrived at the consulate a half-hour early. She had chosen to drive over the day before and stay in a motel close to the consulate so she could arrive promptly at 10:00 a.m. She kept trying to imagine what questions he could possibly ask her. He knew from her application that she had never taught before. *Maybe he just needs to see me, to see if I'm some kind of crazy person.* That made Cate laugh to herself just as a solid, smiling man in a somber black suit came to her with his hand out.

"Do I amuse you already, Cate Kingston?" he asked with an even bigger smile.

"Sorry, I was just trying to imagine what you were going to ask me in the interview. I'm pretty nervous about the whole thing," Cate confessed.

Cate need not have worried. The interview was more like two young people getting to know their new best friend. Darrell talked about Australia and what she could expect, and she told him about college and growing up. The only tough question was the obvious: "Why do you want to take this job and move to Australia for two years, Cate?"

She swallowed hard before she could answer. She didn't want to talk about her dad or the sadness or the anger with this friendly young man. "Adventure." That would become Cate's pat answer when anyone would ask. She wouldn't want anyone to know that burying a part of her felt necessary if she were ever to be Cate again.

Cate and Darrell struck up a friendship that would last for a decade, and Cate would often wonder what happened to him after they lost track when he was reassigned. With Darrell's assistance, Cate was approved within days and needed only to complete background checks (nothing like what she would go through today) and an expedited passport to see her on her way early November 1972. She was first told she would be going to Melbourne in Victoria and read everything she could about the large metropolitan city. It sounded very exciting. Then only two weeks before she left, Darrell called to say she had been changed to Queensland. What? Where? Brisbane? Cate hardly had time to find it on a map and knew very little about it by the time she flew out.

X

"You will not just pack up and leave the country, Cate. That's just ridiculous," Cate's exasperated and angry mother yelled. She had put up with Cate's depression and moping around following her father's death for seven long months, and she really needed to move on, but not to Australia for God's sake.

"I'm going, Mom. I have my acceptance letter from the Queensland Education Department. A contract for two years as a physical education teacher is on its way here," Cate quietly but firmly announced. Cate felt a stubborn pride at making this huge decision on her own.

June stared at her miserable daughter. Cate was so selfish to think she was the only one lost with Ken's death. Being a widow at fifty-four was no picnic for her either. Now Cate was thinking of deserting her as well. Yes, things had been strained between them since Ken's sudden death, and yes, June long ago felt a little resentment of the father-daughter

Ellen Gordon

relationship, but she loved Cate unconditionally, and she needed her now.

"Mom, I love you, but I'm just so sad here. I want to get far away from this stuffy little community, and my college friends are all off doing their own things," Cate tried to explain, but she came off sounding like a whiny child.

Now that the four tumultuous college years were over and Cate had time to reflect on those years, she wasn't all that comfortable with the person she had been. It seemed that maybe she had hurt some people, including Michael and Max. And she was a little wild with the sex and the pot. Fortunately, there were no lasting ill effects, but somehow now she was glad to be leaving the past far behind her—literally.

Andrew heard the news from his mother and called to see if Cate wanted to talk. They hadn't seen or heard from each other since the afternoon in the kitchen months ago when Andrew told her off and walked out. A relieved Cate was so happy to hear his voice. "Yes, come by this evening. I'll make popcorn."

Cate was still dressing when she heard the doorbell and her mom greeting Andrew. She looked at herself in the mirror with a little sigh of satisfaction. She was not sure why it was so important to her that her red hair was shiny and curled or that her jeans and denim shirt fit just right, when after all it was only Andrew. Only Andrew, but that one kiss last Christmas stuck with her.

Andrew was telling June that he had just sold ten wheel loader buckets and had been celebrating with his employees this afternoon. When Cate came down the steps, June and Andrew were still in the front foyer with June congratulating

Andrew on the sales. As Cate approached, she had time to appreciate Andrew's crisp white button-down shirt paired with dress khaki slacks before they acknowledged her presence. How could he always be dressed to perfection whatever the occasion? He probably has designer PJs, Cate thought to herself as she interrupted.

"The kitchen is all yours if you're making popcorn, and the fridge is full of beer. Help yourselves. I have a date with *Travels with Charley*." June was an avid Steinbeck fan and was well into this one.

Once settled with their huge bowl of popcorn between them and a couple cold Buds, the two straddled stools at the kitchen island. "Big decision, Cate. Have you thought how sad your mom will be without you now, so soon after Ken's passing?" Andrew broke the silence.

"I know, I know, I know, Andrew, but I feel like I'm going to explode—I'm angry all the time. And Mom and I aren't really getting along all that well. I need to get out of here."

Cate spent the next hour telling him about Australia. At this stage, she still thought it was Melbourne, and Andrew was impressed with what he heard. Before that last beer was finished, Andrew caught Cate up on his growing business. It was strange to Cate that he didn't mention his first employee, Jack. Cate smiled to herself as she remembered past talks with Andrew where it was all about Jack, Jack, Jack. Had Cate been a little jealous of Jack?

As Andrew stood to leave and call his good nights to June, he held Cate at arm's length and said, "Okay, but if you're really going, promise me that before you go we have one big blowout on the town. Dinner at the Iacomini's, dancing at El Cid, and breakfast at the Bucket Shop. Deal?"

Cate was thrilled. What a perfect sendoff that would be. Was this to be considered a date, she wondered. Whatever it was, she was looking forward to being out with Andrew.

September was flying by. Cate's mom had finally accepted that Cate was going and began to help her sort through what to take. There was a limit on the amount of baggage she could take, so there were some tough decisions. Clothes were the least of her concerns because as a PE teacher she would be in tracksuits, swimsuits, shorts, and T-shirts. And because she had no idea what was fashionable or even acceptable, she thought she'd shop when she got there for fun clothes.

The personal items were tougher. By now her elephant collection had grown to over fifty, with each representing someone special or an exciting time in her twenty-two years. She knew she could only take a few, but the choices were not easy. It hurt that Hubert would have to remain with her mom, who promised to look after him carefully. June knew how much the last gift from her dad meant to Cate. So a couple small elephants from her students while doing her student teaching and several from her roommates to commemorate their adventures would join Petite Red, Dumbo, Pax, White Cloud, Star, and a small pink sachet her mom had given her for the long trip to Australia.

Packing the remaining elephants away for the two years she would be in Australia gave Cate the time to look at every single one and remember the person or the place or the time that the elephant came into her life. She got the idea to record where each one came from in a spiral notebook left over from college.

Years later when she had more than four hundred elephants, the log would be essential to remembering where each treasure came from. She knew that Aunt B would have loved to hear about every single elephant. "Look what you started, dear Aunt!"

As promised, a week before her departure for Australia, Andrew picked up an excited and strangely nervous Cate in his new, ten-year-old Corvette. As she kissed her mom good night and started towards the car with Andrew holding her elbow in mock escort mode, Cate was most impressed. "Have a great night." June beamed as the two walked to the car.

"Since when do you drive Corvettes, Mr. Big Shot?" Cate questioned with a tinge of envy.

"Hey, it's old and has a lot of miles, but I decided to treat myself for getting through my first year with Acme's Attachments," Andrew defended himself.

Andrew's new company was already showing real promise in the heavy equipment attachment business. Sales for his wheel loader buckets were around ten a month, and he was working on expanding the sizes he could offer. It would be another six months before he would leave his job at Highland Tractors. He would leave on good terms with his old employer, who would eventually be one of his best customers.

Cate could not remember a more perfect evening. The lobster at Iacomini's was always Cate's favorite when dining there with her parents. The little bib over her new mohair sweater was a necessity as the warm butter dripped from the lobster claw. They took their time over dinner, mostly talking about old times and growing up together. A crisp chardonnay with dinner and an espresso after rounded out an exceptional meal.

El Cid's was packed, and the band was loud. Cate and Andrew danced until they collapsed onto bar stools around 1:00 a.m. Cate insisted on making a quick stop at her old haunt, the Wildwood.

She couldn't help showing off Andrew to an old lover or two who might still hang out there. It felt so right being with Andrew, and Cate was proud to be out with him. His good looks, charming smile, and hair that fell over his gray eyes caught the eye of girls everywhere they went, and Cate couldn't help but notice.

"Enough," Andrew shouted over the music. "Let's get out of here."

The Bucket Shop was also packed, but by a very different clientele. Most were stoned or on their way, and the munchies had brought them to the only cool place that served breakfast starting at midnight. Cate couldn't believe she was hungry again, but she hoed into pancakes and bacon, washing it down with a beer. She knew she would be cactus tomorrow, but she was having way too much fun to worry now.

When Andrew drove up to Cate's home around 3:00 a.m., they had both been very quiet on the drive home from the city. Cate started to get out of the car, not easy in a Corvette, but Andrew pulled her back into the seat. He put his hands on the side of her face and kissed her. Not a brotherly kiss, and not the holiday kiss from last Christmas. This felt like desire and wanting. Cate felt the heat build down below, just as Andrew gently pushed her away.

Embarrassed and confused, Cate reached for the door handle as Andrew said in a hoarse, quiet voice, "Please take care and come home to us, Cate."

Cate bolted up their front steps and in through the front door before Andrew could even turn the car around to leave. Inside the door, Cate leaned against the hall wall, trying to collect her thoughts and calm down. Thanks goodness her mother was sound asleep, Cate thought.

She didn't want to talk with anyone; she just wanted to be gone. What was Andrew's game, getting her turned on and then just stopping in the middle of maybe the best kiss she had ever had? Is it possible Andrew didn't want her to go to Australia? Well, she'd never know now, because she was getting out of there in one week.

XI

As the time to leave got closer, Cate was on a roller coaster of emotions. She did want to go, but what if this was the wrong thing to do with her life? By now she could have been safely, happily married to Michael or Max or living in a commune with David. Oh no, she scolded herself—she had to move across the world. There was only one person who she could relate to who would be as bold and brave as Cate saw herself now. Aunt B.

One day, just around sunset, Cate drove to Chippewa and parked a few blocks from Chartres. Boldly she walked through the crisp autumn air to the high slope that bordered Aunt B's property. Lights were on in what Cate knew was the magical living room, with the glass cabinets behind worn leather chairs. Uncle Carl had died, and some stranger lived there and was trying to restore it. Maybe she should have tried to stay in touch with Carl, but the family was in shock with B's sudden death, then there were the legal challenges, and Cate felt that talking to Carl would be a type of betrayal. Yet now she would never be inside again or know what happened to the ebony and ivory elephants.

Cate stared up at the big house. "Aunt B, please help me. I want to be like you now. I want to go to Australia and make a new life for myself, but I'm afraid." As Cate turned back to the car, a strong wind came up from nowhere and blew Cate's scarf from around her neck. She felt both a chill on her bare neck and yet a warmth all around her. There was no doubt in Cate's mind that Aunt B was there beside her that night, and that she had made the right decision.

XII

Cate's mom was quiet that last morning before she drove Cate to the airport. June couldn't believe that Cate was really going. Somehow, she thought that Cate would change her mind the last moment or there would be a hiccup with the visa or the contract would be cancelled. Anything to keep her here a little longer.

At the airport, Cate grabbed a cart, a porter at the curb loaded up the four suitcases, and she headed to the Continental check-in desk. As she went through the door, Cate turned to her mom with tears in her eyes to match those of her mother's. At that moment Cate felt terrified and honestly wished she would be going home with her mom. Was she crazy going eight thousand miles away to a new country on her own? But there was no turning back now.

"Call the minute you're safely there and write all the time, Cate. Send me your address as soon as you can." June was practically stumbling over her words by the time they let go of each other. Too soon they would learn what a challenge phone calls between the countries were in the 70's. There was a constant lag in time after one spoke until the other could hear what was said. But at this goodbye, neither had any clue what Cate would experience Down Under.

"Ah, your luggage will go through to LA, where you'll need to pick it up and take it to the Qantas terminal. Wow, you have a long journey ahead of you," the Continental lady behind the desk said gently to the petite young woman in front of her.

Yet a calm came over Cate as she watched her luggage bounce on the conveyor belt toward the waiting plane. It was indeed a long flight with stops in Phoenix and St. Louis before landing in LA to wait for the Qantas flight to Australia. Once in LA, Cate organized her luggage with Qantas for the flight the next day. She kept one small suitcase for tonight at the hotel to dress for tomorrow's flight.

A short taxi ride to the Airport Holiday Inn found an exhausted, unsettled Cate making a call to her mother. When her mom answered, she burst into tears. Exhaustion and the unknown overwhelmed her completely.

Cate slept poorly, but by 9:00 the next morning she was back at the Qantas terminal, eager to find the right gate and get checked in. She knew that her flight was a charter flight organized by the Queensland Education Department for the sole purpose of transporting seventy-five teachers and their families to Brisbane. With her ticket clenched tightly in her left hand and the little suitcase slung over her right shoulder, Cate took a deep breath and opened the doors to the large holding lounge where they would be kept until boarding.

The minute Cate walked through those doors and saw the room full of chattering, laughing families and clusters of friendly singles, she turned straight back into the shy country girl she had tried so hard to leave behind when she went to college. She moved quickly to a couch in the back of the huge room and sat alone, watching the others meet and greet each other. There was such excitement in the air, and it seemed everyone but Cate knew they were headed for a great adventure in the land of Oz.

It was an agonizing five-hour wait before they were called to board the 707. Cate was convinced that every person except her had come with a spouse or a kid or a friend or had at least found a friend during the five-hour wait. Seated by a window, Cate waited miserably to see who would sit beside her for the long flight. She didn't have long to wait.

"Hi, I'm Jackie, and this is Todd. We're from Chicago. How about you?" announced a red-faced, black-haired girl about Cate's age with a broad smile.

"Cate—small-town Ohio."

"This is going to be one great party, ladies," Todd enthused to Cate and Jackie and anyone four seats away. "All we can eat and drink—all free."

And so the journey began. Todd and Jackie had already met and befriended about a dozen people, and they pulled

Cate into the party willingly or not. The Foster's and XXXX beers seemed endless. Cate even had her first Australian Peter Stuyvesant cigarette. No one stayed in assigned seats but wandered the aisles getting to know each other. They partied hard until they had to deplane in Hawaii for a couple hours to refuel. By the time they re-boarded for Fiji, the party mode had faded to sleep mode for most of the plane's excited passengers. As they approached Fiji, the friendly Qantas crew woke everyone up again to feed them, and the party started again.

By this time Cate had met Nate, a math teacher from Maine. They were both a little drunk and a bit nervous about their future destination. To relieve the tension there was a bit of kissing and cuddling before they landed in Brisbane. Cate remembered this last leg vaguely, but she was relieved that she never saw Nate again.

Just before landing, everyone had to return to their original seat. Todd was snoring off his Foster's, so it gave Jackie and Cate a little one-on-one time.

"So you're a PE teacher also," Jackie said, looking a little too intensely at Cate's tiny frame. Jackie was strong, a hockey player and an athlete, Cate thought miserably. What kind of PE teacher was she ever going to be? Hopscotch?

"I'm an elementary PE," Cate defended herself. "Well, I hope that's what I get. I'm not sure I want high school kids."

"High school kids for me. I want to coach field hockey, and I hear it's huge in schools here."

Cate could suddenly feel those all-too-familiar bruises she got while trying to learn, play, and teach field hockey in college.

Ellen Gordon

Touchdown caused the plane full of wound-up teachers to clap and cheer, although Cate wasn't sure why.

Jackie and Todd went off with their new friends who were staying at a different hotel than Cate. "I'll see you at orientation on Thursday, Cate," Jackie yelled over all the excited voices. Cate didn't know any of the people going to the Canberra Hotel in downtown Brisbane, so when they were finally loaded on a bus, Cate took a seat in the back by herself. *I'm really going to have to get better about meeting people*, Cate thought gloomily for the hundredth time in her young life.

As soon as Cate was in her tiny hotel room, she crashed in the clothes she'd travelled in and slept right through dinner. There was no room service, and it seemed the whole city had shut down by 11:00 p.m. A starving, jetlagged Cate waited impatiently for breakfast.

The first day in Brisbane was rest day. Cate really didn't want to be alone all day, so she tried to meet some of her colleagues at breakfast. It seemed most had met last night at dinner and made plans to explore Brisbane on bikes today. She knew she could have pushed out an invitation, but Cate just couldn't do it.

Cate read a little then walked down Adelaide Street to Queen Street, checking out department stores like David Jones and Myers. Sportsgirl looked interesting. Finally, she wandered down George Street and discovered the botanical gardens. In October, Australia's spring, the hydrangeas and jacaranda were in full bloom as well as the soft pink bottlebrush. At a standing-room-only shop, Cate discovered fish and chips wrapped in newspaper. They were salty and delicious, something she had never tasted before.

Sitting on a little park bench, munching on the new culinary delight in the sunshine, Cate felt herself relax. Maybe this was going to be okay after all.

In 1972 Brisbane had less than a half-million people, and watching on this weekday afternoon, it seemed to Cate that people moved slower than folks back home, but they moved with purpose. They mostly looked like Americans, although many of the women had on gloves and hats. Later she would learn that these were women who came from properties in the outback, and this was still the tradition for dressing for the city.

As the day moved slowly on, Cate began feeling sorry for herself again. Cate set about figuring out the time difference between Brisbane and her hometown. At this stage, Australia time was fourteen hours ahead of home. It was 1:00 p.m. when Cate went back to the hotel and called her mom. It was 11:00 at night, but Cate knew her mom would still be reading.

"All's great, Mom. I've met some nice people and have been exploring Brisbane," Cate fibbed. Knowing her mom was so very far away, Cate felt the need to shout into the phone. Then there would be silence for so long that she would start to talk again, just as her mom started to respond. The delay effect was trying, and it wasn't a great call. Even worse, it cost Cate fifteen dollars for just three minutes. Oh, well, at least her mom knew she was safe.

Ellen Gordon

XIII

The orientation was thorough and enlightening for the new Queensland teachers. They heard about everything from road safety: Don't forget to stay on the left side of the road, and watch carefully before you cross a street. Cars are coming from the wrong direction!

They were given a crash course on the education system in Queensland. Each state was responsible for its own curriculum, budget, and teacher training. The teachers were even gently told not to expect everyone in Queensland to love Americans. It seemed there was a bit of suspicion about the morality and ethics of the wild Americans.

What they were not told at the orientation was where they would be posted. "What if we get sent to the outback or the bush or whatever they called it in orientation? Todd would never get a job repairing bikes in a one-horse town," Jackie lamented as they all speculated on what was going to happen to them.

They had been told that many of them would be sent to more remote schools around the state. Not everyone would stay in Brisbane or get one of the larger communities like Cairns or Townsville. Of course, many wanted to be by the water, like at the Gold Coast or the North Coast like Caloundra. Yet several teachers had already heard horror stories of getting one-teacher schools, hours from any real civilization.

Cate had inhaled *The Thorn Birds* by Colleen McCullough, the romantic story of a priest who is sent to the outback and has a steamy affair. The wild, unsettled country described in the story made Cate think of how much she loved her farm and the freedom to roam it growing up. Yet while it all sounded like a magical place to be, Cate was terrified that she might get sent out there alone.

Besides, Cate was already falling in love with Brisbane. With its lazy river winding around the city center, the shops, the ethnic restaurants with so many new tastes to be tried.

The PE teachers, about twenty in all, were seated in a classroom-type setting in the education building. They were handed packets that would tell them where they would be teaching for the next two years of their contracts.

Cate held her breath. With Jackie sitting next to her, they looked at each other then tore open the envelopes. Cate couldn't help letting out a little chirp of happiness when she read Salisbury State School, Brisbane.

Jackie gave her a crushing bear hug as she yelled out loud, "I got a high school in Brisbane!"

All those staying in Brisbane were given a map of the suburbs and three days to find a new home. "Hey, you want to share a place with Jackie and me?" Todd asked Cate as they searched the *Courier Mail* classifieds over cold beer in the Wilson Hotel on George Street. "We're kind of broke, and if we found a house we could share expenses."

"Jackie, do you think that's a good idea?" Cate asked tentatively.

"Hell yes. You're in Salisbury, and I'm in Acacia Ridge High—look how close they are. And look, here is a three-bedroom house in Moorooka, which is close for both of us."

The very excited and hopeful trio rode the 117 bus into Moorooka. Following directions, they were delighted to see how close the house was to the bus stop and blocks of shops. The

Ellen Gordon

three-bedroom, wood-floored, newly painted and papered house was just fine with the three of them. The one small bathroom might be a challenge, but the large yard and working washer and dryer under the house closed the deal.

Cate loved the house. Like most older Queensland homes, it was built high up on sturdy wooden stumps, allowing cooler air to circulate up through the wood floors. Homes did not have air conditioners, and in summer they needed all the cool air they could get. The wraparound veranda had brightly colored chairs and tables scattered nonchalantly throughout. Cate's bedroom was small, but it had large windows covering two sides, giving her plenty of light and a breeze on most nights.

Settling into the house was a lot easier than settling into her new job. While the teachers at her school were friendly enough, they just weren't interested in Cate. They had been warned that not all Australians are American-lovers, and Cate was most aware of resentment from some of her colleagues at the primary school. One day she overheard one of the teachers referring to another "Yank invasion." During World War II, American servicemen arrived in Australia for R&R and evidently had a significant impact on the women. Many married the Americans and moved away. Cate would hear this story many times. What the heck was she supposed to do about that? Plus, there was talk about how Americans were taking jobs away from Australian teachers. That made no sense to Cate. *If they weren't desperate for teachers, they sure wouldn't have paid all this money to get us here*, Cate thought angrily.

The men's and women's staff rooms were in separate buildings. At morning tea and lunch, Cate imagined that every time she walked in to the ladies' break room the conversation stopped. To make it even more difficult, Cate was struggling with the Australian accent. The women would be talking fast and then burst into laughter, and Cate would have no idea what was so funny. This made her even more embarrassed to just be sitting there with a blank look on her face. No one was ever mean to Cate; they just didn't go out of their way to make her welcome.

What saved Cate from complete depression were the kids. They all wanted to listen to her talk, and the older students wanted to know all about America. The only Americans most had ever heard or seen were on TV, and many did not yet have a TV in their home. There was no indoor facility for physical education, so Cate would either be on the oval or in the pool with the grades 1–7 children.

"Cate, no student will leave this school after grade 7 without being a strong swimmer," declared her elderly principal at their first meeting. Fourteen weeks of every school year were dedicated to teaching swimming, and Cate took his demand seriously. Cate would never forget having ten five-year-olds clinging to her body their first days in the pool.

XIV

The first four weeks were difficult for Cate, yet it was hard to stay gloomy living with Jackie and Todd. Todd had started a job repairing expensive bikes in the city and was full of tales about his coworkers and customers. Jackie was loving her PE job and was doing field hockey coaching after school.

There was an endless stream of people through their home, and the weekend parties were becoming legend with their new friends.

After a particularly rough day, Cate came home to an empty house. A box with her name on it was sitting on the front veranda step. When she saw the familiar scrawl of Andrew's handwriting, she grabbed the box and ran into the kitchen for a knife. She hadn't heard from him since that most disturbing night just before she left. She really wasn't sure how she felt about him at this stage.

Inside, it was so carefully wrapped that not one nick marred the soft light brown plaster of the craziest, funniest elephant Cate had ever seen. Her foot-long legs were too long for her body that formed a bowl-like opening. It was the face that made Cate laugh out loud.

The too-big African elephant ears were flapped out to the side of the grinning face. The tag named her Julia, and it was perfect. At once Julia looked shy, drunk, and incredibly sweet. Cate hadn't felt this good in a long time. She knew Andrew knew how much elephants meant to her, and to send this one when she so needed a friend and a laugh was too special.

The note attached simply read, "Saw this and knew it was meant for you. Hope things are working out. Love, Andrew." Cate was pretty sure her mom would have told Andrew or his mom that it was taking a little time for Cate to settle. Huh? Love, Andrew? What did that mean? Big brother love? I miss you, come home love? Cate had no idea, but it sure felt good, and Julia would be with her wherever she would wander in the future.

Maybe it just took time or maybe Julia was magical, but suddenly Cate didn't feel so invisible. Was it just possible that she had appeared standoffish to the other teachers? Cate's chronic shyness could make her seem a bit remote. It all started to change when a grade 6 teacher named Patty asked if she would like a ride to and from school. Cate couldn't afford a car yet, and although the bus service was good, the saved time and money was greatly appreciated. The two would chat a little in the car, but once at school Patty would again act like she didn't exist.

One overcast, drizzly afternoon when Cate had an unusually rough time with the grade 7 boys getting rowdy and out of control, Cate was well fed up with everything and everyone. The grade 7 teacher, Bill Jones, had done nothing to help her with the boys, and Cate could swear she saw a little grin on his face. The nerve of that man.

In the car with Patty, Cate was silent most of the way home, and Patty didn't even seem to notice. As they neared the house Cate couldn't take it anymore.

"What is it with you damn Australians? You're polite and you smile at me, but you don't like me," Cate shouted at a bewildered Patty then burst into angry tears.

Patty pulled the car into Cate's driveway and without a word about Cate's outburst, shouted back at Cate, "Want to play squash with some of us tomorrow afternoon?"

"Yes," sniffed a contrite Cate. "I'd like that." And she fled the car.

The ice was broken that afternoon, although Cate really wasn't sure why her sudden outburst finally got through to someone that she was lonely. First it was squash, then Friday

Ellen Gordon

afternoon at the Salisbury pub, then it was weekend trips to the Gold Coast beaches. Cate became a part of a dozen young teachers and some partners who had a lot of energy, not much money, and could drink copious amounts of beer. While they never accepted Cate one hundred percent, what with her strange accent and Yank habits, they still seemed to like her in their circle.

Cate grew thicker skin because the Aussies were known for their sharp barbs, sarcasm, and innuendo. The Nixon jokes never stopped, nor did their ribbing over her brightly striped socks that she wore with shorts out on the school oval when teaching Aussie students the new game of kickball. They did come to respect the pint-sized redhead who quickly developed into a darn good teacher. And anytime she felt the blues coming on, she had a good chat with Julia. That funny face, and the thoughts of Andrew back home, always made her smile.

Wentworth

I

Cate couldn't believe that she had not only survived, but also had begun to thrive at the end of her first full school year from January to December 1973. The rhythm of her life was not what you could call "fast lane," but there was almost always an adventure to be had on weekends with her teacher pals. Aussies love the outdoors, and a lifestyle of hiking, camping, surfing suited Cate just fine.

Cate's second thirteen-week Christmas school break was coming up fast, and Cate did not want a repeat of her first year's holiday break. Then she was still living with Jackie and Todd, which usually guaranteed plenty of company, but they had gone exploring out of state for most of that first Christmas. Cate had been too broke to go anywhere, having only been in Australia for a little over a month. Why had they brought all these recruit teachers here just before a long holiday? Even if she could have afforded a trip home, she knew she wasn't ready to face Franklin. The sting of losing her dad was too fresh.

But this holiday would be different—Australia was beginning to feel like her home.

II

As the break began, her friends, usually led by Steph, began dropping by to take her along for a barbecue at the beach or a hike in one of the many state parks. Cate couldn't afford a phone yet, so just showing up on her doorstep was the only communication. Steph was a physical education teacher at a nearby primary school. She reminded Cate so much of her good college friend Patty. Steph was feisty, fit, competitive, and quickly became Cate's best friend. Steph was married to Allen, one of the teachers at Cate's school, which meant plenty of opportunity for the girls to bond.

Allen, like most of the male teachers at her school, liked nothing better than to mercilessly tease Cate. It could be American jokes or her outfits or her accent. Fortunately, as the year progressed and Cate's skin got thicker, she began to bite back! For all the teasing, Cate felt she was finally beginning to fit in. Plus, if out with the group, she knew Steph always had her back.

The person Cate could not figure out was Ted Martin. Ted was a conundrum to Cate. He, like the other guys, gave Cate a lot of grief. Sometimes his digs even felt hurtful and harsh. Yet why did he keep coming around and insisting that she join in all the holiday plans? Plus, Ted was the one who on their first camping trip to the Gold Coast taught her to body surf. He proved to be a patient instructor, and to Cate's disbelief he didn't even laugh when she forgot to keep her head down and took a serious tumble under water.

"How could he be mean to me one minute and then be a good friend the next?" Cate debated to herself on the drive back from the coast to Brisbane one weekend.

Cate knew that Ted was from a wealthy family that had put him through the elitist Boys Grammar School in Brisbane. Maybe that's where he got his high opinion of himself and poor opinion of anyone not up to his high standards, Cate decided. His sarcasm was legendary and too often aimed at Cate. She was not taking it anymore and was getting quite sharp with her retorts. The pair bantered constantly, sometimes in a heated volley of insults. Watching this banter was a much-loved pastime by their friends.

"You don't like Americans because we don't like cricket," Cate scoffed back after him after he had been particularly scornful with her country's preoccupation with basketball. Ted considered it a game for sissies.

Ted was first amused by Cate's outburst but retorted with, "Americans don't like cricket because they're too stupid to understand the complex rules."

The others sitting around the beach fire collectively held their breath. The pair was often at odds, but this seemed more antagonistic than usual. Why couldn't they just admit they liked each other? the spectators wondered, not for the first time.

Despite her confusion over Ted, Cate had a wonderful holiday break. Christmas Day found six of the friends camping at the Gold Coast, exchanging little gifts. To no one's surprise, Cate's elephant collection continued to grow.

III

Although they still partied together occasionally, Jackie and Todd had chosen to stick with a group of American friends while, like it or not, Cate was now immersed in Australian culture. Plus, Todd and some of their friends liked to smoke a joint now and then. While Cate had enjoyed marijuana in the States, she valued her job here too much to risk it here in Australia.

One of their peers who were sent to a high school in Rockhampton was caught smoking marijuana with students. It made a big splash in the news, and he was deported. Cate knew if the contract with the Education Department was broken she had to repay the original airfare as well as the initial accommodation to the Education Department. Nope, Cate wanted none of that. Besides, her new Aussie buddies would never think of having a joint. After that incident, Cate became a little uncomfortable sharing the house with Jackie and Todd.

IV

A month after the school holiday, the usual suspects were back at the Salisbury pub for their Friday afternoon ritual. Someone would call out, "my shout," meaning they would buy the first round of beers. Once you got into a "shout," you better stick around until it's your "shout," or you'd be most unpopular. With ten of them around the wooden table in the beer garden, it could be a very long session.

Ted had just grabbed everyone a round and stayed standing when he returned with drinks. "Listen up, mates, I just bought a house," he announced with a puffed-up chest and cheerfully gave them details. He had been living with his brother, who was now going north to take a teaching position in a private school in Townsville.

No one was surprised that Ted purchased a house in Greenslopes. An upper class, older area of Brisbane, not far from Salisbury school but not near students. Ted gave them every detail of his new abode, right down to the hydrangeas in the front yard.

"The thing is, it has four bedrooms and two baths, so I will be advertising for a roommate to help with the mortgage," he finally concluded and sat down.

"Me, me, me." Cate danced out of her seat with her arms waving. The words flew out of her mouth without really thinking it through as usual. "Pick me, Ted. I'd be a great housemate." All Cate could see was her own bathroom. She loved Jackie and Todd, but she knew it was time for a change and just didn't know where to start. She couldn't really afford a place on her own, as she was still saving for a car.

Nine heads, including Ted's, turned to stare at her, open-mouthed. "Are you serious, Cate, or are you just messing with me as usual?" a startled Ted asked.

"Well, if you don't charge too much and you're not messy and I can get a kitten—yes, I'm serious."

Although their friends were amused by Cate's decision, they didn't think it would last. In fact, they started a pool for betting just how long the two would cohabitate. Cate was oblivious to all the doubters, and within three weeks she had made the move.

Cate loved her roomy bedroom, and she bought her first ever furniture to fill it. She had a huge old used queen bed and a dresser to match that she found in a resale store. She bought an old desk from the school that they were replacing. A rickety bedside table and a lamp were the finishing touches.

Cate's bathroom was tiny, just a one-person shower and a sink. Like most older homes, the toilet was in a separate little closet-like room next to the bathroom. With Ted's bedroom far away down a long hall, privacy was not a problem.

V

Cate would always find the American holidays a bit rough when none of her new friends could appreciate the importance of the day. Thanksgiving, July 4th, Memorial Day held no meaning for the Aussies. Never to be deterred, Cate would just invite everyone to her place, well, Ted's place, and throw the appropriate party as if she were at home.

July 4th landed on a Saturday, so Cate had big plans for the day. As she put things together in the morning, she thought of other 4ths back home. A special memory was riding Jack in the July 4th parade with her dad by her side. He had looked so handsome in his volunteer sheriff uniform, riding Sable with the silver saddle and bridle outshining all the other riders.

"No tears today, Cate," she firmly told herself. "This is going to be a special day."

When guests began arriving, they watched a huge American flag fly around on the clothes hoist, a wind-up or -down contraption for drying clothes never seen before by Cate. She had prepared baked beans, hotdogs, potato salad, deviled eggs, and brownies. All this Yankee food would be washed down with huge amounts of Foster's beer.

It turned out to be a perfect afternoon, and though a bit chilly, Cate was in her favorite cutoffs brought from home and topped the outfit off with a red, white, and blue shirt with the American flag sewn on the pocket. Most of her friends made the effort to wear red, white, and blue themselves and put up with Cate describing parades and huge family celebrations into the evening.

Around 10:00 the troops started to leave, with Ted and Cate waving them off. When they were all gone Cate plopped down hard on the sofa with a huge sigh.

"Hey, why the sigh? It was a great party," Ted reassured her and sank down next to her.

Tears were forming in Cate's eyes as she turned to Ted. "I miss home, and I miss my dad," and the tears fell on Ted's sleeve.

Suddenly he was holding her gently and kissing her forehead. Then he kissed her cheek, then her lips. They looked shyly at each other, and without a word clothes were coming off as fast as they could manage. And the coupling that started on the sofa tumbled to the floor and continued until they were both satisfied and smiling at each other.

"Oops," said Cate.

"Yeah—oops," agreed Ted.

Ellen Gordon

After that surprise encounter, they became a kind-of couple. Not a lovey-dovey kind of couple; they each had their own activities and liked their time apart. Cate thought Ted was just fine for the time being, but she really couldn't see anything permanent. And she had no idea what Ted thought, as they never discussed what exactly they did have together. They did share Ted's bed after that night, and it was nice to have steady sex again.

Three years later—Cate and Ted are still together, much to everyone's surprise!

No one won the original pool!

VI

Even though Cate was officially living with Ted, she kept her comfortable bedroom that she had proudly set up when she first moved into his house three years ago. Sitting on the bed with her was Ginger, the kitten grown up and in charge of the household. As Cate absentmindedly rubbed her soft fur, Ginger rewarded her with loud purrs.

"You are a tub, Miss Ginger, and you're only three years old." One of Cate's conditions for moving into Ted's home was that she could have a kitten. She had only just moved in when one of the seventh-grade students brought in a box full of tiny kittens to the staff room at school, hoping to find homes for them. Cate took one look at the box full of six tiny meowing bodies and without thinking picked up the runt of the litter. "I'll take this one, Mathew," she announced.

Now that runt of the litter was obese, Cate had to admit. "Wow, I've had you for three years, and I've been in Aus for almost five," she reflected. It didn't seem possible; it all went so fast. Without thinking she turned to look at Julia, still smiling her goofy smile back at her.

Julia made her think of Andrew, as she often did. Although her mom wrote often, she hadn't mentioned the Jacobs lately. "I guess Mom is moving on, making a new life without Dad," Cate told a bored Ginger.

Dad. "It just doesn't stop hurting, Dad," Cate said a bit louder and angrier than she expected. Ginger dove off the bed and ran for the door. Years and tears were still not mending Cate's heart.

VII

A long weekend was approaching. Cate was trying to remember what holiday they were celebrating this time. She hadn't quite figured them out, even after all this time. The queen's birthday, Melbourne Cup, or Anzac Day? Cate was watching Ted pack a duffel bag for a few days of fishing with some of his rugby pals. In flew a couple pairs of togs (swimsuits), three well-worn T-shirts with the Ballymore logo barely visible, a spare pair of flip-flops, and a large floppy hat.

"Don't forget the sunscreen, Macho Man," Cate teased. "Wait, what will you eat if you don't catch any fish?"

Ted opened the lid of a large Esky cooler. "If there are no fish, it's beer, beer, and more beer."

Ellen Gordon

Cate rolled her eyes as Ted threw the duffel over his shoulder and heaved up the Esky full of Foster's beer and shuffled out the door.

Contrary to feeling left out, Cate found herself anticipating a few days on her own. "It's you and me, Ginger," Cate said to the fluff ball rubbing against her leg. "And that's just fine with me."

Cate glanced at the mirror hanging in the long hall leading to her room. "Look at you, Cate Kingston, all tan and fit. In love with a great guy, with lots of friends. What more could I ever want?"

By the time Cate reached her room and prepared to write a long letter to her mom, a thought crossed her mind and sent up a pesky black cloud. Was she really in love with Ted or was it just convenient to be with him? They did laugh a lot, right? And they did lots of interesting things together, like surfing, camping, and hiking. That was beginning to sound more like boot camp than love to Cate. "What else could she possibly want? She had never lasted this long with a guy, so it must be love," she sighed.

Cate's first years in Queensland went by so fast that when her two-year contract with the Queensland government was about to expire, she knew she was still not ready to return home. The Australian government allowed those who wanted to remain to gain permanent residency and start taking out taxes for the first time. Queensland teachers were paid well, far over what Cate would have been earning in an Ohio elementary school. When the two-year anniversary came and went, she was still with Ted, had a collection of good friends, and was content with her life in Australia.

Plus, Cate had accepted a new position for the next school year. She would contribute to the writing and implementation of a new health curriculum for K–6. While she enjoyed physical education, after five years she was ready for a new challenge. She had already met her new team leader and other writers as the end of this school year approached. Cate planned on doing some reading and prep work over the Christmas break. She hoped that this new position would quiet down the persistent little doubts that she now battled concerning her current life with Ted.

Somehow going home, even for a visit, never seemed to be an option. She had bouts of homesickness missing her mom and the farm, and she wondered how Andrew was getting along with his new business. Cate's mom's letters were newsy, often telling her about her high school friends and their lives.

She heard from Lynn, Barb, and Patty on an irregular basis as they carved out their young lives, as Cate was doing in Australia. They kept promising to come visit one day, but Cate was pretty sure that wasn't going to happen. Australia was just too far away.

In what would be their third Christmas together only a few months away, Ted tried again to coax Cate into a vacation in Ohio for the holiday.

"Cate, you must miss your mom, so why don't we leave right at the beginning of school break—do a bit of travel in the states and be with your mom for Christmas," an enthusiastic Ted offered. "I would love to see snow!"

"Of course I miss Mom, but we write all the time. She's fine—busy, just about ready to retire, I think. She has been such a hard worker; she deserves time off," Cate deflected the

Ellen Gordon

direct question. "But with my new job starting in January, I want time to prepare. I need to hit the ground running on this one."

"Okay," Ted acquiesced, "maybe next year." Lately he had begun to wonder if Cate was tiring of their relationship, and he hoped that a trip to America would bring them closer. She seemed so eager for this new job, which would entail some travel. He wasn't sure that he wanted her starting a new phase of her life.

VIII

The new position turned out to be a bit more of a challenge than Cate imagined. The writing and editing was one thing, but the teacher training was quite something else. When directed to stand before thirty or so of her peers and convince them to adopt the new curriculum, Cate's old less-than-confident personality kept creeping in on her. Her new boss, Lois Jackson, just kept encouraging her and supporting her until the dry mouth and rapid heartbeat began to disappear. As she became more comfortable with the material and the audience, Cate found herself enjoying the opportunity to present new material to fellow teachers. Of course, not all people like change, and the real challenge was getting teachers, especially those who had taught many years, to at least give the new curriculum a test drive.

After the first four months, Cate was loving the work and decided that 1977 might be her best year yet.

The new team was planning their first three-day residential seminar to train teachers not only on how to implement the new curriculum, but also how to integrate interpersonal skill development for children into the classroom. These skills included time management, trust building, communication, conflict resolution, and self-esteem building. At the seminar these skills would be taught through experiential learning, with the teachers actually participating in small groups. Cate felt herself blossoming into a true professional in her field and was looking forward to running one of the small groups for the first time.

Ted was beginning to resent this new enthusiastic Cate. She was different somehow, and he began to think she would leave him behind. "Cate, you are working way too hard and having way too much fun," Ted tried to joke with her. "Spring break is in two weeks, and we have a way cool invitation."

"I'm not sure I can get away, Ted. But I'll bite. What is this way cool invitation?"

Jan and Ian, good friends of Ted's from the rugby club, had invited the pair to spend a week on a working sheep property called Belgaum. Ian worked for the Brisbane city council in the Development and Planning Department. For several years he worked with Robert Grossert, and both Ian and Jan had become great friends with him. The pair were not only surprised, but a bit dubious of Robert's decision to quit his lucrative position to join his family in a business venture in far western Queensland.

"You are going to do what?" an incredulous Ian had demanded of Robert over a couple of Foster's after work one day.

"I told you; we bought an eighty-thousand-acre property—it's a working sheep station. Compared to the properties up north, it's small, but it should carry a few hundred sheep and a few head of cattle. And Jan and you better get your butts up to see me, because I'm sure my social life is about to take a nose dive. The closest town, if you can call it that, is well over an hour's drive."

Given a holiday was approaching, Jan and Ian had decided to take a week to see how Robert was surviving. They had met Robert's parents in Brisbane when they were up from their Sydney farm to visit Robert. They worked that farm before selling it to take on this new venture. They knew they would be welcome and looked forward to the adventure. Immediately they both agreed it would a lot more fun if Ted and Cate could come along. Robert agreed—the more the merrier.

At first Cate protested and started to make excuses until she remembered the Australian novel *A Town Like Alice* by Nevil Shute. Just last year she had inhaled the story of Jean Paget, an English woman who survives a prison camp, makes a well for the small Malaysian community where she is a prisoner, and falls in love with an Australian soldier who is a fellow prisoner. They are true star-crossed lovers, each thinking the other has died before the end of the war.

When Jean eventually finds Joe is alive, she goes to Queensland, Australia, to find him. What she finds is a lovely, thriving town called Alice, but that's not where Joe lives. Willstown is a true outback community with little going for it economically when Joe and Jean finally get together. Jean is determined to make Willstown a town like Alice and does! Cate loved the book for the wonderful love story, but it also opened

Cate's imagination for romance in the outback. She could see herself as an American Jean Paget headed to the bush.

Cate said yes, mostly out of a strong curiosity for what the outback or bush would be like. Ted was delighted that she agreed and hoped that this time away would boost their affection for each other. Too late Ted would be forced to recognize just what a mistake this trip would be.

IX

It was a hair-raising drive, on narrow two-lane unpaved roads, which unnerved everyone except Cate. Still in her dreamtime imagination of the wild outback, she barely saw the trucks pulling four huge trailers fly by, nearly blowing the little Mazda into the gravel on the side of the dirt road. What Cate saw was the wide-open, empty wilderness; this was the bush; this was where rugged men and strong women eked out a living. Suddenly Cate felt alive and excited to get there. She was making the others a little nervous with her enthusiasm.

After nearly eight hours, the weary crew stopped in St. George, population two thousand, to get petrol gas. In their short break they viewed the entire town. There were four pubs, two chemist drug stores, a ladies' dress shop, two farm supply stores, an elementary school and a high school, three churches, a doctor's surgery, a small hospital, two banks, and two small grocery stores. All these miniature stores and schools were packed into six streets. The town was nicely nestled on the Balonne River Dam, which provided much needed entertainment through boating and water skiing. They were all surprised to see a sign pointing to a golf course.

As Cate kicked the red dust off her sneakers before getting back into the car for the last hour of their journey, she smiled at a small aboriginal boy sitting in front of the gas station. Cate had a good feeling about this little bustling community, but she certainly had no idea that one day it would be her home.

There was no MapQuest or GPS systems in 1977, nor were there cell phones. The drive-exhausted crew had to slow down and follow directions to find the mailbox, which was an old rusted barrel. They could barely read the faded letters that spelled Belgaum. A huge hooray went up as they pulled up to the heavy metal gate. Ted jumped out to open it, with Cate bounding right behind him to help.

She couldn't see any sign of civilization anywhere, but she already loved the quiet. Before they had driven a mile, two large red kangaroos bounded across a nearby paddock, getting everyone's attention. All were ready for the adventure to begin.

There were two more gates before they saw any buildings. First, they passed a small wooden cottage with a tiny outhouse a safe distance from its back door. A little further along the red dirt lane rose a large wooden house up on stilts. Especially in the outback, Queensland homes had to be up high not only to encourage rare breezes, but also to discourage snakes, mice, and spiders, all of which were well known in this territory.

As they spilled out of the small car, they were greeted by John, Robert, and Jean Grossert. The warm welcome included cups of tea and homemade chocolate chip cookies. Before plans were made for the next day, the four were happy for a bit of a stretch and to check out their sleeping arrangements in the cottage. Robert had the cottage to himself, and there were two extra small bedrooms for Ian and Jan and his new friends Ted and Cate. Cate threw down her duffel bag onto one of the small single beds in the room Robert gave them and dashed out to bombard him with questions about the property.

"This place is unreal, Robert. Will we see more kangaroos? Do you round up the sheep on horseback? It would be amazing to ride on the property. I just can't wait to see everything," a wound up Cate finished.

Cate made Robert laugh with her babble, but it was clear that he was more the strong silent type who would tire of her barrage before long. He left them to unpack and have a wander around the house paddock with its work sheds and pen of orphan lambs. Shearing had been just last week, and always some of the lambs get lost in the shuffle. This meant bottle-feeding for several weeks. Each lamb meant money, and all needed to be saved. Cate couldn't wait to feed the lambs, so she set off for the sheds before the others finished settling in.

Around 6:00, Robert found the four in the large shed with the guys checking out the bulldozer. Although already old, whoever looked after it kept it spotless.

"That's a Case 450 track dozer," Robert explained. "The rake on the front and the ripper on the back were all made by Dad. He's a genius at making these attachments so vital to land clearing out here."

He went on to explain the popularity of the dozers in the outback. "About fifteen years ago Queensland and the federal government passed legislation that gave World War II vets a block of land in central Queensland, called Brigalow country. All the soldiers had to do was clear the land and set up a farm. Dozers were the hot ticket item, and prices shot up. Now they're saying that in those fifteen years three million hectares, about 7,400,000 acres, of native bush was destroyed. Anyhow, we were lucky to get this used dozer fairly cheap, and Dad fixed it and made the rake and ripper."

"Come on, Mum's got dinner started," Robert said as he herded the four towards the house.

There was enough of a September chill for everyone to appreciate pulling up comfortable old squatter's chairs close to a blazing bonfire. Not far from the fire was the biggest barbecue plate Cate had ever seen.

When she commented on it to Jean, she explained that when they were shearing, which could last several days, they were responsible for feeding the hungry shearers. The large barbecue plate made it a lot easier to prepare their meals and was often used for both breakfast and dinner.

As they settled into the chairs, John came out carrying a tray piled high with thick steaks and lamb chops. All four suddenly remembered that they had not stopped for lunch, so the meat looked good to them. Already sitting on the long picnic table on the other side of the barbecue were big bowls of potato salad, corn, and peas. Everything they were about to eat came from Belgaum.

The conversation was easy as John and Jean talked about their early adventures on Belgaum. Cate felt herself relax as she listened and let her gaze go out over the paddocks that seemed to go on forever. The absolute quiet that surrounded the little group made Cate think of her farm and nights where the Kingstons used to sit around a bonfire down by the creek on Sunday evenings.

Cate's reverie was short lived when all but the three Grosserts were startled by the sudden ear-shattering breaking roar of a motorcycle coming toward them fast. Cate frowned in its direction for disturbing the wonderful quiet.

The cloud of red dust caught up with the rider as he abruptly swerved to a stop about thirty feet from the group. A dog had been perched on the gas tank but flung itself to the ground just before the stop. "And this is Christopher," sputtered Robert.

The man who bounded off the huge motorcycle appeared to be totally covered in the thick red dust, with only his bright blue eyes showing on his face. Who knew what color his hair was under the dust, but it was wiry and cut close to his head. He wore a faded plaid shirt with the sleeves torn off, tucked into a pair of ripped navy Dickeys, the favorite brand of work shorts worn in the Outback. Long tan spindly legs grew out of large work boots, completing one of the strangest outfits Cate had ever seen.

"Your poor dog fell right off—you could have hurt it," Cate burst out before she thought, as usual.

Most everyone, except Ted, grinned at the outburst. *Typical Cate*, he thought to himself. *Just can't keep her thoughts to herself.*

"And who are you to tell me how to drive or look after Mabel?" Christopher countered with raised eyebrows.

"Sorry Chris." Ian spoke up. "Cate and Ted are friends of ours, and Robert was kind enough to invite them to come for a visit as well. Guys," he addressed Cate and Ted, "this interesting specimen is Robert's younger brother. We'll have no dull moments with Chris around."

No one could think of shaking hands with the coating of dust on him, but Ted saluted him and Cate just sized him up. There seemed to be a small indignant spark igniting between the two as they stared each other down. Chris raced up the stairs to wash up for dinner. He lived in the big house with his parents. It seemed the brothers were such opposites that the thought of them sharing the cottage was not acceptable to either one.

While cleaning up, Chris was considering the newcomers. He had met and really liked Robert's friends Ian and Jan. Occasionally, Chris would leave the family farm in Sydney to have a few days with Robert in Brisbane. A few days was about all either could take. Chris was a bit of a loner and much happier and more comfortable on the farm or now in the outback. Robert, just the opposite, was having a tough time adjusting to the solitude of Belgaum. Chris was feeling a little uneasy by the way the girl Cate looked at him, and how dare she question the safety of his amazing Australian sheepdog, Mabel? She always rode with him like that.

Chris at six-foot-two always found short girls amusing. This stranger could be no more than five feet, and the long straight hair made her seem even smaller, elfin-like. Her eyes seemed almost too big for the small face, so when she looked at you the stare was so personal. Oh well, she was either married to that guy Ted, or at least they must've been together. Yet, there was something about her that made Chris want to get back to the party.

The Grosserts had purchased Belgaum two years before. The gameplan was to work hard, spend no money, have a few good years of wool sales, then sell for a profit before returning to civilization. The four of them were all one hundred percent committed to making this work. The bad news was that the first year on the land a drought started, and by now many of the dams on the eighty-thousand-acre property were starting to dry up. That meant the sheep had to be moved from paddock to paddock frequently to keep them in water. It also meant hours of cutting mulga for the sheep to eat. This, added to all the other chores of keeping this place afloat, was more than a full-time job for all four of them.

The barbecue that first night was a great success. Cate couldn't get enough of hearing about Belgaum. All four Grosserts were kind, obliging hosts, and long after dark, when the fire was just coals, they were all settled in over some good Australian wine that the travelers had brought. Eventually, Jean and John went up to their home, and Robert was busy catching up with Ian from their days working together. Jan and Ted claimed exhaustion and headed for the cottage. Cate knew she should go with them, Ted would expect her to, but she didn't want to end the night.

Cate and Christopher talked for another hour, even outlasting Robert and Ian. Chris found more wood for the fire, and they had a last glass of wine. When they finally wound down, and the wonderful silence of the outback washed over Cate again, she reluctantly took the flashlight torch that Robert provided and smiled her good night.

They agreed that in the morning, before Chris' work for the day officially started, he would take her for a ride to stir up some kangaroos and emus. Cate was thrilled, and even Ted's somewhat chilly good night when she reached the cottage could not dampen the wonder of that first evening.

Ellen Gordon

Before daylight crept into the sparse bedroom the next morning, Cate could see Ted's outline in the other single bed, and by his gentle snoring, she knew that he was still sound asleep.

Cate tried to stay still, knowing no one else in the cabin was stirring, but the excitement and anticipation of exploring Belgaum with Chris forced her up, gathering bits of strewn out clothing as she tiptoed out of the bedroom. Cautiously going by their friends' and Robert's rooms to the kitchen, Cate pulled on jeans, a T-shirt, and a baseball cap.

Grabbing her boots and socks, she quietly headed for the narrow back door. Once outside she sat on the front step to pull on the socks and boots purchased just for this trip.

As she adjusted to the darkness, she was startled to see a person leaning against a motorcycle not ten feet from her. She continued to stare in his direction, waiting for him to speak.

"If we get to Plains Paddock in the next fifteen minutes, I can show you the best sunrise in the West," Chris boasted.

"How did you get that beast here without waking us all up? The noise you made on arrival last night was deafening," a confused Cate asked.

"I pushed it, of course, and I'll push back up past the sheds before we take off. By then it will be too late for anyone to yell at us," he laughed.

Cate hesitated for about two seconds before trotting along behind Chris and his bike. For someone of slight build, he sure was strong, Cate decided, watching him push the bike along at a good pace.

Just past the sheds Chris kicked over the motorcycle's engine, and with no hesitation Cate jumped on behind him, hanging on to his narrow waist for dear life.

It was still dark, but Cate could sense the coming of the dawn, with the birds calling out and a breeze picking up as the pair flew down the dusty track. They passed through two gates, which Cate cheerfully opened and closed, before Chris stopped on a high bank of a large dam.

Chris produced a blanket from the bike's saddlebags, along with a thermos of hot strong coffee. Just in time they silently watched the first rays of sun peek up on the horizon. The sky was cloudless, so the rays were almost piercing as they spread out before them.

Cate felt overwhelmed by the beauty of this moment in this amazing land. She slowly got to her feet with the metal mug of coffee between her hands for warmth. Just before daylight in the outback, a chill from the night's dew could still be felt. In just moments the sun dried out the red earth again.

Turning slowly in a 360, with the sun fully up, Cate could see for miles in every direction. She inhaled deeply the smell of mulga and wild grasses and sighed. How could she feel so attached to this land already? It was barren and dusty and difficult, but Cate was already starting to love it.

"Better get you back; I've got sheep to move," Chris said softly, now standing beside her.

Yet they stood there for another few minutes just looking at each other. There was no denying the pull Cate felt towards him, but that was impossible, she scolded herself. As if reading her thoughts, Chris turned and dropped the blanket, thermos, and mugs back on the bike and started it up.

Ellen Gordon

Over breakfast an hour later in the cottage with Robert, Ian, Jan, and a somewhat subdued Ted, Cate tried unsuccessfully to explain the absolute beauty of the sunrise. Everyone but Ted just looked at her with amusement. She gave up and finished her toast.

"I thought we might start the day on the four-wheelers, taking a tour of half of the property," Robert started to explain to the little group, when the roar of Chris' bike cut him off.

"Um, if it's okay, Robert, Chris has to move sheep this morning, and he said I could ride along. Ted, you don't mind if I see you at lunch?" an enthusiastic Cate excused herself before anyone could comment. Feeling more comfortable on the bike now, she jumped on just as Mabel jumped onto her place on the fuel tank. The trio roared off in a plume of red.

Everyone looked at Ted with varying expressions. Embarrassed, he stood and said, "Let's get on those four-wheelers, huh?"

The rest of the time at Belgaum followed a similar daily pattern. No matter what job Chris had for the day, Cate was with him for the morning. All knew something was up when she even went with him to clean out the fly pots. Flies are a great threat to sheep. If they get in their bottoms, they lay eggs, which hatch as maggots, and can eventually lead to death as the maggots eat their way through the sheep. Huge pots full of a honey-like substance are put out in the paddocks, where thousands of flies are attracted and get stuck in the gooey mess. Great plan, but not fun to clean and refill.

Cate rode fence lines with him to be sure there were no holes to be repaired. Sheep could get out, and rabbits and dingoes could get in. They had one near accident when a frightened male emu came charging down the fence line straight at the speeding bike. One three-hundred-pound flightless bird and one flying motorcycle would certainly have an unhappy ending. Chris managed to plunge them into the bush, just as the crazed bird zoomed by.

That may have been the first time they kissed. Fear brings out boldness in the best of us. The kisses led to sex eventually. Sex in the bush with Chris, who was as untamed as the other wildlife, was daring and exciting to Cate.

By the end of the stay at Belgaum, it was obvious to all that there was some sort of bizarre connection between Cate and Chris. As the four crawled back into the tiny blue Mazda, everyone, including John and Jean, was shaking their head at the pair. Cate had her consulting job with the Education Department to return to, and Christopher was as tied to the property as he possibly could be. He had no money; everything the property earned covered their meager living expenses then went to pay off the mortgage as fast as possible.

The truly star-crossed lovers said goodbye, barely hiding their sadness from the others. Ted never said a word about Cate's behavior. They weren't married, and truthfully they hadn't really been getting along as well as their first years together. What they did have was a lot of fun, energetic friends who were always up to something every weekend. That made it easy for the two of them to just hum along with the crowd for days on the beach or hiking in the parks or impromptu "barbies." There wasn't a whole lot of chatter on the ride home, and all four were delighted to part at the end of another long drive.

Cate still shared Ted's bed, but they both knew their relationship was falling apart. She thought her heart was broken. All she could think about was Chris and Belgaum. She wanted desperately to be back on the land, to inhale the sounds and smells of the outback. Chris wrote long, lonely letters to her, declaring his love and describing his days on the land.

All four of the Grosserts continued to work from sunup to sunset just to maintain, and Cate loved hearing Chris describe moving a herd of a hundred sheep with just Mabel to help him. The more he wrote the more Cate knew she was falling in love with him.

"Cate, I have to take the kangaroo hides into Toowoomba to sell next month. Care to meet up?" Chris drawled in one of their rare phone calls. One of the few ways for Chris to earn extra money was to hunt, skin, and sell kangaroo hides. When he shot a roo, every bit of it would be used, not just the hide. The meat would feed the sheepdogs, and the huge bones would clean their teeth. People didn't realize that the kangaroos competed with the sheep for feed on the property. Culling them was not only a source of income; it kept the population down, especially critical in drought.

"Of course I'll be there," Cate quickly answered. Yet when she hung up and the arrangements had been made, she wondered why she felt a little reluctant to meet Chris in Toowoomba. What they had on the land was wild and intense. Sex in the soft grass by a dam in a hundred-acre paddock was an experience Cate would never forget. Being in the outback was something indefinable to Cate, and yet she longed for it. Often she would fantasize what it would be like if her dad were still alive and he came to Belgaum. He would ride horses and hunt with Chris. Then sadness reminded Cate that if her dad were still alive, she would never have come to Australia.

X

Chris found them a small, tidy room at the Wentworth Hotel in downtown Toowoomba. It was a pub with ten small rooms upstairs, popular with outback travelers. The pair met in the cozy lobby and decided to have a beer before heading to their room. Both were a bit anxious and out of their comfort zones.

"I've missed you. I have no idea what happened to us that week, but you changed my life." Chris stared into his beer glass as he spoke.

"It was insane and a bit scary," was all Cate could think to say.

They finished their beer, and feeling like a couple of naughty teenagers, they climbed the worn wooden stairs to their room. Chris sat in the only chair in the room and pulled Cate onto his lap. "Look, a real bed, Cate. We don't have to do it in the grass or against a mulga tree or in the old herder's hut."

Cate snuggled closer and giggled. "Maybe we should do it on the floor—that's more like what we're used to." The tension was broken, and they both relaxed.

"Oh no, I paid hard-earned kangaroo hide money for this bed, and we're going to use it," Chris commanded. And so they did for two days, barely coming out to eat or grab a few beers. Mostly they talked about Belgaum, whenever they were actually talking. Chris would have no understanding of Cate's world, and besides, it was his world that Cate longed for now.

On their last morning, reluctant to stir from the afterglow of sex, Chris reached down into his rucksack. "Close your eyes; no peeking. Okay, open them."

Sitting on the pillow next to Cate was a cheeky pale pink elephant leaning on its side with its trunk high in the air. Wide-eyed and with a huge grin, this barely a handful of an elephant made Cate squeal with joy as she kissed his tiny head. "Chris, he's perfect. I'll call him Wentworth. Cate had forgotten that she had told Chris about her love of elephants and how her collection had grown in her five years in Australia. Chris remembered and found this little guy in an antique store in Toowoomba before Cate arrived. He watched her face when she saw Wentworth and could tell how genuinely she loved this tiny surprise.

It was time for Chris to start his eight-hour drive home. Cate kissed him and watched him climb into his huge yellow Holden ute. A ute, or utility truck, looks a bit like a pickup in America, but with a long, low back.

Toowoomba was enough of a country town that the heavy kangaroo bar on the front and the kangaroo hunting spotlights on the rooftop didn't look out of place. Yet Cate couldn't help thinking that Chris' ute parked outside her suburban home might raise some eyebrows.

The spark between them was stronger than ever, and they had no idea what to do with this attachment. They talked about living together on the property. At the far end of Belgaum was an old house that the family used when shearing on the west end of the property. Beside the house there was a free-standing building with four rooms and bathing facilities for the shearers. The shearing shed was nearly identical to the one by the family homestead at the other end of the property. They dreamed of fixing up the little house and living happily ever after there.

Yet both knew it was just a fantasy. Chris could barely afford to cover his own expenses, let alone support her. And Cate did appreciate her Brisbane lifestyle now, and the teacher's pay was quite good. When they parted that day, neither held any real hope for being together, but Cate did promise that the next school holiday she would spend most of it with him on the land she longed for.

XI

The two-week August school break was approaching, and every teacher was making plans. "So what are you planning for the break?" Ted asked while the pair wolfed down bowls of muesli before heading to their prospective schools. "A bunch of us are going camping on Fraser Island. If you come along, you can share my tent. Wink, wink."

"Ha ha," Cate retorted. They hadn't had sex in months. In fact, not too long after the Toowoomba weekend, Cate moved back into her own bedroom. Ted hadn't even commented, so Cate assumed he was just fine with that. They still hung out and enjoyed each other's company as well as the whole gang of friends. "I'm going to Belgaum for most of the break," Cate declared a little too loudly.

"You're kidding, right? Please tell me you are not falling for the bumpkin of Belgaum." Ted's tone was cruel and deliberate. "I know he writes to you, but what future is there with him?

And you wouldn't survive six weeks on the property. No beach, no squash court, no movies, no concerts, and no friends." He'd built himself up to quite a fury.

His words stung, and Cate felt the moisture in her eyes. What right did he have to dictate who she should love or where she should live? Her anger was rising too, but then she stopped herself and wondered, *Did I hurt Ted by suddenly moving out of his bed and his future? Why is it so easy for me to leave people behind and never consider how they might really feel?*

"Sorry, Cate, that came out all wrong. It's just that I know you better than you think I do, and you are too much for that boy-man. Of course he wants you. He's alone in the middle of nowhere. Please, just be careful you don't commit to something that's just not right for you."

"I'm sorry too, Ted," although neither one knew why she said that.

The ten days on Belgaum were some of the best of Cate's life. Chris and Cate were up while it was still dark, so there was time for an enormous breakfast of eggs, lamb, baked beans, tomato, and toast. Robert had relented, and they were staying with him in the cottage. Cate sensed he was tolerating her for Chris' benefit, but he was sure she'd never be a permanent fixture in his life. She was a distraction to Chris when his work was needed every day.

After breakfast they would jump on the bike with Mabel on board and head out for whatever work needed to be done that day. One of the best days was when they were moving sheep from Plains Paddock to Dark Forest Paddock, a good eight-mile drive. As the last sheep moved into the paddock,

Cate saw a small bundle curled up near a log. The other sheep were long gone by the time Cate got off the bike to pick up the snowball lamb. It bleated its hunger and fear with its little tongue sticking out. Cate called her Selma, and they took her back to the nursery with a few others to be bottle-fed by a thrilled Cate. She was proud to have saved the lamb and was pleased to look after it while she was there.

The pair ate their evening meals with Robert, John, and Jean in the big house. Jean was originally from England, and to Cate she seemed out of place in this rugged environment. Her hands were swollen with arthritis, and when she did laundry with an old-fashioned wringer machine in cold water, Cate knew her hands suffered even more. But she never complained about the hard work and was an excellent cook for the men. Cate enjoyed her time with Jean, helping clean up after meals and hearing about England, her move to Australia, and meeting John, the love of her life.

"I think I've put on ten kilo in ten days with your wonderful cooking, Jean," Cate complained as she helped herself to a piece of apple pie after dinner one evening. All four at the table just looked at her. She didn't have an ounce of fat on her; in fact, with all the outdoor activity, she looked thin.

While Jean was somehow elegant even in this harsh setting, her John was every bit an Aussie outdoorsman. Cate couldn't help but compare Jean and John to Chris and herself. Like his dad, Chris was a little rough around the edges. But that's what Cate loved about him, right?

"So when are you going to come live on the property, Cate?" John asked out of the blue. "You're a good worker, and we could use an extra hand," he teased.

Cate was blindsided and truly couldn't think of a thing to say. Chris rescued her. "We're working on it, Dad."

Back in Brisbane, Cate was miserable. She tried to explain how she felt to her best friend Steph, but not even Steph could comprehend why Cate would want to give up her life there in Brisbane to live in isolation and even danger. And honestly, how could she give up Ted for a guy with no future and no money?

"Steph, when I'm on the land with Chris, I am so very content—it's like coming home—I'm meant to be there. It's how I used to feel on our farm back home. I like to jog out into the bush by myself and, sure, sometimes I'm scared, but mostly I'm just so overwhelmed by the beauty. I love Belgaum, and I love Chris. I just don't know how to make it work—yet," Cate sighed.

By now Cate had made a very positive impression on those in charge of the new health curriculum she had been helping write and implement. The implementation was nearly finished, so by the end of the year Cate would be looking for a new project. She'd already asked if there was any chance of a phys. ed. position in St. George, hoping to find the perfect solution to having the land and a job. Unfortunately, the phys. ed. teachers in the high school and primary school were a married couple planning on staying in St. George for a few years. Cate had given up on a job coming through and was considering a position with the education department's Drug and Alcohol Program Unit. It would be a similar curriculum development project for high schools throughout Queensland.

Then came the best surprise phone call that Cate could imagine. "We heard you were interested in getting a position in St. George, Cate?" asked the voice of a southwest region inspector, Lawrence Kirby. Cate had met him a few times at conferences, and she knew he knew of her background in health education.

Cate caught her breath. "I am, Mr. Kirby."

"You have quite a bit of experience in curriculum development from what Lois has told me." Lois was the team leader on the health curriculum project and a true mentor to Cate. Lois had helped her overcome her terror of public speaking and turned her into a good trainer for the project. And she'd become even more; ten years Cate's senior, she was a close friend.

"Thank you. I've enjoyed working with Lois, but what does that have to do with St. George, if I may ask?" Cate could hardly control her excitement. Her heart was racing, and she held her breath.

"There is a new project being trialed in about ten schools in the state. It's called the Alternative Program, designed for students who want a high school diploma but either can't or won't do the work required. St. George has been selected, mainly because of the new principal, Steve Paul. Honestly, he's worried about his SAT scores being dragged down by kids who fail. If they're put into this program, they can still graduate in a two-year program if they do the work, but their grades will not count in the school's rating." Steve Paul was obviously keen to make this happen in his school. As an up-and-coming principal, he had no intention of being stuck in St. George for long, and success of a pilot program would greatly boost his career path.

"I'll do it." So typically Cate—words were out before the brain wrapped around the significance of the decision. Time after time in Cate's life she had jumped into something—a new relationship, a new home, a new job, without much thought, and this was no different. In a five-minute phone call, Cate's life was turned around once again.

Trying to reach Chris that night meant going through the St. George exchange, a slow, sometimes impossible process. To be a telephone operator on a country exchange was a position of power. One person controlled all phone calls to over thirty properties.

Each property had a hand ring phone, and a specific series of rings meant the call was for them. If the operator was especially busy, especially tired, or especially didn't like you, your calls could be more than erratic. Fortunately, Sally, the operator on duty, was very pleasant to an overexcited Cate, who was trying to reach the Grossert property. "I'll put you right through, dear. No one else is on the line right now," Sally proclaimed.

The Grossert family was gathered in John and Jean's home discussing the next day's work when the unexpected call came through. "Who on earth can that be?" exclaimed John as he rose to answer the loud series of rings.

"Oh," a startled John spoke into the phone. "It's for you, Chris."

The family watched Chris' face as first it grew a wide smile realizing who was on the phone, and then watched him collapse into tears. So overwhelmed was he by the thought that Cate was coming to live with him, he couldn't stop crying. Cate hadn't expected that reaction. She was all smiles and laughs and plans—no time for tears for her.

In a few weeks it would be the thirteen-week Christmas holiday break. She would move up then and have time to settle in before starting her new job in January. She talked so fast, Chris couldn't keep up with her, so that when his tears ended in a hiccup, all he could say was, "Hurry up here, Cate."

When they rang off, Cate sat on the back steps of the house she still shared with Ted and thought about the phone call. She couldn't put a finger on the uncomfortable feeling that somehow the call was unsatisfactory. "Silly me," Cate scolded herself, "this is all that you've wanted for months."

As for Chris, he turned to face his bewildered parents and brother. They had no idea what Cate had said that set him off like that. Now profoundly embarrassed, Chris just muttered, "Cate's coming to live with me," before heading out the door and onto his motorcycle. He had to get away, to think, to ponder how on earth they were going to pull this off.

Crystal

I

True to plan, Cate had her worldly possessions packed and ready to ship to St. George by the end of the first week of school holidays. The night before she drove to her new life, the gang held a huge going away party for her at Ted's house. She was going to miss this crazy crew, especially Steph and Ted, but they all vowed they would come up on school holidays and chase sheep with her. Cate knew they thought she had lost her mind, yet over the few years they had known her, they knew there was no stopping her once her mind was made up.

Cate made it to St. George around 3:00 the next afternoon. The eight-hour drive by herself was at once exhausting and exhilarating. On Chris' advice, she had traded her little Corolla in for a Ford Falcon, already equipped with a roo bar. There was no denying the comfort and safety of the large car for this long drive. As she pulled up to the gas pump, she could swear that the same little aboriginal boy was sitting on the curb smiling at her. She took this as a welcoming sign.

Most of the teachers were away for the holidays, but she had instructions on how to find her little cave of an apartment. Set up on stilts, the building was divided in two. She would learn shortly that the other half was inhabited by Julie, a home economics teacher at the high school. Most of Cate's possessions had gone straight to Belgaum, including her precious elephant collection. She had so carefully packed all eighty of them for the trip to the outback.

Cate took a two-minute walk through her teacher's accommodation. "Well, I guess it could be worse," she assured herself. "I could have to live here full time." Now more anxious than ever, Cate wanted to get to Belgaum and Christopher.

As she drove over the Ballone River bridge headed south, it seemed somehow symbolic that she was crossing into a new world. Cate tried to shut out any anxiety she had over the new job. For now she only wanted to focus on the next six weeks getting to know the land and her man and his family.

Cate was sure that John and Jean liked her, and they wanted Chris to be happy, but she was also sure that they were probably taken aback by her sudden decision to move in with him. Even in Cate's mind when she stopped long enough to reflect on her leap of faith, there was that rascally little cloud of doubt. And if the parents were puzzled by the impending move, Robert was annoyed beyond belief.

"How dare this crazy Yank think she can just plunk herself down on our land and in this family?" a somewhat bitter Robert complained to his dad. "I bet she doesn't last six months out here."

But Cate was a steamroller of energy and determination to make this work for all of them. They took possession of the little white wooden house at the far end of Belgaum, and Cate set about making it a home for the two of them. After only two weeks the ecstatic couple moved Chris' meager possessions and furniture to their own small piece of the property. Chris' bed, a table and two chairs, a well-worn couch, and two lamps were the only furniture, and leftover cooking utensils from shearing with Cate's dishes and pans completed their basic needs.

Even Christmas Day was a workday on the land. Chris and Cate were in South Paddock at first light. Robert had discovered a hole in the fence that needed immediate mending. Cate in bib coveralls and a T-shirt worked side by side with Chris until the fence was whole again.

They just had time to race home, shower, and head to the main house for Christmas dinner. Cate didn't need or want anything for Christmas. She was sure she had everything she needed.

II

Cate sat cross-legged on the rough, unpainted boards of the deck at the south side of their battered home. Now four weeks into the school break spent on Belgaum, Cate was more in love with the land than she could have imaged. Maybe her favorite time was just as the solid blackness fell over Belgaum, and the gigantic sky opened to a million bright stars. It took Cate's breath away every time she witnessed this miracle of the outback.

A letter from her mom lay beside her this evening, and the news about Andrew made her just a little homesick. It sounded like the Jacobs and her mom were as close as ever again. Cate figured it had been a bit awkward after her dad's death. No one knew what to say or do to make it better for June or Cate. They all missed him, but no one as much as Cate, she thought.

Andrew's company was turning into a successful small but growing business. He left his longtime job and organized his first apartment near the plant. June's letter said he was working 24/7 but extremely pleased with himself. "Huh," Cate said out loud to herself. "I just bet he is pleased with himself. Too busy to write to me obviously." Yet she couldn't help wondering if he ever thought of her.

Cate's reverie was broken by the heavy thud of the huge feet of an approaching kangaroo. Cate named him Big Joe. It wasn't the first time the more than six-foot red roo had come to drink from the bore drain by the house. The gentle slurping went on for just a minute before Big Joe retreated into the blackness. This was the magic, the mystical existence of Belgaum. Cate knew Big Joe was aware of her nearness, yet he was neither afraid nor as aggressive as the big kangaroos could be.

"I don't ever want to live anywhere else, Big Joe," she called after the ghost of the kangaroo.

The complete silence of the outback was broken by the very faint hum of Chris' motorcycle, still miles away. *He'll have three gates to open and close before he gets to our house paddock,* an excited Cate thought. Just time to pop a couple cold beers and meet him at the top of the stairs. Life seemed so simple and perfect that first year.

When had the doubt about her future with Chris crept in?

III

As the English expression goes, Cate's world was going "pear shaped." As the end of the 1979 Aussie school year grew closer, Cate was finishing her two-year commitment to write and teach an alternative class curriculum to twelve unmotivated and now dearly loved teens. Sadly, the alternative program was not the only thing finishing. It hadn't hit Cate all at once; rather it was just a sad, gradual realization that she was falling out of love with Chris in their second year together. Over and over she questioned herself. *How is this possible? I was desperately in love with him just two years ago,* she would argue with her conscience. Leaving Belgaum would break her heart, but Cate knew the only way she could stay was to marry Chris, and she couldn't marry without the love she once felt for him.

Cate was never happier than when she was roaming the property on horseback. Chris had picked out a tall sturdy bay named Harold for Cate when she first came to live with him. Harold was an amazing horse, afraid of nothing. Over her many rides the two of them had encountered wild boar and snakes and been caught in sudden violent storms. In every adventure Harold stood his ground and returned Cate safely to their home.

She could feel her dad's presence when she rode alone through the open paddocks. She would never stop missing him or their rides together. Cate loved to imagine the two of them exploring Belgaum together. He would have loved this outback wilderness as much as Cate. If only she loved Chris as much.

IV

"What's wrong with me?" Cate sternly shouted out loud. It was a Saturday, and Cate had grabbed her huge Australian bird book before saddling up Harold. With the book tied on the back of the saddle and water in the saddlebags, she headed to the bush. She decided on Bore Paddock today. There was a small dam with plenty of shade for her and grass for Harold. Fortunately, at the end of Cate's first year in the outback, the drought had broken, making life a little easier for people on the land.

The stillness of the bush might frighten some people, but the tranquility soothed Cate, especially that day, with so much on her mind. She sat quietly on the edge of the dam, the bird book unopened, as she tried to figure out what to do with her messed up life. It wasn't long before her reverie was interrupted by a flock of noisy pink and white galahs. They swooped down, nearly filling the branches of an ancient Australian gum tree. Cate didn't know how it got started, but for a person to be called a galah meant they were a bit silly or stupid. Maybe it was all the loud chatter these lovely parrot-like birds made that got the whole galah thing started.

Never mind the birds, Cate reminded herself. Think. She tried to remember all the good things about Chris and how desperately she was in love with him in the beginning. She had to be with him, had to be here. It couldn't just be the land, could it? It couldn't possibly be that she was that shallow and self-centered, could it? Cate really didn't like where this internal conversation was going. "Aaagggghhh," she screamed at the top of her lungs, sending the galahs squawking their displeasure as they disappeared.

Ted had called Christopher a man-child once in anger, which hurt Cate a great deal at the time. Yet now sitting in this bit of paradise reflecting on why it was all falling apart, Cate began to understand. Chris had never had to live on his own. He was always on the family farm in New South Wales, right out of high school and now on this property. He either didn't want to or wasn't given the opportunity to taste the outside world as his brother Robert had done.

One Saturday morning as Cate was clearing their breakfast dishes and mumbling a bit about how having a dishwasher again would be nice, she heard a crash from the tractor shed. She watched Chris as he jumped the garden fence calling out her name as he ran to her. He was crying, and between sobs he said, "Dad will kill me. What should I do?"

Chris had left the tractor in gear when he jumped off to retrieve a shovel he needed for that day's work. The tractor took off on its own, crashing through the tall shed door and running over Cate's tiny scooter. She didn't know whether to laugh or cry. It seemed so improbable, but his distress was real.

She felt a bit like his mom, or his teacher, when she said, "You call your dad, tell him what happened, and find out about insurance." It seemed straightforward to her, but his mix of fear and lack of taking control was the very first inkling that maybe she would be doing more of the "taking care of stuff" than Chris.

Harold was eager to head back to House Paddock where he roamed around free once unsaddled to cool down. Cate walked with heavy feet from the shearing shed where she kept the saddle and bridle to their little house. She knew she had to tell Chris how she felt, but how? Chris was sitting on the narrow wooden top step cleaning a rifle as she approached. Seeing the rifle reminded her that they planned on kangaroo hunting that night. Cate swallowed hard. Her courage was temporarily gone.

"What paddock are we going into tonight?" Cate asked, trying to sound enthused.

Chris looked at her for just a moment. Did he sense something?

"Let's check out Burn Paddock. We haven't been in there in a while. I need to get at least ten more hides before we head to Toowoomba for our Christmas break," Chris declared while heading to the ute to load up for the night.

A kangaroo hunt begins at dark. Just like deer, this is when they are most active and sensitive to light. On top of Chris' ute was a bar with four large spotlights that could be turned one-eighty with a handle inside the cab. A good team of roo hunters had a spotter, handling the lights, and a shooter to take the animal down.

Cate was quite an accomplished spotter, a skill developed over the last two years. Chris let the ute roll along slowly on its own through the paddock while Cate slowly turned the spots to startle a kangaroo.

They were in the paddock only a few minutes before a large red roo stood on its back legs and stared into Cate's light. Chris, standing on the driver's seat and head out the top of the ute, took careful aim, bringing the prize to the ground with a perfect shot.

"That skin will bring us some good spending money, Cate." Chris gushed with the adrenaline still pumping.

The next part of the hunt was not Cate's favorite. Chris expertly cut the hide in a way that when connected to a chain and the ute, a gentle pull forward pulled the hide from the kangaroo's body. She did appreciate that every bit of this animal would be used. The hide sold, the meat cut up to feed all the sheep dogs on the property, and the bones to keep the dogs' teeth healthy.

After taking down three kangaroos, though none as large as the first one, Chris declared he'd had enough for one night, and they headed back with the night's bounty. The next morning Cate knew Chris would expect her to take the three hides to the little shed between the house and the shearing shed. There she would carefully rub coarse salt into the hides to preserve them. As the weary pair climbed the stairs to their little abode, Cate decided the next day would be soon enough to tell Chris that she was leaving.

Well, at least Robert will be happy with the news. He said I wouldn't last six months, but I made it two years, an exhausted Cate thought as her head hit the pillow.

V

It took Cate all day Sunday to finally find the words that would break both of their hearts.

"Chris, I'm going home at Christmas—back to the States to see my mom." Cate breathed out slowly and watched his face.

"You know I can't afford the cost or the time off right now. I thought we were going to have a few days back in Toowoomba over the Christmas break. Back to where we began." His voice was both tense and hurt.

"I'm sorry. I need to go home. I need to sort out some things." For several minutes only the buzzing of the ineffective window air conditioner could be heard.

"Are you going to marry me, Cate? You're wearing my mother's engagement ring—you said yes only six months ago. Are you going to marry me?" Chris' voice was now raised and angry, but his eyes were damp.

"I don't know—I honestly don't know." Cate barely managed to get the words out. Slowly she went down the steps to the garden. Seeing the six small trees they were determined to grow in this uncooperative soil made Cate feel even worse. She couldn't make herself look back at him. In the huge Ford Falcon purchased just for her new life in the outback, Cate headed back to St. George and her tiny apartment. Although she had this apartment from the start, more nights were spent at the property than in the town.

It was over an hour's drive back to town, and it was almost dusk. The worst time for the kangaroos to be on the road. Cate wasn't a mile away from their home when the tears started to fall, nearly blinding her. She felt more than heard the heavy thud of something hitting the bull bar on the front of her car. Cate was terrified.

She knew that if it was a hurt and suffering kangaroo, the right thing to do was hit it on the head with the tire iron. Feeling sick to her stomach and trying to swipe at the tears, she started to get out of the car. Just then the mature gray

222   Ellen Gordon

male kangaroo stood up, shook itself off, and bounded into the bush.

"What next?" Cate thought in utter misery. It took a few minutes to gather herself and for the shaking to stop. Okay, sobbing and driving at night with roos on the road was not going to work.

It was a great relief to cross the bridge over the Ballone River into St. George. The thought of the tiny one-bedroom "Cave," as she had dubbed the residence, somehow cheered her up. Her teaching life, her town friends, life in the Cave, and drinks at the RSL were all so separate from her life with Chris at Belgaum, and right now she was glad for that separation. Was it possible that this dual life of town versus property had anything to do with loving Chris less? Why hadn't she ever invited him into town to party with her teacher friends?

Cate had tried to get Chris to go to tennis outings with other property owners on Sunday mornings. It was always a mixture of young and old, wealthy property owners, long-established owners, or newcomers like Chris and his family. She bought Chris tennis gear and everything, but it just never worked out. He was uncomfortable out of his own environment, and soon they dropped out. Was she ashamed of him and his lack of social skills?

Plunked down on her green vinyl couch decorated by the Queensland education department, Foster's in hand, Cate was once again forced to examine her predicament. If she wasn't going to marry Chris, then she had to find a job somewhere other than St. George. No way could she live so close to Belgaum and not be a part of it. Plus, there really wasn't any position there, now that the alternative program she had created was not to be continued. Evidently students like those she had instructed the last two years were the guinea pigs for a trial program destined for failure.

In six weeks the term would end, and Cate was about to leap off yet another cliff. How many times now had she absolutely known what she wanted and then it wasn't what she wanted at all? First Michael, then David, then Max, then Ted, and now Chris. She really thought that she wanted to share a life with each one of these men, and now she had no one. Thoughts of Andrew flitted through her weary brain.

VI

The official transfer out of St. George and back to Brisbane came two weeks before term ended. Now that it was official, the toughest talk of her twenty-eight years would take place with Chris at Belgaum. It was a Friday afternoon, and some of her soon-to-graduates, or the "Dirty Dozen" as they liked to call themselves, were in no hurry to leave the classroom.

Just two years ago Cate stood in this tiny classroom and waited for the twelve young men and women to come through the door dragging their feet with sullen looks on their faces. These kids had never had any success in school. Each one had a different motive for being in this class. Andy's parents owned a local pub, but all Andy wanted was to be a mechanic. He needed a high school diploma to get an apprenticeship. Marie and Carol both lived on properties and would become jillaroos, but it was becoming more difficult to get into a program without a high school certificate. Aboriginal students'

Ellen Gordon

parents were given a stipend if they stayed in school through grade 12. So the class was a real mixed bag, but they all did want to get a high school diploma, and somehow they had put up with her for two years. Each of the twelve did receive their high school diploma. Cate was very fond of all of them, even those who made her life a misery at times.

Yet that day she needed the stragglers to move along. Cate had asked Chris to meet her at 5:00, and they were both dreading this meeting. When Cate pulled through the House Paddock gate, she didn't see Chris' bike and began to worry that he would stand her up. She knew her courage would only hold up for so long.

As always the house was unlocked. Cate had only been back a couple times since the day she told Chris that she was going home for Christmas. She had to pick up her clothes and a few personal items. Usually she would come when she knew Chris was out on the property.

In the sink was Chris' plate, knife, fork, and white enamel mug. He would have had his lamb, eggs, and two pieces of toast washed down with hot sweetened tea well before daylight. Just looking at them gave Cate a lump in her throat. How many of those big breakfasts had they shared before heading out to work on the property together?

Out of habit Cate headed for the deck, where night after night she would wait to hear the distant roar of Chris' bike then see the pinpoint light heading towards her. Here she could clearly visualize the happy couple. He would hop off his motorcycle almost as fast as Mabel his Australian sheep dog did. Mabel first—she must be fed, watered, and tied up. Then he would leap the fence that kept their little garden safe from rabbits, wild pigs, and kangaroos. Cate would meet him at the top step for hugs and kisses before they shared a beer and talked about their very different days.

It was still light when Cate heard the familiar roar and watched sadly as Chris came down the red dusty lane that she had walked a hundred times to the shearing shed. He didn't stop to tie up Mabel, just marched towards her. Cate noted that he didn't jump the fence like he used to. It seemed the joy and the little boy had left him now.

They sat in wooden chairs on the deck, not really looking at each other. Cate had carefully planned her words, her apology, her it's-all-my-fault speech, but when she saw his face when she handed back his mother's ring, the words stuck in her throat.

Chris got up abruptly. "I'll be right back—stay there."

For only an instant Cate pictured him returning with his rifle, killing her and then himself. It was a relief when he returned promptly with only a small package.

"I bought this for you—it was to be your Christmas present. I bought it the last time we were in Brisbane. Every time you look at this elephant, Cate, you will remember just how much you hurt me." He didn't say those words in anger, more like he was stating a fact.

Cate took the small felt box and left. There were no tears now, just relief that it was over. She knew for sure that she was a horrible person for what she was doing to him, but she had to move on, and so did he.

Back in the Cave, Cate opened the soft blue box to discover a one-inch snowman-like Swarovski crystal elephant. It had two crystal balls for body and head with teardrop ears and tiny black crystal eyes. But what gave him his personality was a long slender trunk that stretched up and over the back of his head then up in a graceful sweep. Chris thought Crystal would remind her of the pain she caused him, but as the light shone through the beautiful crystals, all she could think of was her time at Belgaum and how very much she would miss it for the rest of her life.

Cate sat Crystal next to Wentworth on the slender shelf over her kitchen sink. They were like tiny bookends of her last three years that began with meeting Chris at Belgaum with Ted and friends and ended today with the horrible rushed goodbyes.

VII

Going home for Christmas holidays was a first for Cate since leaving America seven years before. There was always some adventure to keep Cate Down Under. Now with the break-up with Chris, a new job she was very lucky to land the last minute was starting in January, and the thought of settling back in with Ted, even as friends, made seeing her mom and friends look very appealing.

As soon as her meager belongings were dropped off at the rambling Queenslander that Ted now owned and shared with a couple other teachers, Cate flew home the next day. She was genuinely glad to see her mom and to spend time catching up. They had a lot to share.

VIII

Cate sat on the frozen ground next to her father's headstone. "Hi, Dad, I'm home. Mom and I are getting along just fine. I still miss you so much, Dad." She laid a bright red carnation on the clean snow and felt tears trickle down her chilly cheeks. This was the hard part for Cate. She had to adjust to life back home without her dad. She had hoped that time would have softened the pain of losing him, but now it felt as fresh as the snow that fell that morning.

A few days later, Cate was trying to catch up with some of her old high school friends. Some were married, some even married and divorced. It was a small community, and Cate's mom knew just about everyone. It was strange to Cate that no one called her first, and it seemed most were too busy to even grab a coffee. She was deep in thought about how things had changed or she had changed, when the phone woke her up.

"Cate, it's Andrew. Want to grab a drink tonight?"

"Do I ever," Cate declared, suddenly happy again.

They met at the Hilton Lounge. Andrew was already occupying a private booth when Cate bounced in. "You look great, Cate. Australia must agree with you." Andrew observed Cate's soft yellow sweater and black cargo slacks. *Yellow is a good color for our little red head*, he thought to himself.

Several hours passed with the two both eager to share and to hear what each had been up to. Cate was genuinely interested in Andrew's manufacturing company, which now had forty-five employees and could barely keep up with orders for his wheel loader and excavator buckets. Plus he just made the first prototype of a coupler that would allow an operator

Ellen Gordon

to switch attachments. He planned on getting a patent on it as soon as possible.

"Oh my gosh, my Andrew is going to be rich," Cate blurted then felt suddenly shy for saying such a ridiculous thing to him. Andrew blushed, but he didn't disagree. He seemed so grown up, this now bespectacled handsome man that she had known all her life. They used to laugh at their parents who made it obvious that they wished there would be more than friendship between the two of them. Cate wondered now why there wasn't a spark or even a little flirtation.

It was a pleasant evening for both. Cate realized just how much she had missed her big brother and mentor. She wondered if he was seeing anyone. He hadn't commented after she told him the whole sad Belgaum story, and she really didn't want to pry.

The four weeks were flying by, with Cate continuing to enjoy time with her mom, Andrew, and his parents. She did finally see Patty and Lynn from her college days. They were both teaching, so it was fun to swap student stories. Patty had married her high school then college boyfriend Bob, who was now teaching at the private boys school Villanova, and he was of course the football coach. With their teacher's salaries they would never be rich, but they were happy.

"Patty, you and Bob are the best couple I know. I may be coming home next year for good and then we can hang..."

Cate couldn't finish the sentence because the screams of the girls drowned her out. "Are you serious, Cate?" they shouted at the same time. "You'd really leave Australia. Oh we will have so much fun."

It was the first time Cate had said it out loud. "I'm coming home," sounded so strange, yet somehow right. Her mom was being subtle, but Cate knew that as she aged she would want Cate near her.

Once again Cate was at a major crossroads. If she came home what would she come home to? She loved her friends, but they had their lives. It was all too much to figure out, so Cate did nothing.

Andrew stopped one night flushed with excitement. "I have to see a dealer in San Francisco next week. I know you are flying out of LA, so come to Frisco with me for a couple days. My business won't take long; then we can explore the art galleries. I know you're a Salvador Dalí fan, and there are plenty of dealers there. What do you say, kiddo?"

Momentarily speechless, Cate just stared at him. They had been having some fun get-togethers with family and on their own, and she had found this new confident, successful businessman to be a bit full of himself. Yet Cate couldn't suppress the little chill of excitement that forced out a "yes" before she thought any further.

"And it's my treat, Cate. I've been in some of the galleries I mentioned before, and I'm thinking of investing in a Dalí piece, and you can help me pick it out. Good to go?"

As Cate tried to finish her packing, she sat on her high school bed and reflected on the visit that was almost over. When she arrived she had not made a final decision to come home in a year, yet now she was committed to return. Her college buddies were delighted with her decision, yet Cate was still stinging from the lukewarm reception from her high school buddies. She had finally managed to see them all, but only because she persisted. Cate knew they were still in Michael's circle of friends, and he was married to someone named Sue, but still it hurt, and she hoped it would be better when she moved home to stay. She might even be asked back into the Thursday night euchre games.

It was strange saying goodbye to her mom again, but she knew she would be back in just one year. The big question on both their minds was, What was Cate going to do when she came home?

IX

Cate was relieved and yet disappointed that Andrew suggested that they don't tell his parents or Cate's mom about their plans. She understood that they might either frown on such an adventure or be over the moon that they were getting together. Yet it felt a little uncomfortable to keep it a secret. Was he ashamed of her?

When the pair arrived in the San Francisco airport, one of Cate's bags was lost. Not even that hiccup could put a dent in Cate's excitement. They sat together in first class, something Cate had never done, and made plans for their two days together.

The Supershuttle whisked them away to the Savoy hotel on Geary Street. The lobby was old, sedate, and elegant. When Andrew went to the desk to check them in, Cate held her breath. She didn't know if she was relieved or disappointed when she heard that he had booked two adjoining rooms.

"Here's your key, Cate." Andrew beamed down at her. "See you in the lobby in twenty minutes?"

"Okay, see you shortly," Cate agreed. The old-fashioned skeleton key opened to a corner room with lots of natural sunlight bouncing off the pale blue gray walls. A colorful quilt comforter stretched across the double bed. There was barely room for the soft comfy-looking chairs and the bedside table. Cate quickly put out her cosmetics and freshened up her lipstick. On her way out she looked once more at the double bed. What had she thought? That Andrew would get them one room with one big bed and that he would throw her down onto it the minute they arrived? Well, maybe.

The streetcar ride to the Wharf, exploring the little shops, eating fresh oysters, and just sitting by the water watching lazy seals made their first day perfect. They had wandered into Austin Gallery just as they were about to close. When Andrew told him what he was interested in, the man cheerfully agreed to stay open and show them several of Dalí's pieces.

After an hour, Andrew and Cate had narrowed down his choices to three of Dalí's works. They agreed they would return the next day to make a final decision.

They climbed up Lombard Street, the most crooked in the world, and knew they'd had enough playing tourist and looked for a quiet place for dinner around 8:30. They wandered into a small crowded hole in the wall called Charley's. A guitar-playing singer entertained them for almost three hours. The singer was happy to play several of their requests, including Men at Work's "I Come From the Land Down Under."

"Perfect, perfect, perfect day," Cate bubbled as they got out of the Savoy elevator on the third floor. Cate had a very pleasant buzz going and did not want the day to end.

Andrew pulled her close and gave her a brotherly kiss on each cheek. "You, miss, are drunk, and I'll not take advantage of someone under the influence." Andrew laughed. "Well, at least not tonight," he added. "Big day tomorrow—sleep." He turned Cate's key in her door, put the key in her hand, and gently shoved her inside. "Lock up."

Cate playfully went to check the connecting door, but it was locked on his side. "Darn," she giggled. She could hear him moving around, turning on the TV, but she remembered little else about the evening until she heard a tap on the connecting door six hours later.

"Let's go, sleepy head. We're going to taxi over to Sausalito, one of my favorite communities across the Golden Gate Bridge. Hurry up—see you in the lobby." Andrew sounded way too awake and happy for the slow-moving Cate. As she dressed she debated whether she was disappointed or relieved that Andrew had made no advances. Did she want to have sex with him? And what would that do to their years of friendship? Cate had no idea what that man thought of her.

Sausalito was wonderful. They left the taxi just across the bridge on the water front. For the next few hours they wandered the small streets lined with shops and galleries. It was like a little world of its own, so laid back and slow moving. They drank some bold red wines in a little café on the waterfront before heading back over the bridge to their favorite little hang out, Charley's. While they munched burgers and drank beers they compared thoughts on the art they had seen so far.

"Let's go back to Austin's and have them pull out the three we really liked the most yesterday," Cate suggested.

"No, to me it's down to 'The Temptation of St. Anthony' and the 'Divine Comedy,'" Andrew declared.

They spent well over an hour looking at the two pieces and discussing them with the gallery manager. It seemed Andrew and the manager spoke the same language, and it was obvious that Andrew was enjoying himself immensely. The "Divine Comedy" was part of a series, and being an EA, it was more valuable than the other. It was also much softer in color and subject. It was not a typical, wild Dali by any means. "Temptation" on the hand was a 100/300 bold, large painting. Of course, Cate would love it because it had obscured, rather shapeless elephants in it. Cate felt so grown up giving her opinion and listening to Andrew and the manager.

At around 4:00 they looked at each other and said at the same time "The Temptation of St. Anthony." They both laughed out loud. It would make a fine addition to Andrew's small but growing collection. They were totally pumped as Andrew paid and made shipping arrangements to his home.

"Let's celebrate and have a picnic," Andrew enthused.

They found a smart deli with wonderful blue Camembert and smoked Gouda cheeses. Three types of cold cuts and lots of olive were topped off with a loaf of French bread and creamy butter. They were packed into a sturdy grocery bag. "One more stop," Andrew called over his shoulder as he lifted the bulging bag.

A bottle of Dom Pérignon was purchased at the Savoy lounge. "Please bring it well chilled and put it on ice before bringing it to 304, please." Andrew directed.

Cate's eyes grew wide with anticipation. A picnic in Andrew's room? Her heart thumped wildly in her chest as they got into the elevator. "That's okay, isn't it Cate?" Andrew whispered as he bent down to kiss her lips.

Cate put her head on his chest, hoping that would suffice for a response. He unlocked his room and gently pushed her in, just as he had done to her in her own room the night before. It wasn't a corner room, so there wasn't as much light, but the colors and art on the walls were similar to Cate's room. Cate plopped down on one of the soft chairs and looked at Andrew as he took off his tweed jacket and sat down across from her.

"Now, what the hell are we playing at, Miss Cate?" Andrew inquired with raised eyebrows and a serious voice.

The knock on the door startled them both. The already chilled champagne was carefully set on the little bedside table, along with two crystal glasses. A bowl of mixed nuts completed the tray. Andrew rose to give the waiter a generous tip before locking the door behind him.

Suddenly Andrew was no longer her big brother or her mentor but this slender athletic man who was now taking off his shoes.

"I have no idea, Andrew," Cate whispered, "but let's have a glass of champagne and toast to your purchase today." Cate was trying to divert the conversation to something safe.

They had one glass of champagne then stood at the same time, each watching the other as they slowly took off their clothes. There was no need for words as they enjoyed searching each other's naked bodies with approval. Andrew turned to the double bed, and Cate followed.

Both were experienced lovers, but there's nothing as delicious as exploring a new lover's body, and they were doing just that. For a time Cate was oblivious to anything but the eager touching of her body by large soft hands. Her skin tingled with appreciation, and as the tension of the ache between her legs became too strong, she let out an involuntary moan.

Taking this as his cue, Andrew thrust himself into her wetness with a moan of his own. They moved in frantic unison and pleasure until Andrew exploded into a dreamy Cate. She hadn't cum, but she didn't care. The act, the joy, the wild coming together left them both breathing heavily as they lay side by side.

"Here, put this on." Andrew handed Cate the button-down shirt that he had been wearing. "Let's have more bubbles."

Cate would have liked to linger naked beside him in the bed a little longer, but she sensed that he may have been a little embarrassed. Why would he?

When she hopped the plane down to LA airport the next morning, Cate was somewhat confused. They had such an amazing time, but they hadn't had sex again or even discussed it. What they did was go back to Charley's and dance until 2:00 in the morning.

Andrew would be staying in San Francisco for another few days on business, so he rode down the elevator the next morning with Cate and walked her to the waiting cab. He kissed her forehead and smiled. "See you when you get home next year, kiddo."

Ellen Gordon

X

Qantas flights out of LAX were always late at night. Normally that suited Cate just fine. They would feed you way too much then you would crash for eight or so hours before they'd feed you again. This time sleep eluded her from the time she climbed into her window seat over two pleasant and pre-occupied sheep farmers from New Zealand until the time they touched down in Brisbane thirteen hours later. Cate was wide awake.

It seemed all her supposed adult life she had been making rash decisions and then regretting them. She had wanted to be a hippie and live in a commune with David, she had wanted a solid respectable life with Max, and of course she had planned on marrying Michael and living in the small community she grew up in. None of that worked out so well, did it? Then to top it off, what about losing Belgaum and Christopher? Why couldn't she just be happy, content, and stay put with someone?

Suddenly going back to America seemed like another plan that wasn't so well thought out. Was she committed to returning now that she told her mom and friends? And what about Andrew, what's going on there? She didn't even know if she liked him anymore, so why did she have sex with him? Did that mean anything to him at all? They really did have a wonderful time together. Maybe he was better as a big brother and friend.

"I will drive myself crazy," Cate spoke through clenched teeth then realized she had said it out loud.

"Are you okay, miss?" the farmer in the middle seat shyly asked.

"Well considering I've just messed up my life once again. Considering I'm going to a new job that I'll only have for one year because I'm crawling back to Ohio. Considering I just had sex with someone who has been like a brother to me all my life. And considering I'm about to share a house with an ex-boyfriend. Yes, all things considered, I'm just peachy," Cate whined like a spoiled five-year-old. Then feeling mortified with the outburst, she flipped on her side and stared out the window. Not another word was exchanged with the farmers, and as soon as was allowed they gathered their gear and raced down the aisle.

XI

Cate was both terrified and excited as always when she jumped into something brand new. "Is there a pattern forming here?" she mumbled sarcastically to herself. Her career path changed as fast as her love life, and now she jumped again. It was more than a little weird knowing that the new job and sharing a house with Ted again was just a twelve-month journey. How much trouble could she possibly get into in just one school year?

Five teachers had been selected to take on the newly established role of curriculum liaison consultants in the Brisbane region. That title was quite a mouthful, Cate thought. Each consultant would be given five high schools to service. The job description was a bit nebulous, so when the twenty other consultants who were to cover the state converged on the Gold Coast Resort, all were equally clueless.

The first evening was a blur of paperwork, school assignments, general introductions, and a full agenda for the next four days. Cate retired early after dinner.

As always, being the only American in a new group of Aussies, even after seven years, brought out the uncomfortable country girl once again. She knew there would always be the few in the education department who resented the "Yankee Invasion," as she had heard it called. The fact that the Americans didn't have to pay taxes to either country for two years did upset some of her coworkers. Then there were always those who loved to bring up some American blunder.

Early the next morning, a nervous Cate dressed in her favorite black sweater—called a jumper in Australia, which always amused and confused her—with a white T-shirt underneath. She worked hard on her now long red hair to get the wave out of it. Then she pulled it back with a black ribbon.

"Okay, Cate, let's go get 'em," she encouraged herself in the mirror without a lot of conviction.

She'd said hello to the girls she knew on her team and went to get a coffee. She passed a man with his face buried in the *Courier Mail* morning paper. When she returned with her coffee, the brightest blue eyes that she'd ever seen, except her dad's, were watching her.

"Hello."

"Hello." Cate kept moving. She was a bit shaken with the similarity of that man's eyes and her dad's. Shortly Cate would come face to face with those brilliant blue eyes again.

"Okay, listen—the Brisbane team is to go to the Pineapple Room to meet there with Sue Benson, who will be your supervisor this year. You all met her last night at introductions," instructed the program advisor.

The five moved cautiously and quietly as they entered the small conference room, which was all set up with packets with their names typed in bold blue letters. Cate looked across her table at the already familiar blue eyes but quickly looked away. Next to him was a man named Greg who she had met last night. She remembered him as loud and bold. Thankfully Sarah and Gwen took their seats near Cate and then cheerfully turned and greeted Mr. Blue Eyes as Colin.

Sue wanted them to spend some time getting to know each other, and Cate knew the dreaded "getting to know you" games were headed her way. *Why was this always necessary?* she thought. *Just let us get to work*, Cate sighed to herself.

"I came from the States as a phys. ed. teacher then worked on a new K–6 health curriculum and spent a year training teachers on the program. Then I had two years teaching an alternative class to year 11 and 12s in St. George." By the time Cate finished, she was bright red and breathless, having not remembered to take a breath.

"Crikey, is there any job in the department you haven't tackled?" roared Greg, making Cate even more self-conscious.

When the others finished their introductions, Cate let herself look up, and there were the perfect, disturbing blue eyes staring at her again. He had a huge brown beard, which

Ellen Gordon

seemed so out of place on a soft, almost delicate face. The hair on top of his head was gone, leaving a ring of soft short and tidy brown hair.

The next few days blurred together with school selection. Cate's base was to be Richland High, wherever that was; then she would be responsible for three other high schools in that area. Each consultant was given information packets about their schools, including size, principals, special programs, and calendars to read each night.

It sounded to Cate that they were to be the go-to guys. If a school wanted to write a grant for new computers or get some specialty training or needed a speaker for a class, they were to assist in their endeavors. The curriculum liaison teachers could make that happen. Yikes, thought Cate.

"Do you think you're going to like this job?" Gwen asked when at last the final session was over. Cate was feeling quite exhausted from the constant conversation, planning, and studying of her new schools.

"I think so. I mean, it sounds like we can make this position valuable to the schools, and I guess that's the challenge. I do wonder if it's a position with value enough to justify salaries," Cate pondered. She was a little sensitive at reactions from other teachers after the alternative program she had just completed in St. George. It didn't look like it was going forward in any schools this year.

"What a strange thing to be thinking, Cate. Of course we're going to be valuable and unique in the system."

Gwen and Sarah were a pair of true Aussies in Cate's mind. They were sharp-witted, not afraid of a good double entendre, outspoken on any subject, and basically happy souls. She was so glad she met them and that they would be teammates.

Greg on the other hand remained loud and sarcastic, often making Cate the brunt of his never ending comments on Americans. Cate knew he was just trying to be funny and was probably a nice guy, but she found him exhausting. Why couldn't he pick on someone else?

She hadn't had an opportunity to talk much with Colin. Well okay, she tended to avoid him when possible. She had no idea why, but she felt shy in his presence. The last night of the seminar, the five got together with Sue, their highly efficient taskmaster, to relax over a few beers. She gave them a pep talk, assuring them they would be successful and then left them to meet with other supervisors.

Cate was seated between Colin and Gwen when a loud debate between Sarah and the ever-babbling Greg broke out over Rugby League versus Rugby Union. Cate was sure that Greg would have to be a rough and tumble League fan and was surprised that he favored the more highbrow Union.

Colin ignored the noisy debate and leaned close to Cate. "I've seen you before, Cate."

Startled, Cate gave a little involuntary jump. "Really? No, I don't think so." Cate was thinking to herself that if she had seen those eyes before surely she would have remembered.

"It was at Toogoolawah School. You were there to meet with Principal Davis about the new health program. You came into the staffroom, and Davis introduced you," Colin gushed with a smile. "All the guys in the staffroom were most impressed."

All Cate could think of was how she could have missed those eyes, if his strange story was true. She did spend a day at Toogoolawah, and she could still remember the tiny staffroom full of teachers.

"Wow, you have a good memory. That was several years ago, before I moved out west," was all Cate could think of to say.

Colin just smiled at her and joined the debate over another beer before they all called it a night.

XII

Cate was settling in to life back in Brisbane, although it still seemed odd that this would all be over and she'd move on again back to the States. During this time she naturally thought a lot about Andrew and their time in San Francisco. She had also been making an attempt to connect more with her mom as the year progressed, making sure to call at least every couple weeks.

Thank heavens the phone connections were so much better then—no delay when talking. Sometimes it felt like she was tugged between two very different worlds with very different people.

One Sunday morning, Cate caught up with her mom on a Saturday evening back in Ohio. Her mom had been playing tennis and was meeting friends later. Cate had been giving her mom the latest on her job, new friends, and living with a crazy bunch of teachers when her mom interrupted her.

"Oh my gosh, Cate, you won't believe this. Andrew is gay." Her mom's voice was full of excitement with the news.

"What?" Cate exclaimed, much louder than she intended.

"Yes, isn't it amazing? Evidently he has been living with his plant manager and business partner Jack for the last few months. He came out to his parents when they moved in together."

"Wait, wait, Mom, what do Karen and Harold think of such a rush affair? I mean, it's so sudden. Are you sure?" Cate croaked out the words.

"Oh they're fine with it, sweetheart. They say they've never seen Andrew so happy, and they really like Jack. I can't wait to meet him next weekend."

Cate was in shock. It was six months ago that they'd shared a magical few days in San Francisco, and she thought—what had she thought about their little affair? Somehow its importance was diminishing, certainly in Andrew's eyes.

"Are you there, Cate? Are you all right?"

"Just peachy, Mom." She swallowed hard. "I'm happy for Andrew." Even to herself, she sounded anything but happy for Andrew. How could he have had sex with her if he was gay? Was she just an experiment, a last fling on the straight side?

After a while, Cate started to put together clues to Andrew's sexual orientation. Hadn't he always been the best dressed, ahead of all the fashion trends, even in college? Did he ever seem to date in high school or college? His attachment to San Francisco made more sense now. The only puzzle was why they had sex and why, if they were supposed to be so close, he didn't tell her long ago.

Over the next few miserable days, Cate began to realize just how much she had been counting on Andrew being there for her when she returned. Maybe not even dating, just being there like he always used to be. How could he be gay? How could he love some man? She had nothing against gay people, but why did Andrew have to be one of them? Cate realized that this news had seriously taken the glow off her return home, but it was too late to turn back now.

XIII

Cate truly liked the new job, all the new people and all the new challenges of satisfying her customers—the teachers— was just what she needed to keep her busy. Other than being a resource and making things happen, there wasn't a whole lot of paperwork outside school hours.

Cate started running, playing squash, and even began to enjoy hanging out with Ted and her old friends again. Anything that would help push Andrew and his new status out of her mind was good to Cate.

After one of their monthly staff meetings the five walked out together, leaving Sue to finalize their reports. Gwen, who had a new boyfriend that she'd met at one of her schools, suggested they organize a night out including all of them and whomever they wanted to invite.

"Come on, guys. Let's all go to the Red Parrot at the Hilton to dance this Saturday. James and I are planning on it."

"I'm in," called out Sarah.

"Not me," Greg roared. "I do not dance."

Six pairs of eyes turned to Cate and Colin with raised eyebrows. Sarah and Gwen had been urging them both to go out for some time, but both had dodged the suggestion. Cate really did like Colin, but starting any kind of a romance at this stage seemed futile. Plus, she knew he had a pretty bad breakup just six months ago and was still hurting from that.

Reluctantly, under severe pressure the pair nodded in unison and then smiled at each other.

Friday night before the big event, Gwen and Sarah mysteriously cancelled. Cate couldn't decide whether to be angry, if it was just a game to them, or to be a little excited over going out alone with Colin. She called Colin to see if he would like to cancel also.

"Hell no. I'll meet you at your place at 8:00. Then we can take the train in and taxi home. Okay?"

Colin knew where she lived because she had the team over for champagne—well bubbles—one Friday after work. She'd dubbed it a "verandah sit." A place to unwind on a Friday afternoon.

Because their old Queenslander sat next to the Sherwood Railroad station, it was great fun to watch people getting on and off the trains. The girls were especially cheeky giving the men coming and going a rating of one to ten. Heaven knows what Colin and Greg must have thought of that activity!

Right at 8:00 he pulled into their driveway and onto the lawn so other housemates could come and go. He drove a rugged Land Rover that one day Cate would name The Beast and love to drive.

Colin wore a gray shirt with a thin black tie and black slacks. She liked the look, and she was glad that she'd decided on the red skirt, white top, and little red, green, and black jacket. She decided they made a dashing couple.

She wasn't sure why, but she was glad that Ted and the other roommates were already out for the evening. And for once

Ellen Gordon

none of her ex-pupils from St. George were staying with her. Since their graduation, the homestead was like a revolving door for them. Some had come to Brisbane for work or to shop or just to check up on Cate. She loved them, but for once the silence was nice.

They hopped the 8:15 into the city. The carriage was full of people of all ages going to movies or clubs or the theater. Because of all the noise around them, Cate and Colin were pretty much silent until they were on the city street and headed to the Hilton on Queen Street.

Magic happened that night. The pair danced and drank until 2:00 when the Red Parrot closed. They caught a cab back to Skew Street, talking all the while about nothing and everything. Cate made a pot of Bushells tea, which they drank seated side by side on the little kitchen bench.

Colin shared the full painful story of his breakup with his previous girlfriend. They had gotten through college, started solid careers, and he assumed that within a year or so they would marry. Evidently Sharon saw her future looking decidedly different, with her focus on studying law in Melbourne and staying there to practice in criminal law.

Colin had no idea how long that idea had been brewing or when it was she'd planned on telling him. They were both teachers, and as the last semester started she bluntly told him it was over between them—she had other plans. The end of eight years of commitment.

Obviously, Colin was still carrying a lot of pain and regret. Cate decided not to lay her issues with Andrew on him, instead changing the subject to their coworkers and how the program was progressing.

Daylight peeked through the kitchen window before Colin stood to leave. He gave Cate a gentle kiss on the lips. "I had a great time, Cate. It's been a while since I've had some fun." Cate waved as he carefully backed out the Land Rover, dodging the cars of her roommates who had all returned while they talked.

Cate giggled to herself. "I wonder what Ted thought when he saw the car still here." She flopped down on her bed for a few hours' sleep while dreaming of the man with the extraordinary blue eyes.

XIV

The months were flying by for Cate. It was the end of September, and with only a few months to go before she left Australia forever, she wanted every single day to count. She was playing a lot of sports, running most mornings with Ted or one of the others, and saw Colin on a regular basis. It was a strange relationship for Cate, mainly because Colin had never initiated sex with her. She was far too stubborn to suggest it herself, but it left her a bit unsettled. Was there something wrong with her, or did he still pine for his old girlfriend?

As Thanksgiving approached, Cate just didn't feel like making a huge meal this year. There was such an odd assortment of guys living at her house; she just didn't feel up to it. She was pleasantly surprised when Colin asked her to come to his home in Esk for Thanksgiving dinner with some of his friends. Cate had never met any of his friends and assumed they were friends of his when he had a partner.

"Your friends are terrific, Colin," Cate yawned, so full of turkey, cranberry, mashed potatoes, corn, bread rolls, and three kinds of pie that her head was nodding. "Do you think they liked me?"

Ignoring her question, Colin pulled her close to him and kissed her in a way he'd not kissed her before. It was a demand. Cate felt the stir between her legs and felt his heart beat fast against her breast. He led her to his bed, undressed her too fast to save two buttons on her skirt, and was deep inside her before she could catch her breath. He felt so good inside her, and she desperately wanted him now. But he pulled out and put his mouth where his penis had just been a second before.

Cate thought she was an experienced lover—she certainly had enough sex in her life—but never had any act sent such shivers, such aching, before a release so powerful she cried. As he entered her again this time for his pleasure, she felt herself cum again with him.

Both were speechless at the almost violent yet so totally satisfying act that just happened. They laid in the darkness holding hands until they both fell into a deep satisfied sleep.

XV

"Oh man, did you hear that Sharon is trying to get back with Colin?" Greg couldn't resist being the one to run that by Cate.

"So? What difference should that make to me?" Cate tried to keep her voice steady. "I leave the country in just three weeks, so Colin can see whomever he wants, Greg." She knew she shouldn't care. Although they were still seeing each other, the fact that she was leaving was a big dark cloud over their heads. If she wanted him back and he still loved her, maybe that was for the best, Cate tried to convince herself.

The weekend before Cate was heading back to America, Ted, Sarah, and her old pal Stephanie decided to throw a farewell party under the old Queenslander that had been Cate's home that year. They invited anyone who even knew Cate and wound up with a swarm of about fifty people.

Cate was overwhelmed by the presence of so many people who had crossed her path in the eight years she was in Australia. There were students and two teachers from St. George. She wondered for not the first time if Chris knew she was leaving the country or if he cared. The entire gang of primary teachers was present, sharing plenty of stories. Of course the whole consulting team, including their leader, joined the fun. Ted was especially in great form as host and spent most of the evening entertaining the party with stories of Cate's escapades.

Cate knew her greatest flaw was her impetuousness. Her impromptu decision making and speaking without thinking had gotten her in plenty of tricky situations. Now here she was about to give up an excellent job that she loved and leave all these good friends and a possible relationship with Colin. She really didn't know what to think about Colin. They still saw each other, but there was a distance that wasn't there before, and Cate could only imagine it was the girlfriend.

One of the strains on the relationship of Cate and Colin was a result of them working together. They would discuss a program or an idea together, but when they got into a meeting with the others, Cate turned silent. Colin would look at her for backup on what they had discussed, but Cate would avoid his eyes. She couldn't explain it to him, but she felt suddenly muted around the other team members. What did they think of her relationship with Colin?

The last few days before D-Day as she now called her departure, Cate was wrapping up her precious elephants to be sent on ahead of her to her mom's. There were over eighty of them by now, each a memory of the person and the reason it was given while there in Australia. Tears fell when Crystal and Wentworth were carefully put in the container. She would always miss Belgaum and for years after dream of somehow buying it and returning to it.

When Julia was ready to pack, Cate wondered yet again what on earth she would say to Andrew when she saw him. She still felt humiliated and silly for thinking there might have been something between them. She wished Julia would just stop smiling at her.

Ten of Cate's friends came to the airport to push her through the gate. She'd had a few beers and was feeling sad and reluctant to go. She looked at the familiar faces, including Colin's, and nearly panicked. At the last moment Colin pulled her back away from the others.

"Would you like a visitor in America?" he asked as he hurriedly kissed her cheek before the others pulled them apart. Did he just ask to come to America to see her?

"Yes, yes, yes," she shouted over all the final goodbyes while stumbling through the huge metal doors.

Savant

I

"I must be insane," Cate mumbled to herself as the Qantas 747 rolled down the runway, preparing for takeoff to LA. "I spend eight years making a life for myself in Australia, and now I'm leaving?"

As she settled back into her comfy seat in premium economy, enjoying her little upgrade from economy, Cate couldn't help comparing this flight to her first to Australia in 1972. That flight out of LA took thirty-two hours with stops in Honolulu, Fiji, New Zealand, and Sydney before finally finishing up in Brisbane late at night.

With this nonstop flight, Cate would cross the international date line, picking up a calendar day on the way. The 747 should touch down in LA about the same time she left Brisbane, a mere thirteen hours later. Most of Cate's belongings were being shipped and wouldn't arrive for a couple weeks.

With the easy flight over, Cate cleared customs, picked up her two bright yellow suitcases, and headed to the Continental airline counter. She eagerly hopped a 9:30 a.m. flight to Cleveland and home.

On both flights Cate reverted to her "pretending to read so don't talk to me" routine. She tried not to dwell on what she left behind, instead focusing on her future. She knew she would have to stay with her mom while she got herself a job and a car. Her superannuation, Queensland government's retirement plan based on years of service, gave Cate a small cushion to get started, but she knew it wouldn't last long. The future was one big question mark in Cate's mind.

Cate had butterflies thinking of the reunion with her mom. They had gotten along fine the last time Cate was home, but that was just a brief visit, and she'd been busy with her friends. The prospect of living together again was probably making both women a little anxious.

"Cate, Cate, Cate," June called to her daughter, with her toes dangerously close to the "do not enter" red line.

Mother and daughter moved rapidly toward each other, both dissolving into smiles and tears. It was as if both realized that this was a momentous day, a strange beginning with an undefined end. Bags were quickly collected and the airport exited, with the pair talking non-stop all the way back to her mom's new home.

"Did you ever suspect that Andrew was gay, Mom?" a very curious Cate asked.

"Not really. Your dad and I did wonder why he never dated. We even wondered why he never asked you out. You were always such good friends, well, most of the time once you grew up," June laughed.

"Well, I certainly didn't know, and I can't help being angry with him that he never told me," Cate complained. She could never tell her mother about San Francisco, so she bottled up the confusion and anger until she could talk with Andrew. She planned on giving him an earful.

June had champagne, hummus, cheese, and crackers ready for a ravenous Cate. When they had finished the bubbles,

Cate watched her mom clear the dishes and glasses. June looked good, Cate decided. At sixty-two, she was still trim and fit from weekly tennis with friends. Cate assumed she had taken it up again after Ken died. Once again Cate wondered how her outdoorsman dad and this highly educated professional ever found each other, married, and kept it together all those years. The familiar ache of missing her dad instantly overwhelmed her.

Cate knew that after two years of getting Ken's affairs cleared up, her mom had sold the farm that she loved so much and missed all this time in Australia. She told Cate when she planned to sell, and Cate had held her tongue. She knew she couldn't expect her mom to keep the horses and the farm going on her own. She even felt a bit of guilt. If she hadn't gone to Australia, would she have stayed with her mom and helped to keep the farm going? They would never know.

Cate liked her mom's modern condo in Medina and knew June had always preferred city life to their rural home. She'd retired last year and obviously was enjoying this new life.

"I think I'll drive out to Seville, Mom, just to say hello to Dad," Cate offered softly.

She saw her mom pause for just an instant then shake it off. "Okay, see you around 7:00 for dinner. I'm making your favorite pot roast."

Cate sat on an old blanket she brought from her bedroom. The ground was frozen next to her dad's grave. "Hi, Dad. I'm back for good and still missing you," she whispered. The tears felt hot on her chilly face. "I'm going to take care of Mom, I mean, when she gets old, Dad. I know you would want me to do that. I wish you were here. I wish we still had the farm and the horses. I feel so very lost coming home like this. What am I going to do with myself?" Cate was suddenly feeling very sorry for herself.

"Ahem," came a deep voice from behind her. Cate jumped up, totally unaware that there was anyone in the cemetery but her.

"Michael?" Cate was flabbergasted.

"Well, your mom told Sue, and Sue told me you were coming home today. I just figured that you would be here."

"Wow, I'd forgotten how fast news travels in small-town America," Cate exclaimed, a little more sarcastically than she meant.

"Same old Cate." Michael smiled. "I just came to say hi and welcome you back. You know I married Jenny Logan the same year you left? Yeah, we have a boy and a girl now."

Cate swallowed hard. She knew if they had stayed together they would have been miserable, but seeing him looking just as handsome as ever, with that damn crooked smile, made her remember happier times. "I'm happy for you, Michael," was all she could manage.

Cate had developed the hiccups and a running nose from the crying and wished that Michael would stop looking at her with a small smile. "I still wish we'd given it a try, Cate." An awkward pause came between them. "Anyhow, we're having friends, mostly people you know, over for a New Year's Eve party—we'd like you to come, Cate."

It was too much for Cate. Being there talking to her dad, and Michael showing up inviting her to his home with his wife and family. "I'll think about it," Cate called over her shoulder as she fled to her car before the tears came back. In the car she saw that Michael was still by her dad's grave. Did he come to talk with Ken also? Somehow the thought made her happy as she drove slowly back to her mom's for pot roast.

II

The first few weeks back home were a bit surreal for Cate. Her possessions had arrived from Australia, but there really was nowhere to put them. The boxes stood in the corner of the guest bedroom in her mom's new condo. Christmas was almost there, and Cate had a serious case of the holiday blues.

None of her high school friends had bothered to call, making Cate think they had moved on with their lives and didn't need her friendship.

Her college buddies were in town for the holiday, and they planned on a Christmas Eve lunch together. While Cate wanted to see them, she knew it wouldn't be the same. She had lunch with Patty and Lynn when she was back last year, but then she was still adventurous Cate—starting a new job, about to have a dirty weekend with Andrew, and looking forward to the future. Now here she was with no job, no man, and living with her mom.

What Cate was really dreading was Christmas Eve at Andrew's parents' home. Even the long-standing tradition of eggnog and fabulous catered canapés didn't excite Cate this time. She'd been home three weeks, and Andrew had not called or stopped to welcome her home. Now she was going to see him for the first time since she learned about his boyfriend.

Ugh, just saying "boyfriend" in her head made Cate feel sick to her stomach. How could Andrew be gay? She'd known him all her life. She'd kissed him. Hell, she had sex with him. Cate couldn't help the anger and confusion she felt.

And the worse part was knowing that she would no doubt be forced to meet Andrew's precious Jack at the party. What on earth would she say to them? Did Andrew tell Jack about their "thing" in San Francisco? Cate herself wasn't sure what that "thing" was, but there was definitely something going on in San Francisco. He hadn't even bothered to call her since she came back. It was a full-blown self-pity party for Cate.

"Mom, do you really want to go to Harold and Karen's this Christmas Eve? Doesn't it still seem a little odd going on our own?" Cate asked.

June studied her daughter for a long moment. Such a beautiful young woman yet seemingly clueless that life had gone on here while she was away. She knew that losing her dad was devastating, and now she thought Andrew had deserted her as well for his lover. *Grow up, Cate*, she thought to herself.

"Sweetie, I told you that I've been seeing Jason Coleman for over a year. He and I met on the tennis court. It's not what your dad and I had, but it's nice; it's fun. We've traveled together some, and well, he'll be there tonight."

Cate stared at her mother. Her mom was going to have a date for this traditional family event? Why was everything so different now? No one seemed to care about her feelings anymore. Cate just walked out of the room, too overwrought to speak.

III

Lunch with Patty, Barb, and Lynn was better than Cate expected and just what she needed to perk her up. She gave them expensive soaps and spa gifts while they combined to give Cate a pair of matching elephant salt and pepper shakers with multicolored pastel patterns across their backs. Cate loved the little pair and loved her friends. "They will be perfect in my new apartment, wherever that may be," Cate declared.

In the next two hours the girls reminisced at the Sheraton Inn in Cuyahoga Falls. There were a lot of insane, fun times to dig up and a few Cate would love to forget. Naturally, the girls wanted to know if she had kept in touch with Max, David, Michael, or any of the others from her hippie phase toward the end of their college days.

Cate couldn't bring herself to tell them how all the relationships had ended badly, but David's was certainly the most dramatic. They hadn't seen each other for a while; he was off to Maine to get religion or start a farm or something. Cate had just burned bridges beyond repair with just about everyone she knew after her dad died.

Right after Cate's dad died, David had stopped by the apartment out of the blue to ask if she wanted to go to a party. Things at the apartment were a bit tense with Barb and Lynn, mostly because of Cate's strange behavior. She was either in tears or moping around complaining about something or inhaling a bottle of wine. If only someone understood the pain of losing her dad, if someone could just console her, Cate was sure she could get through it.

"Okay, David, I could use a good party right now," Cate had said, trying to sound enthusiastic.

The party was more like an impromptu campout well out in the country. There were at least thirty people Cate guessed when they pulled up in David's ancient VW Kombi. As usual he knew everyone, and since he'd been away, he had a lot of catching up with his friends. That was fine with Cate. She found a quiet spot away from the others and accepted two joints on her way to escape. She smoked the first and felt the sense of relief she'd been looking for, and she wanted more of her pain to go away. By the time she finished the second joint, Cate was almost comatose. Because of Max and school, she hadn't smoked dope in several years. She struggled to her feet and in her addled mind decided she wanted David, and she wanted to have sex with him right then.

She staggered around the party calling his name. Most of the partiers were almost as stoned as Cate, but others laughed at her. Finally, a young girl in dreadlocks pointed her to a small pup tent on the edge of the group.

Cate tossed open the flap to see a naked David with an equally naked girl she remembered as Sonya enjoying an enthusiastic reunion. Mortified, angry, embarrassed, she was just too mentally drained to take any more.

"What the hell do you think you're doing, David? Get me out of here now." Cate continued to scream at him as he slowly came out of the tent, still naked and still aroused.

"I'll take you home when I've finished here. You're stoned and talking stupid," David angrily said back in a calm voice. With that he went back in the tent and zipped up the fly.

The girl with the dreadlocks came forward. "I'm sorry. I assumed you knew he was doing it with Sonya. They go way back," she explained kindly. "I'm leaving. I'll give you a ride if you like."

So that was the un-glorious ending of a relationship that had been Cate's first act of rebellion and freedom. Dreadlocks and Cate didn't speak much on that ride back to her apartment, but she often thought how grateful she was to this girl who she never saw again.

No, she wouldn't be sharing that tale of woe with her friends; that was for sure.

Cate spent most of the time telling them about her Australian adventures. Barb, Patty, and Lynn were enthralled with the tales of the outback and life on the property with Christopher.

"Oh my gosh, Cate, there is no way I could live out there with all the snakes and spiders and wild pigs and bush men!" Patty declared. Her life had been organized years before and was going right on schedule. She loved her class at Springfield Elementary, she loved her Bob, and they were hoping to start their family soon now that they had their house. Even the thought of that long plane journey made her shudder.

"I think it's great that you did it, Cate. I mean, I think I was brave landing on the West Coast by myself, but you—wow— here's to our most adventuresome friend," Barb stated loudly with a clink of their wine glasses.

"The big question is, Cate, what on earth are you going to do now after such a grand adventure? Franklin or even Medina must seem very small after all your travels," Barb asked with concern for her friend.

"I haven't a clue, ladies." Cate sighed deeply. Feeling that little sense of doubt about her decision to return to Ohio creeping into her mind.

Shortly thereafter, there were hugs and a few tears. Cate promised that as soon as she could afford it she would fly to San Diego for a visit with her friend. Barb's advertising job had introduced her to a lot of people, including her new man, Freddie.

Freddie was with a startup company and had a very profitable future ahead of him, if all would go to plan. To Cate it sounded like Barb had landed in the perfect place. She was genuinely happy for her good friends, but it made it all the clearer that Cate was the only one with a dubious future.

IV

The purchase of a stunning red dress perked up Cate's mood immensely. She knew sometimes redheads avoided red because of the clash. But that was exactly what Cate liked. From the minute she tried it on at Higbee's, she knew this formfitting dress was perfect for her. If she was going to face Andrew on Christmas Eve, she was going to look perfect.

"Oh, Cate, you look so beautiful. No, you are so beautiful," June exclaimed when Cate appeared in the hallway. "Are you ready to go?" she asked gently.

"As I'll ever be, Mom," Cate sighed.

The Jacobs' home was as familiar to Cate as her own old house on the farm. When decorated professionally for the holidays, it looked like a movie set. Cate had spent so much time there growing up, arriving felt like a second homecoming. Cate looked at the barn as a valet took her mom's Lexus. How many times had she ridden here with her dad and tied up Jack and Sable in that barn? Cate sighed and followed her mom into the red front door with a perfect silver wreath.

Harold and Karen rushed to hug and kiss Cate when she entered the large living room full people, most she'd known all her life. "Welcome home, darling, you look fabulous," Karen gushed. "So good to have you back where you belong—we've missed you, Cate."

Cate loved this couple, and their sincere love of her made her feel completely comfortable being there until she saw Andrew standing in the doorway to the dining room, staring at her.

"Come here, Andrew, and see who just arrived," Karen demanded of her reluctant son.

Andrew came slowly across the room. He couldn't deny that Cate looked like a fashion model, and he was busy trying to keep flashbacks of San Francisco out of his head. "Cate, it's great to see you home," Andrew announced somewhat stiffly.

"Thanks, Andrew. I'm off to get some eggnog," Cate muttered and made her exit to the dining room, where the elaborate spread of canapés used to amaze and tempt her in Christmases past.

Andrew and his mother turned from each other nearly as fast as Cate moved on. Neither knew what to say to the other about Cate's rudeness. Karen had no idea that the two had ever been anything but like brother and sister, and she certainly didn't know about San Francisco. She couldn't understand

Ellen Gordon

what seemed to be a coldness between the two. She couldn't believe that Cate would condemn Andrew for being gay.

When Cate had several canapés on a tiny Christmas china plate, she turned to the other end of the room to see her mom chatting with a tall, thin man, whose long sandy-colored hair curled just at his collar. The face was pure "boy next door." June and the man were smiling at each other, obviously at ease with each other. Before Cate could escape, her mom called her over.

"Cate, come meet Jack." Her mom smiled. Cate knew her mom was trying to get this awkward moment out of the way by introducing Andrew's lover sooner than later.

Cate felt physically sick to her stomach as she headed across the room. She suddenly wished that she didn't have a plate full of canapés in her hand, because she was sure she'd never eat them now.

"Hi, Cate. Your mom has been telling me about your time in Australia. Andrew and I are hoping to get there and sell some buckets within the next few years. You'll need to be our consultant." Jack grinned at her.

It was clear to Cate that Andrew had never talked about her to Jack, because he was obviously just learning about her. She smiled and weakly and replied, "It was great fun, but it's good to be home. Nice meeting you, Jack. Please excuse me. I see Mrs. Carmichael."

At that moment nothing could be further from the truth. It wasn't good to be home, and she longed for Australia and her job, and she wondered what would have happened with Colin and her if she had stayed. Still, she hoped she didn't sound rude to Jack and her mom. How could she have anything against him, except that he had the love of someone she thought she loved? What a mess. Cate was glad she saw Mrs. Carmichael.

Cate gave her a big hug and kiss on the cheek. She was one of June's oldest and dearest friends, making her like a grand-mother to Cate for years. She was in June's book club and her bridge club, so she had been in their home frequently as Cate was growing up. There was something solid and reliable about Mrs. Carmichael, and Cate needed that badly right now, when everything else in her life was topsy-turvy.

"Promise me that you will come over soon and tell me all about Australia and what you're going to do next," Mrs. Car-michael insisted as she held both of Cate's hands in hers.

"I promise." Cate grinned, just so happy to be with someone who had always been on her side.

The rest of the evening dragged on with Cate avoiding An-drew and Jack, not that the happy couple would have noticed. The only positive surprise of the evening was meeting her mom's date. It even sounded weird saying it inside her head.

She was prepared to dislike him just on principle, but there wasn't anything to dislike. While he was the exact opposite in every way of her dad, it was easy to see why June enjoyed his company.

Jason was tall, well over 6'2", with steel gray hair that gave him the distinguished look of a college professor. In reality he was a retired high school principal, who loved tennis, travel, cooking, and apparently her mom, Cate decided. He didn't try to impress her or ask her endless questions about Australia, like so many people were doing. He did tell her that if she were interested in teaching here in the area, he might be able to give her some good contacts.

"Thanks for that, Jason." Cate nodded. "I just don't know if I want to go into the education system again. I didn't actually teach much in Australia. After a couple years in phys. ed., I worked on curriculum development and teacher training. But thanks, I'll keep that in mind."

Cate was happy for her mom. They looked good together, and she never wanted her mom to be alone. "So, here's my mom with a great guy, and I have no one," Cate lamented to herself.

V

"Phone for you, Cate," June called up to Cate in her bedroom, where she was contemplating whether to take Jason's suggestion and try the education route. No other prospects were on the horizon, and her funds were running low after purchasing a used Honda Accord. Jason had helped her find it, and he had checked it out thoroughly for her before she made an offer. The car was burgundy on the outside with a beige leather interior. Even with fifty thousand miles, the car looked like new. Cate named him Charles.

When she headed to the phone, Cate hoped it would be one of her high school buddies calling to welcome her home. It seemed odd that no one had tried to connect in over a month. Patty, Barb, and Lynn were back to their lives, and Cate was feeling quite alone.

"Hello?" Cate spoke into the phone, hoping she sounded upbeat and not bored to tears like she really was.

"Cate, it's Andrew. There's something I want to talk with you about. Okay if I come over around 7:00 tonight?"

Totally off balance, Cate could only manage a surprised "okay." And with that, Andrew hung up on her.

What on earth would he want to talk about? Maybe he'd explain why he didn't bother to tell her that he was gay and had fallen in love with a man or that San Francisco meant nothing or why he wasn't even enough of a friend to welcome her home. Angry tears ran down her cheeks.

After a few minutes, she dried her eyes and wondered aloud to herself, "What if he broke up with Jack now that I'm home? What if seeing me on Christmas Eve made him realize the mistake he made? What should I wear tonight?"

Bridge club was that night, so Cate's mom was out when Andrew arrived. Cate wondered if Andrew knew that June would be out tonight. Andrew's mom was in the same club, so he would probably know. When the doorbell rang, Cate's stomach did flip-flops.

Dressed in faded jeans, a light blue button-down polo, and a navy sport coat, Andrew looked just like a model out of *Esquire*. Why hadn't she ever noticed how perfectly he dressed for all occasions? Suddenly she ached for him to hold her and tell her everything would be just like it used to be. If nothing else, she wanted her big brother back. She was afraid that San Francisco had made that impossible to go back.

As soon as they sat across from each other in the comfortable living room, Andrew jumped right in with his mission.

Ellen Gordon

"Cate, I have an offer for you. I ran it by Jack, and he agrees it's a smart move. You know that Jack is my plant manager and business partner as well as my, um, lover, right? There would be no Acme Attachments if Jack hadn't agreed to come on board at the very beginning." Andrew paused to take a breath.

"Anyhow, my company is growing fast. We're up to ninety-five employees now, and I haven't a clue how to handle them. We have no one to work on personnel issues or safety training. Your mom told Jack that you've done a lot of adult training and problem solving for schools in Australia. I'd really like to give you a job," Andrew finished suddenly, nearly out of breath.

Cate felt cold and embarrassed at her earlier thoughts of them getting back together. She hated that this offer was coming from Andrew and Jack together.

"Well, say something," Andrew demanded. To Cate he sounded disappointed, that maybe she should be jumping up and down with excitement.

"Exactly what would I do? I've never worked in manufacturing," Cate cautiously inquired.

"I have no idea really, but I need someone who knows how to work well with people. I need an employee handbook, so our attorney tells me. I'm not paying him $250 an hour to write the stupid thing. He can review it, and he would assist with the legal aspects. Then someone needs to train the employees. Oh, come on, Cate. I thought you'd be so pleased. You need to get to work. I can't pay big bucks, but you'll have benefits," Andrew finished and looked crestfallen at Cate.

In spite of her shock and disappointment, Cate couldn't curb that old excitement and rush of taking on another new challenge. *Here I go again*, Cate thought to herself. *I'll just jump right in and make it up as I go along.*

"Okay, I'll give it a try," a dubious Cate told Andrew.

"That's terrific. And thank heavens you won't have to report to Jack or me. You'll report to Tim Harding. He's Accounting and Quality Control. Great guy. You'll like him a lot."

"Okay, I'll do my best," Cate rather solemnly promised. "Oh, and congratulations to you and Jack. You must have fallen pretty hard, pretty fast," Cate said, hoping her voice was steady and there was no hint of sarcasm.

"No, actually, it wasn't immediate love. Jack was in my John Deere class in Iowa years ago when I first went to work for Highland Tractors. He was in sales at the time at a dealership in New Jersey. Anyhow, we became friends over that week and stayed in touch. When I was getting ready to start my company and I told him about it, he came to Ohio to talk about it. Well, that was the start of Acme Attachments and eventually our love," Andrew finished.

Cate looked at Andrew through different eyes just then. Who was this man so sure of himself and so successful and so clueless to what Cate was feeling?

"Come to the plant Monday and meet with Tim. He'll get you set up. I'm really glad you're home Cate. Your mom really missed you," Andrew called out as he headed for the front door.

Cate stomped her foot and threw a pillow at the closed door. "Arrogant, selfish, egotistical man."

VI

Cate worked hard all her life at not letting others know just how shy she was and how she found polite chitchat uncomfortable. In every new situation, and she'd put herself in many new situations so far in her life, she had to cope with a dry mouth and fast beating heart while smiling and making eye contact.

Now she was looking across the desk at Tim Harding, who seemed to have no more idea why she was here or what she would be doing for the company than Cate did.

But he dutifully filled her in on what they manufactured there, how many employees they had, and little bit of history about how Andrew grew this business from nothing. It was obvious that he held Andrew in high esteem, which somehow annoyed Cate more than a little. Didn't anyone care that Andrew was gay and his lover was their plant manager? Evidently not, so she kept nodding and reminding herself that she really needed this job.

Tim took her on a tour of the offices and plant, stopping to chat along the way. He obviously had the respect of the employees by the way they greeted him. Cate guessed he was in his early fifties, with close-cut gray and black hair. His skin was dark and rather leathery, so she assumed most of his career had been in the outdoors—a contractor would make sense.

"Welcome, Cate," smiled the cheerful receptionist secretary named Debbie. "We can certainly use another female around here," she declared. "It's Carole in finance, me, and you. The other ninety are all guys. Are you single?"

Cate liked her immediately. "Single, and I'm just fine with that." Cate grinned back at her.

Meeting Carole was not as positive as her introduction to Debbie. Carole was a bit overweight and wore a lot of makeup. "What on earth will you be doing here? We don't need another person on payroll right now. Things are a bit tight. What was Andrew thinking, Tim?" she questioned him as if Cate was not even in the room.

Feeling offended and under attack, Cate couldn't help herself. "I'll be writing an employee handbook and training everyone on it—you know, like a personnel director's job." Cate wasn't even sure what that job title entailed, and she wasn't even sure where that came from, but it shut Carole up for the time being.

As their tour continued, Cate was greeted pleasantly by four engineers as they looked up from their drawing boards or computers. Cate knew that Andrew's company manufactured things that fit on construction equipment, but that was about the limit of her knowledge. She felt some excitement stir to learn more about the products.

Men in blue work slacks and shirts, with their name and the company logo, were spread throughout the ten-thousand-square-foot manufacturing plant. There were dozens of stations, all doing different processes to the large steel rolls. There were welders, cutters, assemblers, all too busy to do more than nod as Tim and Cate passed. Still Cate could feel the curious eyes following her around.

Tim stopped suddenly and turned to Cate. "I like that title, personnel director. If it's one thing I need around here, it's someone to deal with people issues. There are endless issues with the medical insurance, uniforms that don't fit, or a new hire or someone to let go." He was looking at her in a completely different light. "And I liked the way you stood up to Carole. She's a great accountant, but a people person she ain't. Let me show you to your office."

VII

For the next two months, Cate created her new position as personnel director of Acme Manufacturing. She had introduced herself to vendors that she would be responsible for—office supplies, insurance, uniforms, temp agencies, and attorneys. There was plenty of low hanging fruit with some of these vendors who had never had anyone question their fees or services before.

Her first big win was with the contract for the uniforms. The renewal was coming up, so Cate spent time talking to the men about their preferences. What a can of worms. Many of the uniforms had buttons missing or they would be given the wrong pants size or sometimes just not come back at all.

Cate selected two other uniform vendors who gave solid bids. Armed with comparable or lower prices, Cate went into serious negotiations with the current vendor.

Cate got the current vendor to lower the price slightly, but more importantly, no contract would be signed until the complaints stopped. Even Carole was forced to acknowledge the coup without a smile and only an abrupt, "Good going. The guys think you're amazing."

"How did you do it, Cate?" asked Frank the lead man in shipping. "I've had the correct uniform with no holes and all the buttons for a month now."

"Pure talent, Frank," Cate boasted.

The men on the plant floor loved her. Not only was she easy on the eyes in their all male work world, but she was genuinely interested in their work. She got herself a uniform just like theirs, with "Cate" on the pocket. Steel-toed shoes were a must, as were safety goggles and ear plugs. Every week she found time to stand by with one of the employees, listening and learning about their piece of the work on attachments. When she was working with Jason, a young welder, she saw that his gloves, designed to keep hands safe from sparks, had holes in them. Cate did the research and found a far safer, superior product for the welders. Wins like this were making her not only liked but also appreciated for her work.

Cate worked late nearly every night. There was so much to learn, and she was making a start on the employee handbook. Around 8:00 one night after she had been there almost five months, there was a gentle rap on her office door.

"In," she called, assuming it was Tim, who often worked late like she did.

"Hey Cate," Andrew called softly. "Tim tells me everyone is singing your praises."

Andrew was on the road almost nonstop now, getting contracts with major equipment manufactures like John Deere and Komatsu. Cate had only seen him a few times and always with Jack by his side.

Jack had tried to get to know Cate, but she couldn't let herself relax around him. "I wanted to let you know how much that means to Jack, me, and the company."

"You're welcome," Cate replied, keeping her head down and focused on her work. "Thanks for giving me the chance," she added coolly.

"I was a jerk, wasn't I? I know I just kind of blew you off when you got home. No excuse, but Jack and I were brand new, and honestly I was a bit embarrassed about San Francisco."

"Embarrassed?" Cate stared into those perfect copper-colored eyes. "Embarrassed? You are a jerk, Andrew Jacobs." As usual the mouth was ahead of the brain. Andrew was her boss, and she was in his building, and she just called him a jerk.

Andrew stood up slowly, shaking his head. "I'll say it once again. Grow up, Cate."

He shut the door quietly. The sting of the tears and the sting of his words were too much for Cate. She threw an eraser as hard as she could at the door, just as it opened again. There stood Carole. The eraser barely missed her head and landed in the hall.

Carole stared at her for a few seconds. "What did Andrew want? Did he fire you?" she questioned with a little too much enthusiasm.

"No, just a little disagreement."

"You knew Andrew before you went to Australia, didn't you? Did you ever go out with him, before Jack, of course?" Carole continued to push with nasty sneer on her face.

Cate felt she was in treacherous waters now. "No, Carole. Andrew and I grew up together. His parents and my parents were very close friends."

"So that's how you got this job then? Because your parents and Andrew's parents were good friends?"

"That's a very mean thing to say, Carole, but even if it's true, I love this job, and I know I'm doing a good job. That's what Andrew came to tell me," she could say truthfully.

"So let me get this straight. You're crying because Andrew came to congratulate you on your fine work. Ha." With that, Carole slammed the door on her way out of Cate's office.

Cate was beyond miserable. Was it true that Andrew just gave her the job because of her parents? Or was he just feeling guilty about the way he had treated her when she came home? She put her fists to her forehead and shook with anger and disappointment. Andrew didn't fire her, but it would be a long time before he stopped avoiding her.

VIII

After almost a year on the job, Cate had her own apartment and joined a gym, hoping to make some new friends. The loneliness was the only thing that Cate couldn't conquer. Her old high school friends, although less than forty minutes away, didn't make any effort to get Cate back in their circle. They hadn't even asked her to one euchre night. She knew that she hadn't been all that nice to them when she first came home, because things were so confusing with Andrew, living with her mom, and trying not to run back to Australia.

Coming home after yet another long day at the plant, Cate threw the mail on the table before noticing a bright blue card. "May I come see you now?" was all it said, and it was from

Colin. The thought of seeing him again was all warmth and excitement and wonderment. They had written a couple of times, but the letters were mostly newsy, and neither hinted at any kind of future. Cate splurged on a phone call to Australia that night. "Yes, yes, yes."

It was a cold, snowy Friday night in November when Cate jumped into Colin's arms at the Cleveland airport. He looked exhausted, but the smile and the sparkling blue eyes told Cate how glad he was to be there. He'd taken two weeks long service leave, even though in a month he'd be on his long summer school break. It didn't escape Cate's thoughts that the man must have really wanted to see her!

After all that time at Acme, Cate had not taken a single day off work, and she was there most Saturdays and even a few Sundays when needed. When she told Tim a friend was coming from Australia, he insisted that she take some well-deserved time off.

"Take as many days as you like, Cate. You practically live at this place, and I think we can survive a few days without our star executive," Ted teased.

IX

"How could these two weeks be going by so fast?" Cate complained to the naked Aussie in her bed. Back in Australia there had been a definite spark between them, but to Cate this was different—better. It felt like they had been together a long time, not just a couple of weeks. Cate loved his sense of humor and marveled at all the stuff he seemed to know.

Without being pompous, quite the opposite, he was simply the most intelligent person she had ever met.

Cate didn't want to take too much time off from Acme. There were insurance contracts coming up soon, and she needed to do her homework. Some days Colin would go to the plant with her, where Debbie in reception had fallen in love with him and would cheerfully keep him occupied while Cate worked.

"Want to come out into the plant with me?" Tim asked Colin one afternoon when he saw him standing at Reception. "You look like you might need rescuing from Debbie. She can talk your ear off."

That started an instant friendship between Colin and Tim. Colin's natural curiosity had him soaking up all the information that Tim enjoyed explaining to him about their products. After an hour walking the plant and seeing all the steps to create the buckets and couplers, Tim invited Colin back to his office.

"Cate told me that Andrew just picked up a contract with John Deere to provide 150 buckets, couplers, and forks for the 550 wheel loader. Congratulations, that must be a real boon to the bottom line," Colin told Tim as they settled into his office.

"Yep, they are going to the military, so it will be a special color and has to be the highest quality. It means hiring at least five associates in welding and burning, maybe more," Tim was happy to explain.

"I know this sounds a little strange, but knowing a bit about Cate's work here and the business you're in, I found myself reading a bit about your industry before I came over. Australia has started investing a lot of money in infrastructure, so the construction industry is growing fast. I read an article on how steel products, like forks and buckets, are being brought in from Brazil. Have you ever looked at Brazil? I know the forks are one product you don't build, you purchase," Colin questioned.

Tim studied Colin for a few seconds. He knew him well enough to know that Colin would not bring up a subject if he did not know something about it.

"I haven't heard or read anything, but Jack is in charge of purchasing. Let's go see if he's in today," Tim suggested.

The pair found Jack on the plant floor inspecting ten buckets about to ship for a 410 backhoe.

"Got a minute, Jack? Colin here has a question or maybe a suggestion," David shouted over the noise of the plant.

"Sure, let's go to the conference room so we can hear ourselves talk."

When the trio was settled in comfortable chairs in the quiet conference room, Jack addressed Colin. "It's good to see you again, Colin." Cate had introduced Colin to both Andrew and Jack on one of the rare days they were both in the plant. Although things were still a bit unsettled between Andrew and Cate, they were both glad for an opportunity to show there were no hard feelings. While nothing was said, Cate felt relieved that little tantrum seemed to be forgotten.

For the next forty-five minutes, Colin shared what he had learned about the Brazil steel market and made notes of the questions that Jack posed. At the end of the impromptu meeting, Jack and Colin shook hands. "Come back to us with more definite information, such as a contact in Brazil, and we may just be interested in looking at a proposal," Jack concluded with a friendly smile.

Tim and Colin found a restless Cate talking to Debbie at Reception.

"And where have you two been hiding?" an impatient Cate inquired.

"Your brainy man was educating Jack and me on steel from Brazil, if you must know," Tim teased.

X

Cate was pretty sure her heart broke the morning she watched Colin disappear down the jetway on his way out of her life again. When Colin was here, they didn't really talk about the future because there seemed to be no future for them. They took each day they had and enjoyed it to the fullest. The two weeks were full of laughing, exploring, and loving.

Just one week after Colin departed and Cate was still moping around missing him, he called. "Cate, I want to come back. I want to spend my school holidays with you. We need to figure this thing out. I'm just not that good without you," Colin finished and held his breath.

"Yes, yes, yes," Cate practically shouted into the phone.

Colin arrived the second week of December. He seemed a little preoccupied with some project he had brought with him. Cate assumed it was preparation of some sort for his consulting job with the Queensland Education Department. This worked out perfectly because Cate was busy at work leading up to the holidays.

On the Friday two weeks before Christmas, the party to thank the employees for their demanding work was in full swing. To Cate's immense relief it seemed to be going great. She'd organized a money machine, where employees got thirty seconds in the booth to grab as many dollar notes as they could capture. It was fun to do and just as much fun watching.

Two tables were full of all sorts of catered food and drink. Cate always marveled at how much this crew could eat. And since all machines were to be turned off until the next Monday, Andrew even provided cold beers as well as sodas.

Andrew started a tradition of giving every employee a turkey at Thanksgiving and at Christmas. When it was time to hand them out, Cate stood in the back of the festivities and watched Andrew greeting every employee as he handed them their turkey. She was sorry they were no longer as close as they once were, and she did realize that she was wrong to blow up at him. Maybe one day he could be her big brother again.

As well as a turkey, Christmas bonuses were given based on their time working in the plant. Preparing the list and amounts of the bonuses had been a huge and satisfying job for Cate. They were a loyal bunch, and they appreciated that the working conditions and hourly wage at Acme were above the average for that area. Plus working for Jack, Tim, and Andrew was a bonus. They demanded a full day's work and focused on quality, but they were always fair. Cate loved thinking of the joy that the bonuses would bring to the men's families. By 3:00 that afternoon all ninety employees were headed out the door for the weekend, lugging their turkeys and their bonus checks.

Cate and Colin quickly and easily fell into a routine. Both early risers, the coffee was brewing by 6:00 every morning. Some days Colin would drive Cate to the plant then continue working on his project or take the time to explore the area.

Cate was amazed how comfortable he became driving on the right side of the road—opposite to what he was used to. Or some days he went to the plant with Cate and spent the morning with Tim on the plant floor. It amused Cate that he was so interested in Acme and had become friends with Tim and several of the workers.

On Christmas Eve the plant was shutting down at noon. Cate and Colin were on the plant floor wishing everyone a Merry Christmas. The workers always had questions about Australia for Colin to answer. The most common one was always, "Are there really kangaroos running in the streets?" Cate was half listening to Colin describing a koala to John, one of their welders.

She looked over at the door to the offices, and there was Andrew leaning against the wall watching her. He looked curious and puzzled. Cate assumed by now he had heard that Colin and Cate were an item. Could that possibly upset Andrew, that she also had found love? Once again, she wished they were brother and sister again.

Well, let him wonder about Colin and me, thought Cate, and she turned back to the departing employees.

Back in her office, Cate rushed to gather coat, purse, and the four wonderful elephants that various staff had given her for Christmas. She almost missed a company envelope with her name on it. Inside was a payroll check made out to her for one thousand dollars. A yellow Post-it note said, "Thanks for all you do, Cate." Had Andrew come to give her the bonus personally, then found her with Colin? Well, she would certainly enjoy the bonus, and it felt good to know that Andrew appreciated her work.

Ellen Gordon

Tim and his wife Lorain invited Colin and Cate to a holiday party between Christmas and New Year's. Cate was more than a little nervous attending an event where some of the engineers, the sales team, and their families would be there, plus a lot of people Cate did not know. And if Jack and Andrew showed up, what would she say to them? Talking to these people at work was okay, but Cate was never at her best at this type of social function. Yet, not wanting Colin to know her fears, she put on her familiar fake brave face.

Halfway through the evening, Cate decided that she would never have to fear another social function as long as Colin was by her side. He kept his eye on her, and a casual arm around her shoulder was all the support she needed to relax and enjoy the evening. When Andrew joined them in the kitchen where they were helping Lorain, Colin jumped into a discussion with him about the Cavs basketball team. Basketball was new to Colin, and they had enjoyed a game the week before.

The conversation was easy, and Cate felt that love she had all her life for Andrew. And now here he was happily chatting with her lover. Colin's natural easiness with people drew them to him, and it looked like Andrew was warming up to him as well.

To celebrate New Year's Eve, Colin and Cate went to Iacomini's for a long dinner and some dancing before heading to Cate's apartment at about 11:30. It had been a wonderful evening, and while sipping champagne, the pair was sleepy and felt comfortable just to watch Times Square on the TV and wait for the ball to drop. Cate was toying with the small gold elephant charm on the chain around her neck. She called him Savant, and he had been a wonderful surprise from Colin on Christmas morning. This elephant would always represent the start of their life together. The last of the ten best elephants in her life.

At the stroke of midnight as the ball dropped, Colin dropped to one knee before her. "Cate, I have two things to ask you. One, will you marry me? And two, would you be okay if I started a business here?"

"But, Colin," Cate started to interrupt.

"Cate, I think I'm onto something with Brazil. I've found a company that manufactures forks, and they would be very interested in manufacturing the forks Acme needs for the military order. I've given them the specs, and the quote they've given me for a container load is one hundred dollars less per fork than Acme is paying now.

Colin's enthusiasm was contagious. "When will you know it will work? When will you tell Andrew?" Cate said while hugging him.

"How about you set a meeting ASAP with Tim, Andrew, Jack, and you, of course," Colin hugged back.

"Hey, wait a minute. What about question number one, Cate?" Colin realized they had both gotten caught up in the idea of a business and that the marriage question was still up in the air.

Cate was never one to hesitate or to think things through too carefully. "Yes, yes, yes."

XI

"I want a shot at making this Brazil thing work, Cate," a serious Colin told her over coffee the next morning. I'll resign from the education department. With what I'll get from my superannuation, I should be able to bankroll the first trip to Brazil to see the forks getting made then bring a setback for testing. If Acme is satisfied with the product, I'll only take a small percentage from the first container until we get more orders."

Cate was excited and scared at the same time. What would this mean for Cate and Colin if the business failed? She knew she loved him, but it was happening so fast.

Colin was wrestling with a bottle of Chandon wine. "Let's do this together, Cate. I don't want to live away from you ever again."

When the cork popped, Cate repeated her yes to the new business and yes to him staying and yes to marriage proposal.

XII

Colin returned to Australia just long enough to sell all he had, including his beloved Land Cruiser, The Beast. His resignation as a consultant surprised no one, but it felt good to know how much he'd be missed. There were lots of promises to visit and lots of good lucks. Those who remembered Cate chuckled that he might need some good luck.

Cate was a little jealous at how quickly the men of Acme accepted and respected Colin. He paid his own way to Brazil twice to meet with the owners of the steel manufacturers and to watch the first prototypes be built.

To Colin the Brazilians and Brazil itself reminded him of Australia. In spite of the language barrier, he grew quite fond of the owners, their workers, and their families. From the beginning they included him not just in the factory, but in their homes as well.

He stayed in a tiny motel room in Mococca with a narrow single bed and one lamp on a small dresser. Each morning he would wake up to the smell of a dark, strong thimble-sized coffee that was served with his generous breakfast of fruit, bread, and cheese.

Six months later the first container of forks was ordered and paid for by Acme, with Colin receiving his percentage from the Brazilians for the purchase. This arrangement would continue for two years until Colin started his own fork tine business called Freeroll. Andrew was not interested in being a fork tine company and was content to buy containers of forks at discount prices while Colin was getting a bigger share of sale price and taking the risks.

Somehow because of Colin's success with the tines and the impact it was having on his company, Andrew not only became quite fond of Colin but also felt all barriers dropping between Cate and himself. It felt right to have her back in his life, and Jack adored her.

XIII

Watching Jack and Andrew across her patio table one perfect and rare September Ohio evening, Cate wondered when Andrew and his partner became such a huge part of her life again. She knew a lot of it was because Acme and Freeroll had continued to grow, and the success brought the four of them together both at work and socially over the past four years. But now they felt like family. Andrew was her big brother again, and she loved Jack nearly as much.

By now Acme had made Andrew and Tim multimillionaires. They were the most successful wheel loader and excavator attachment company in the US, with 250 employees in two plants.

While not yet in their league, Colin and Cate were enjoying sales well over a million each year. With low overhead because Colin worked out of their condo and kept the inventory warehoused close by, Freeroll was promising a strong future for the happy couple.

They had married in St. Croix with only Andrew and Jack as their witnesses. The house they rented called Windswept sat high on one of the island's mountains and provided a perfect 180-degree view of Christenstaid and the farm valley below. Now several years later, their love was even stronger.

XIV

Cate wondered what the "Three Musketeers," as Cate called Colin, Jack, and Andrew, could be up to. Many times Cate would walk into the room, and the conversation would go dead, and the trio looked like little boys with their hands in the cookie jar. It was funny at first, but now it was getting a bit irritating.

Cate speculated that the men were looking at houses. Jack and Andrew had purchased an old Tudor home in Shaker Heights, Cleveland, and were busy restoring it to its original beauty. Colin enjoyed working with them and along with Cate would spend a Sunday afternoon covered in sawdust or paint.

Colin and Cate had been discussing getting their own home for about six months. Then suddenly Colin seemed to go cold on the idea. Cate was bewildered and not pleased that he came to this decision to stop looking without her input. Now the three of them were up to something, and Cate feared that Colin had found a house and was going to surprise her. What if she hated it?

"Okay, you clowns, what have you been up to? Always whispering and ignoring me." Cate pretended to pout. "Colin, you're not gay too, are you? Because you sure fool me," she taunted.

The men laughed but continued to stare at their plates. "If you're not doing anything on Saturday morning, we may just show you something, if you can behave until then," Colin announced.

"Impossible," Jack and Andrew chimed in together.

XV

Cate was up at 5:30 on Saturday morning, unable to sleep another minute. The anticipation over what the men had been up to was killing her. She was more convinced than ever that Colin had found a house, and she was terrified that she would hate it. "I will not be buying any house unless I love it," she vowed to herself as she jumped into jeans and a polo shirt.

Finally after tea and toast, Colin stood and headed to the car. "Okay, Cate, time to meet the guys."

As they drove out of Fairlawn in Akron, where they lived for the past few years, it seemed to Cate that they were headed west towards Medina, towards her mom's home. Her mom and Jason Coleman had been married for three years now, and they had decided to live in her mom's large condo instead of Jason's house. *Oh no*, Cate thought, *I don't want to live in Medina*. It was perfect for her mom and Jason, with everything they needed right there, but it was growing too fast for Cate's taste.

Cate's stomach began to do flip-flops once they jumped on 71 South and then exited at 224 West.

"Colin, where are we going?" Cate stammered with some agitation in her voice.

Colin ignored her, and they drove in silence the next fifteen minutes. When Colin pulled up the car in front of Chartres, once the most magical place, now looking forlorn, there stood her mom and Jason, Jack, and Andrew. Before Cate could move Colin grabbed her hand and said, "For better or for worse, Cate, we now own Chartres."

"Andrew brought me here one day when he heard it was back on the market. After your uncle Carl passed away some redneck got hold of it and just let it start to fall around him. Another owner tried to get the place back to its original shape, but he ran out of money and had to sell."

Colin looked at Cate, who hadn't moved but had gone completely pale, as if she might faint. Had he made a terrible mistake buying this place for them to call home?

"I told Aunt B that I'd buy it someday. I told her that just before she killed herself. And now it's ours? Oh my God, Colin, I love you so much." They hugged tightly then got out to face the others.

Jack was the first to speak. "Cate, we're going to get this place back to where it was. Andrew and I can't wait to be a part of it."

Cate hugged each of them one at a time. Clinging to her mother, she whispered, "How could you not tell me?"

Cate held her breath when Colin turned the big brass key and opened the squeaky oak door, and she stepped back in time. The front hall pictures were gone, but she could see the yellow outline where they had once been. She could visualize every single piece of the missing art.

Down the long hall Cate moved as in a daze. When she stood in the archway to the room that she always loved the most, she saw that the glass shelves that had held those magical little pieces were empty. The worn leather recliners were replaced by stiff fabric chairs. It was all wrong, all gone. Cate felt overwhelming sadness.

She turned slowly to the gigantic fireplace that she used to read inside of when she was little. There on the magnificent wooden mantel stood the family of five ebony elephants.

"Amadi, Amara, Ayo, Anuli, Adanna," Cate whispered to herself.

"How's this possible?" Cate spoke to no one in particular. "Aunt B told me that they would always be mine." With that, at last the tears rolled as Cate relived that last afternoon with her aunt. Colin wrapped her in his arms and let her cry it out. Later they would tell Cate how the elephants had been hidden, probably by Aunt B on the night she killed herself. They were in a place where only a curious toddler would go. They were carefully wrapped in Aunt B's ancient costumes then placed under all the massive clutter of the upstairs closet. Under the costumes, magazines, hats, and wonderful props from an age long gone, the elephants had rested for fifteen years. Was it pure luck that Andrew found them when exploring the wonderful contents of the closet?

Ellen Gordon

One Year Later

All of Cate's amazing elephants were proudly displayed in the glass cabinets that once held Aunt B's crystal in the long dining room, on the shelves that once held B's miniature collection, and throughout Chartres. Each elephant held a memory of someone or somewhere that touched Cate's life.

The ten best elephants that defined Cate's life to this point each had a special place at Chartres. Petite Red, Pax, White Cloud, Dumbo, Crystal, and Wentworth had top shelf positions in the glass cabinet behind Cate's new leather chair. Beside her chair, Hubert happily held her evening glass of wine, with Colin in the leather chair close by. Julia and Star held prime spots in the tall glass cabinets in the formal dining room, which once again held dinners for twenty of their friends. Savant for the rest of her life would hang around Cate's neck, a daily reminder of their love.

Cate knew that Aunt B was still in that house. She felt her presence everywhere, like a soft breeze when there were no open windows or when one of the ebony elephants moved from its place on the mantel. Cate had longed for adventure and love when listening to her aunt's wonderful stories, and now she had both.

Ellen Gordon

About the Author

Ellen Gordon's extraordinary career, both here in the US and in Outback Australia, gave her plenty of material for *Ten Elephants Ten Memories*. As an educator, curriculum developer, adult trainer, HR executive, and executive vice president of a manufacturing company, Ellen was fully occupied until retirement. Now with husband Colin, her time is spent volunteering, traveling, writing, and gardening in their Bonita Springs, Florida, home.

Look for Ellen's next novel, *The Canal*, coming out next year.

Ellen Gordon

Ellen Gordon